Hunt

Simon Maltman

To Shyler,

Hope you enjoy it,

all th best,

Simon

"It's nearly time we had a little less respect for the dead, an' a little more regard for the living."
From *Juno and The Paycock* by Sean O'Casey

Prologue

It was 1990. Early Spring, I think. Not long before I got out, switched sides and became a tout. I didn't see that coming. I also didn't see the bullet before it whizzed past my head. It had been just me and Sullivan in the back room of McGovern's Pub in West Belfast. Then we had a little uninvited company. Apparently, their agreed dress code was balaclavas, blue jeans and leather jackets. Probably paramilitaries- UVF or UFF. Cops don't wear balaclavas. Not on official duty, anyway.

Sullivan already had his gun out. I threw myself down as one of the intruder's bullets caught in the wooden beam to my left. It sounded like a whipcrack. There were two of them. Sullivan's Glock roared from beside me. The bullet tore through the first man's leather jacket, before he crumpled onto filthy floor.

Now there was only one.

I had my Colt in my hand. I rolled halfway under the table as the second man aimed his snub-nosed pistol at me.

He pulled the trigger.

Misfire.

I put a bullet in him. Centre mass. The Colt's boom was thunderous in close quarters. My attacker went down, but he wasn't dead... yet.

Before I was even on my feet, Sullivan crossed the room and kicked him in the head, over and over again. Cordite swirled around them like embers from a bonfire. Sullivan was brutal, unforgiving.

I looked away.

I'd already lost my taste for it all, long before that night.

Part 1: Everybody Knows This Is Nowhere

Chapter 1

Nine years later...

I suppose it was close to midnight. I'd been living in Beaconsfield for a few years by then. It's a one-horse town in Pennsylvania where the horse had long been shot and sent to the glue factory. I'm Irish, and I know one-horse towns. When I was a kid, places like this at home had horses that shot back at you.

Here, I lived in a little clapboard house on a street on the edge of town. It was very quiet that night. It was always quiet. I stumbled up the road after a few beers, but I wasn't steaming. If I told you that as I approached my home, engulfed in blackness, I had a bad feeling, you might tell me that's nonsense. Well, I *did* have a bad feeling when I was a few hundred feet away, and I can't explain it any more than that. And I was right to feel it. Maybe it's a part of you when you've been on the run for as long as I was.

I stood there swaying a little, pushed the thought away, and was grateful for an evening breeze sweeping through the humid night.

Just being stupid.

I slotted a cigarette in my mouth, squinting up towards the moon as I focused on making the lighter spark. Then I trudged on towards home.

There were only a few thousand others living in the whole of this backwater town.   Half of them made their living from apples or chickens. If the chickens ever fought back, we'd be outnumbered a hundred to one. If the chickens threw apples at us, they'd not run out of ammunition until the new season. My place was the last on the left on a small street. Beyond it was a kind of no man's wasteland covered in people's old junk and thriving weeds.

I took in a long draw as I made it to my front yard. I tried to keep it tidy enough, but it wasn't much; a patch of scorched grass, a mailbox and white fencing yellowed from the heat. I'd painted it only the year before. The summers got too hot, and I would be happy if spring was to stay for most of the year. Tonight, the moon cast an otherworldly glow over the street. The town looked best like this. I looked back, up at the distant church spire looming above all the other smaller buildings. Much better this way. The glare of the hot daytime sun too easily showed up the imperfections. And surely there were many. The people there were mostly okay, but it was a poor place. A place like many others that existed quietly and didn't care if anyone knew it was there or not. It surely wasn't somewhere anyone would choose to visit. In my coarse youth I may have unkindly referred to such a place as a dirty hole.

I glanced at my rusted mailbox. *Michael Dempsey* was etched on it in black. My name is indeed Michael, but my second name is Walker. I'd always figured if they ever got close enough to me, having the same first name wasn't that big an issue. I'd fought against changing it. The advice had been to go for something completely random. At least I could hold onto that one thing. But as Bernard Shaw once said, "Life isn't about finding yourself. Life is about creating yourself."

I tossed the butt away, with a half effort to get it in the old soup tin I kept on the front porch. It was already starting to overflow. I missed, but didn't care. I'd sweep up in the morning. It was 1999 and I reckoned that tin had sat there since maybe '96. Pulling out my key, and now at the door, the unsettled feeling came back, and I knew. I *knew* there was somebody inside. Some defensive mechanism in my brain was telling me there was another human being inside. Maybe more than one. I can't explain it, but it's saved me more than once in the past.

I sobered up good and quick, in part anyway. If they had found me, had come for me, then I needed to get myself together. I tried to shake off the night's drinking and just *think*.

Perhaps the boredom of life was making me imagine things that weren't there. That had happened more than once too, particularly recently. My life, for the most part, had become one long, solitary monologue inside my own head.

It wasn't like I could go and get help either. What would I tell anyone? *I've got a bad feeling. I'm too scared to go into my house.*

No. There wasn't anyone I could go to anyway. Nobody knew who I *really* was. The cops weren't an option either. That wasn't going to happen. I was on my own.

I looked about the yard for something to use as a weapon. Nothing doing. I scanned the house in my head. My gun was in my bedroom upstairs and that was at the back of the house. I'd have little chance of getting there if they were already inside. They would be professionals. They would be prepared.

I thought about lighting another while I looked up and down the empty street.

I couldn't just stand outside all night. As quietly as I could, I slotted in the key, turned it and pushed the door open.

Nothing.

I silently closed the door behind me, and my eyes searched the room, adjusting to the lack of light. My living room looked like it always did; a little messy, a few dishes needing cleared, some dust in the air.

Maybe I *was* imagining it all.

I padded quietly through the room, then into the kitchen. Everything looked as it should. I stood at the foot of the stairs, cocking my ear for any slight noise. I couldn't hear anything. Above me was my bedroom, the spare room and a small bathroom.

Then it came. A creak.

I knew my house and it did creak sometimes. But this was the unmistakable creak of a foot walking over the floorboards in the bedroom above me. No doubt about it.

I froze.

Now I really was sober. I swallowed hard, my throat dry, and crept over to the cupboard under the stairs. I reached in and pulled out my hurley stick. If you don't know what hurling is, it doesn't really matter. It's a bit of a rubbish game. You just need to know that I now had a long lump of ash wood with a curved edge in my hands. It was the best I could do.

I waited.

Then the thought struck me like an anvil. Why wasn't I dead already? It should have been the easiest thing. Just two men could handle it. One waiting upstairs on lookout, one hiding behind the

4

door. A compressor on a revolver, two in the back of the head as I came in, job done. That's how I would have set it up.

Strange.

If they had come for me, I should be dead ten times over by now.

I couldn't just stand there all night, listening for creaks, clutching my hurley stick in a baseball pose. I caught my reflection in the ancient mirror on the wall. I'd now passed forty, but fifty was still far off. I stood six feet, two inches, and my body hadn't gone to hell just yet. It'd be a while before I started to stoop. I was still trim, strong. I'd always been strong. From the cradle 'til whenever death finally came, I knew I'd have to be. And I could handle this. Whatever it was. I had a lifetime of violence to fall back on. It wasn't my first rodeo.

I climbed the stairs.

Chapter 2

Halfway up the staircase, I heard another creak.

Then another.

I made a few creaks myself, then I heard damn well full-on shuffling, and even someone whispering.

I wasn't just imagining it all.

What was going on up there?

The bathroom door was open, and I could see that it was empty. Both bedroom doors were shut. I hadn't left them that way. I came to the spare room first. I held the hurley loosely in my right hand. With my left hand I twisted the handle and kicked the door open. The room was dark. I took a step inside as my eyes adjusted. There was only a desk and shelves in it, a few bits and pieces from a life on the move. Nowhere for someone to hide and nobody was trying to. My ears pricked up at more noise from my bedroom beyond. The sound of the window latch opening? I stepped out and strode across to my bedroom door. I took a breath, swivelled the handle, and kicked it, hard.

The door swung open. Inside were two men, both young, black, with their hoodies up, partly obscuring their features. One was stood to my right at the end of my bed, my small portable TV in his arms. The second was a little larger than the first, straddling the windowsill, one leg hanging out. He had my little metal money tin that I kept in my bedside cabinet in his arms.

"Get the hell out of my house!" I yelled.

The first guy dropped my telly and moved to run around the side of my bed. I pulled back, took a swing and cracked him across his left arm with my hurley stick. He cried out, scrambling away towards the far wall. The second guy began to squirm awkwardly out of the window. I lunged around the right side of the bed and swung the stick down onto his knuckles. He yelped, lost his grip and tumbled out through the sash window. I tried to grab for him, not to save him, but to pull him back in to be given a good hiding. Behind me, the first guy crawled desperately across the bed, fleeing through my bedroom door. The second guy half fell, half jumped onto the little lean-to, a few metres down. Then he tumbled off, landing awkwardly on the gravel below.

At the side of my house was parked a twenty-something-year-old station wagon with wood panelling along the side. It was empty of people, but the back door was open, and I could see a small pile of some of my few possessions inside. Suddenly the first guy sprinted towards the car. He paused to help his buddy to his feet.

I put a hand on the sill. I sure as heck wasn't going out after them. It wasn't worth it. Part of me was far too relieved that it hadn't been who I thought it would be. Just a couple of stupid punk kids.

"You're dead, do you hear me?" I shouted out after them. I rather enjoyed hearing the Belfast growl in my voice.

They didn't stop to look up and clambered into the car. The first guy pulled out the choke and then the lights shot on. As the tyres squealed, I leaned out of the window, aimed and flung my hurley like a spear. It soared through the air and crashed off the windshield, a large crack instantly forming and spreading out across the glass. Dumb luck rather than skill on my part. The car flew noisily backwards, out onto the road, turned and screeched away.

"Wee bollixes," I said under my breath.

I jogged out of my room and back down the stairs. I didn't even feel that angry, I knew it could have been much worse.

I rounded the outside of the house. There were tyre marks zigzagging the ground and petrol fumes still hanging in the air. There was the faint sound of an engine revving in the distance. Pulling out another cigarette, I lit it quickly and filled my lungs. I bent down and picked up my hurley. It wasn't even damaged. Damned hardy Irish wood. Maybe hurling wasn't such a bad sport. Maybe it needed given another chance.

I exhaled. I shook my head.

Quoting O'Casey to nobody, I said, "The whole worl's in a state o' chassis."

Chapter 3

"Mix this up for me, will you, Michael?"

"No probs, Pete," I said, and started setting up the colouring machine.

I worked part-time in the local garage, mostly doing body work. I hadn't slept much the night before. It took a few turns of the clock and a few more whiskeys before I managed a couple of fitful hours. I had discovered a small pane of glass had been knocked through in my backdoor. I'd boarded it up none too tidy with a two-by-four I'd sawn in half. Then I'd done a quick reccy around the house to see what was missing. I already knew about the VCR I'd spotted in the back of their car. Along with that were videos, CD's, a portable radio and even my small coffee table. They must have done a few runs to their car before I got home. The second of my rather clumsy intruders had managed to take my money tin with him, despite his skydive out of my bedroom window. That was the biggest loss. It contained my emergency money. There was close to a thousand dollars in there. That was a lot to me.

There wasn't a lot of money coming in. But then, I didn't need much either. I was on my own and had been for a long time. That didn't look like it was going to change any time soon. I had been a member of the IRA for a decade and had done a lot of bad things. I'd performed tasks that seemed justified at the time. I'm not sure what I think about them all now. For several reasons I eventually found myself on the other side of the war. I wanted peace, something that we now seemed close to, finally, in 1999. I had worked secretly for The Brits against my former friends for over a year. I had become a rat. A dirty tout. A lowdown, rotten *traitor*. Now I'd been on the run for years, living out here for four of them. It's a strange life. Maybe mine more than most. That money in the tin was my escape money, if I needed it. I hadn't touched it in all those years.

I'd taken *the King's shilling* alright.

I knew what I was.

But I hadn't spent a penny of it.

"I've the machine set, Pete. How 'bout I put on a wee brew?" I said.

"Yeah, coffee would be good," he said gruffly, straining with a wheel crank.

Sweat lashed off his face and his bulky, ebony arms were perspiring too. I went into the grubby little back kitchen and flicked on the kettle. I got on well with Pete. He was a good guy. A family man, quiet, but with a big heart to match the size of his body. I hadn't told him about the break-in. I hadn't told anyone and wasn't planning on it. I had already decided not to take it to the Troopers. The closest station was up in Pilton, about fifteen miles away. We didn't even have a local sheriff or anything like that. I still couldn't get my head around all the various branches of law enforcement in the States. Too many layers and confusing lines of authority. I'd been brought up to avoid *any* peelers as much as possible. That still hadn't changed. The last thing I wanted was to draw any attention to myself. Back home, almost every small town and village had a police barracks. And not too far away would be an active army barracks too. Most of them were surrounded by huge solid walls and barbed wire. They needed to withstand car bombs and even artillery fire. God forgive me, I'd attacked more than one in my time.

I worked on two cars during the afternoon, mostly alongside Pete in an easy silence. A classic rock station churned out some good tunes as we worked: early Fleetwood Mac, Led Zep… it suited us both. I glanced at my own car, perched unceremoniously on blocks in the corner. It needed a new head gasket and Pete was going to install it for me on a quiet day. That motor was my one indulgence: a dark orange 1974 AMX Hornet. I loved that car. Since my life had all gone to hell back home, it was my closest thing to family. My own family would have liked me better if I *was* dead. Insubordination in the community was enough to have you banished, being a traitor was something else entirely. For that there was only one outcome.

"You time for a swift half before dinner?" I asked as we each made a passing effort to remove a few layers of grease and paint from our hands at the end of the day.

"I'd love to Mick, but Ella has dance class and Ashleigh has a late shift. Rain check… tomorrow, buddy?"

"Dead on. No probs."

I'd just go for one myself anyway.

***

It was after nine and I'd had the one and a good few more besides. I was seated out the front of Nelson's, one of the two pubs in the village. One was less dingey and rough than the other, but I preferred Nelson's. Nobody ever bothered me, and I bothered nobody. My table was out on the pavement, or *sidewalk* I suppose I should say. There wasn't much more than the one main street in Beaconsfield. After that were housing estates scattering out in all directions for a few miles, including my own current dot on the world. The whole town was only about five miles square, if you didn't count the fields beyond. They spread away from the town like a spiderweb crack in a pane of glass. I had been sitting, mulling over what to do next. Okay; I was brooding. I was aggravated. Most of the stuff that I'd lost wasn't that important, but the money I couldn't so easily write off. I might need it. Why should some kids get to break into my gaff and nick my money? I threw back the rest of my pint. There was a pleasant bubbling fizz on my tongue. I lip up, put my head down and sauntered off to the west side of town.

If Beaconsfield had an underbelly, it was the west side. It wasn't very far. There was a railway bridge going over a small creek. Alongside that was a crossroads leading to the two poorest neighbourhoods. There was a strip of three shops, all closed at night, where kids would hang out. For the most part it was just skateboarding, a spot of vandalism and some drugs. I figured if I was to have any chance of locating my unwelcomed ne'er-do-well guests, it would be a good place to start. I was already there after about a half an hour's walk. I approached the strip of shops from Oaksbridge Lane, just beyond the old stone bridge. It was getting dark, but still warm. I was dressed in my oil-stained grey T-shirt and old blue jeans. I was glad of the respite from the heat of the sun. I'd been sweating buckets in the garage all day. Only one streetlamp there wasn't broken, throwing an orange glow across

10

the tumbled down row of shops, some adorned with a fresh splash of graffiti tags. There were three groups of youths scattered around. I didn't recognise any of them from the night before. Almost all were young black men; just boys some of them. They all looked like they'd already had hard lives, though some were probably not yet out of their teens. My pasty white face was always out of place in this town and now it stuck out even more like a busted finger. Also, it probably didn't help that in the sun I turned a lovely pinkish hue.

A kid of maybe fifteen bounded up to me, jumping up from the kerb where he had been sitting with two others.

"Yo, man, you tryin' to score?"

"No, I'm good. I'm just after some information," I said.

He tilted his head at me, his eyes wide like a puppy's, but his face weathered. "You a cop?"

"No, I'm not a cop. I just want some information. I can pay a few quid."

"What are you, Scottish?"

"Irish."

He shrugged. "I guess you *is* a cop. We ain't no stools here either. What is it you wanna know anyway?"

Two massive guys, maybe mid-twenties, sidled up beside the kid. One was probably bigger than the other, but I couldn't have told you which one. Built like 'brick shithouses', we'd have called them back home. I threw my cigarette down and exhaled upwards, like I was maybe going to howl at the moon. I looked back at them. The trio looked at me with hard stares.

"Last night two guys broke into my place, stole from me." I cast a glance at the two big guys. "I want to find them."

"And they were brothers?" said the one on the left. He had a gold cross hanging in front of his tattooed chest, his top shirt buttons hanging open.

"Yeah, if you mean they were black," I said.

"You a racist?" said the one on the right. He had more hair than the first guy. It hung floppily across his scalp, in part concealed by a red bandana.

11

"No, I'm not racist. Most people in this town are black. I couldn't care less what colour anyone is. But I want my gear back."

They seemed to consider this, then the young kid started up again.

"We ain't gonna tell ya nothin' like that even if we did know. And I ain't even sayin' we do. Get the hell outta here man."

He said it in a low voice, suddenly looking angry. He seemed to grow older too. Was he in charge here? Good grief. He was just a child. Lurch and Tyson were answering to him?

"Like I said, I got a few dollars. They don't need to know where I heard it from."

"We said get lost," said Lurch, taking a step towards me.

I loosened up my body. It looked like they wanted to prove something. Maybe I had intentionally come looking for a way to release some of my own tension. Still, I wasn't going to take it out on them unless I had to. Besides, I was rather out of practice.

"Listen, you guys don't need to put on the hardman routine. I've seen it many times before and I've knocked down bigger guys than you lot. 'Youth is wasted on the young?' Bernard Shaw? Nothing? Okay." I held my hands up in mock frustration.

Tyson suddenly took two steps forwards and shoved me hard in the chest. I barely reacted. And he didn't manage to move me.

I exhaled, keeping the red mist at bay. Very restrained really.

"I'll let you have that one. I don't want to damage your chiselled good looks. Now back off before I drop the pair of you."

Lurch must have been feeling left out, taking a step and moving to shove me on the right shoulder. I slipped through his swing, grabbed his arm with my left hand and pulled it behind his back before launching a hard right into his face. He went pale, let out an incongruous yelp for a man his size and fell on his ass. Turning back, Tyson swung a hard right. I ducked it and he stumbled off balance. I sprang up in one swift movement, landed a solid uppercut to his chin. He faltered just before I hit him again with a left to his face and a second uppercut with my right. His legs buckled and he went down, almost out for a ten count.

I glared at the kid. He glared back, unmoving.

"I won't hit a little kid, your mumma might come and kick my ass for you," I said. The other two stayed crumpled on the floor. The groups of youths scattered around had all stopped what they were doing, staring at us. Nobody made any move towards me. Casually, I lifted out my smokes and lighter.

"Thanks for your times fellas, very neighbourly of you," I said, then turned and walked into the night.

Chapter 4

I slept better that night. I did have a couple of whiskeys before bed again, so maybe that helped too. Maybe it was the walk and fresh air. Bull. I knew it was really the scuffle. I hadn't needed to hit anyone for a few years. So much for keeping a low profile. But it had felt good. I'd made no progress. And I was pissed off not to have made any progress. All I had to show for it was a couple of sore knuckles. But still, the release alone had been worth it.

I was due off work the next day and slept in until after ten. I brewed up a pot of coffee and reached to turn on my radio. I cursed out loud, remembering it had been nicked. I took my coffee with a few slices of toast into the living room and switched on my main TV. At least I still had that one and my basic cable. A couple of hours whizzed past. I went for a walk afterwards. My car was still in the garage, so the options to me were fairly limited. I made a loop of the town and ended up back on Main Street. Beaconsfield has two eating establishments. One is a guest house with quite a fancy menu, linen napkins and the like. I strolled past it and went to the diner. It was a greasy spoon like thousands of others across America. It had all the trappings. Formica tops, red plastic booths and the constant mustiness of grease and fried fat hanging in the air. There were plenty of empty booths to pick from. Santana played his recent track *Smooth* on the stereo. It was okay, but not like his early stuff.

"Hello, Michael. What will it be today?" asked Holly.

Holly was thirty-something and seemed to work there most days. She had smooth skin the shade of a new vinyl record. She was attractive, despite the garish red and blue uniform and absence of makeup. I'd a notion on more than one occasion of asking her out, but I heard she was going out with the manager of the guesthouse across the street.

"Well Holly, I'm feeling adventurous. Stan got any of those nice cuts of back bacon in?"

She raised an eyebrow, looking up from her notepad. "He's got the kind he always has."

14

"Well, I feel like living dangerously. Give us three slices and a pancake stack, and refill that syrup jug, would you? I'm lashing it on today."

"Maple?"

"You know it."

"I'll bring you the bottle."

"Works for me," I said.

She strode away towards the kitchen and I 'people-watched' out of the window. Everybody appeared to be merrily going about their business. They all seemed to have some sort of purpose. I wondered what that was like. Beaconsfield wasn't a bad place to hole up in. Quiet, predictable, and after the life I'd led, that had to be a blessing. Well, until two nights before. I reached over for a newspaper left abandoned and flicked through it. Thankfully it wasn't a local rag full of the monotony of driving convictions, deaths and agricultural news. I learned that it was due to be a dry day, that computers *probably* wouldn't crash at the turn of the century and that Oliver Reed had died. The first two things were pretty good, I was sad about Olly Reed. He was a fine actor and I had happy memories of courting a few girls seeing the *Musketeer* movies in my youth. I'd have to have a drink to him later.

I flicked on through the pages to see if there was any news from back home. Relative peace was in its infancy and there was still daily paramilitary activity, albeit with new names like "The Orange Defenders" and the "*Real* IRA." I didn't know who these new jokers were. 'Real' IRA, like the 'Real' Ghostbusters? Things had not been plain sailing by any stretch. It was all still going on. Punishment beatings, folk put out of their homes. There had been three pipe bomb attacks on ordinary, peaceful Catholics by loyalist thugs too. There was a piece in the paper about the Omagh Bomb the previous year. Republican terrorists had carried it out, despite a substantial seventy-one percent of the population voting for The Good Friday Agreement. The agreement had meant a ceasefire and the release of all political prisoners on both sides. For many, this had been the hardest part to swallow. For me, my feelings were more mixed than most. Then out of nowhere, as peace was close, the town of Omagh was blown apart. The killings in Omagh had disgusted almost everybody, me included. Twenty-nine ordinary citizens had been murdered, including a young woman, pregnant with twins.

I turned to something lighter, scanning the entertainment pages. *The Matrix* was topping the movie charts and a new *Star Wars* movie called *The Phantom Menace* was doing well at the box office too. I'd seen it and thought it was a bit wick. When my lunch came, it was good, and I stayed for two further cups of coffee and a slice of key lime pie. And I got to have another chat with Holly, which was nice.

I was stuffed. The grub was enough to keep me full for the rest of the day. I had a few beers across the street afterwards and chatted briefly to some locals I'd gotten to know a little. Then I headed home. My mind couldn't offer me any solutions for what I should do next in trying to track down my money. Maybe I should just let it go. I'd already stuck my head too far above the parapet the night before. I threw myself down onto the sofa. I fired the telly back on and flicked between episodes of *Friends* and *Frasier*. I looked for something else not starting with F when I got bored, but found nothing that interested me. I pulled myself up and decided to have a look through my old things from home. I kept them all in my spare room. I treated myself to a single malt Bushmills, bringing it up with me. I hoked around in the cupboard up there and found my half-broken CD player that only ever played upside down. I slotted in Neil Young's *Harvest Moon*. The laser did its thing and Neil began to serenade me about a blonde on her Harley Davidson. It was his twenty year follow up to *Harvest* and is a pretty decent record. I sat on the floor and pulled out my shoebox full of memories from Ireland. I finished my drink.

I only got as far pulling off the lid. The picture on top was an old black and white photograph of my parents. It was them on their honeymoon. I breathed out heavily. My parents were both still alive, so far as I knew. But I was dead to them. I was in no frame of mind to look through these things, it was too painful. I put the lid back on and ran my head over the cold cardboard, a deep knot in my gut.

Reaching across to my bookshelf, I picked up an old olive-coloured hardbacked anthology of Yeats. I'd had it since school days. I ran a hand over the spine and gave it a sniff before beginning to flick through it. I read a verse here, a verse there.

I couldn't concentrate on it.

It hit me afresh, as it had done many times before; my old life was no more. Everything I had once been was now gone. All I had left was the belief that I had done what I had to, what was *right*. *Right* whenever the only other option seemed worse.

That's what I had always tried to do, more or less. But was that enough? Who knows? I sat up on my knees and turned to look at my framed original copy of the Irish Declaration of Independence from 1916. It hung on the wall behind the door, beside a few other pictures. Some of these I had owned for a long time, others only since I'd started my life in America, such as it was. The poster was extremely rare and there was only a scattering of copies known to be still in existence. I had been presented with it following my induction and subsequent rise through the Irish Republican Army. Whatever my views now on the struggle and the way to achieve independence, it was something I never could have parted with. The Rising was still justified in my opinion. Much of what I had done was too. But it didn't mean I thought we should fight forever no matter the cost.

But there was something very wrong.

The declaration was missing from my wall.

Chapter 5

I stared at the empty space, willing it to reappear. My head swam. I unfolded my legs and sat down on the floor with my feet out, dumbfounded. Had I not checked on it after the break in? I mustn't have.

Stupid.

How had I missed it?

I had been too busy thinking about the money, thinking about my damned CD's. I released my anger on the CD player, pulling out the power lead and tossing the little machine across the room.

That wasn't going to make it play any better.

Why hadn't I checked on the declaration sooner? It was by far the most valuable thing I owned. Far more valuable even than my car. It also had an unquantifiable emotional link for me. But more important than all of that, it could be dangerous. It was the only thing that could potentially be connected directly to who I was.

Where the hell was it?

I got up and paced the room. Nausea swept through my body. Panic caught hold of me. I hurried to my bedroom and pulled out the wooden box that housed my gun. Flipping the lid and looking down on the grey steel of my Colt M19 made me feel a little better. At least it was where it was meant to be. I couldn't remember the last time I had opened the box. I lifted it out, reassured by the weight of it in my hand. I tried to always keep it fully loaded. Twelve rounds and one in the chamber. I clicked the safety on and off. The Colt had been another gift from my *seniors* during my early days with the Provos. It had been smuggled into Ireland in the 1970s and then owned by a fallen comrade before my time. It meant a lot to me back in the day, and it still did. I sat there clutching it, feeling the lowest I had felt for a long time. In many ways I had slipped into a world of just *existing*. Barely even that. Now this.

I sat like that for a long while. I don't cry. I'm not trying to act macho. It just isn't in me. But I felt close to shedding tears then. Eventually, I dragged myself up, went downstairs and cracked the seal on a new bottle of special reserve Jameson. I can't remember much about the rest of the night, but I do know that I slept with the Colt underneath my pillow.

The next morning, surprisingly, I awoke full of purpose. Aside from the hangover, I felt pretty good. I wasn't exactly brand new, but I was okay. I had a plan. I wasn't due in at work, but I called into the garage around ten to see if Pete had had a chance to finish off working on my car. He had. Finally, something going right. I walked down to the garage and thanked him with a solid handshake and the promise of a few beers soon. I went across to my baby and patted the still pristine dark orange side of her. She really was a thing of beauty. Speeding away from the town, the freshly tuned engine responded like God created it himself. I was okay. I was in control.

It was a hot day and I wound my window down and cranked up the stereo. I slotted in a cassette copy of *Freakey Styley*, the 1984 album from The Red Hot Chili Peppers, and their finest album in my opinion. The bass held together the laidback funk coursing through me as After about forty minutes, I turned off the freeway onto the main road into Pilton. Pilton is the closest "big" town. It's about three times the size of Beaconsfield geographically and almost six times it in population. I didn't go there very often. Sometimes I went for a change of scene to browse the record stores and bookshops, and to consume fried foods in a different diner. It reminded me a little of Derry back home. The North's second city, and the natural centre of the Republican movement that I had once lived for. I was there for good reason. Recent events had given me a wobble, but I was back on track. That's how I deal with things. I make a plan and I follow it. Simple.

I parked in a multi-story lot and headed off on foot towards the town centre. It's much more urban than Beaconsfield with several shopping streets, a cinema, a couple of little theatres. There are no skyscrapers. Nothing above seven or eight storeys. Outside the centre are several churches, then a variety of housing areas. Some on the up-and-up, some not much more than slums.

The first part of my plan was to work out where any of my stuff might be. It didn't matter what I found first. Any of it would do. I wanted to get back to the source, then I could try and find the declaration, and ideally the cash too. The chances were that nobody would recognise at first what the poster was. They probably wouldn't know what to do with it. I figured that I had a small chance at finding my video player, maybe some of the CD's and videos even. All that mattered was getting a start on finding that declaration. I guessed that the only way two thieves would get an easy return on any of my stuff would be to pawn it. Simple way to remove it from any connection from them as well. Pilton was the only decent sized town nearby and somewhere that I knew had a few pawnshops. If they'd gone that route, they would have done it fast. A quick sale with no come back.

A search through the phonebook informed me that there were three in total. If I was wrong about it, I was no worse off. And I had no other place to start. I visited the first two stores and had a good rifle through them both. They each contained everything from jewellery to guns. Vinyl to hardcore porn. I didn't find anything that obviously belonged to me. I saw a few of the same CD's and became momentarily excited, but nothing about them convinced me that they were actually mine.

The third store was on the slightly rougher side of town. The shop was small and looked crammed, the main windowpane smeared with dirt. Displayed behind the glass were a great many things, including my poster from the 1916 Rising.

Chapter 6

Bingo.

I strolled past the window and got out my Marlboros to settle my rising nerves. I couldn't believe my luck. It's like when you're a kid and fancy a girl, ask her out and she says yes. Or when you're walking down the street thinking about someone and next thing you know you run into them. I smoked to the end of the block, puffing hard, working out what to do now. Then I threw the filter down, crushed it underfoot and headed purposefully back to the shop. I glanced at my poster in the window, then pushed open the grubby door. A little bell rang above my head. Inside was stuffy and stale with tobacco residue and dust. A well-built white guy in a grey vest, with tattoos covering his thick biceps, was lighting up a fresh Marlboro Red behind the counter. The small shop had nobody else inside. The man nodded to me, and I nodded back before pretending to take an interest in a rack of vinyl. He actually had a few good discs. But that was not what I was there for. I moved on to a rack of CD's and videos. Grouped together were a few of the same ones that I had lost. This time I reckoned they *were* mine. The scratches and remnants of sales labels were familiar. The man busied himself on his computer, ash cascading from his cigarette over the keyboard. I crossed to the other side of the store. There was an untidy pile of video recorders beside a couple of worn, half-strung guitars. I recognised the player on top and lifted it up to give it a once over. It had a couple of dents that looked the same, and a part ripped barcode on the side, just as I expected. It was mine.

"You lookin' anything in particular?" the man asked, raising his eyes above his computer screen.

I put on a half-smile and narrowed my eyes.

"Sort of, yeah," I said.

I stepped across to the counter. He got down off his stool and faced me. I'm a tall guy, but he had an inch on me and much thicker arms. I looked him hard in the eye until he looked away.

"Sort of, like, what?" He crushed the end out in an overflowing glass ashtray like he wanted to push the butt through it.

I licked my lips. "How much of your stock do you figure is stolen?"

He squinted at me and his whole face hardened. "What are you? A cop? Nothing's stolen in here."

"Now then, I know that's not true," I said, then sparked a cigarette of my own. "I reckon you know it's not true as well."

He continued to eye me suspiciously, "You law?"

"Do I look or sound like law?"

"Get the hell out of here then." His hoarse voice grew louder.

I ignored that. I swivelled and pointed across the store.

"That's my video player, some of my CD's, videos…" Then I clocked my CD player. A laugh escaped my throat. "And there's my flippin' CD player too."

I turned back to him.

"This is bull," he said. "I can vouch for all this stuff. Now get the hell outta here."

He reached under his counter for what I presumed was some form of deterrent. A baseball bat or a shotgun. I whipped my fist across and laid a hard right into his bulging arm. It was like punching a tree, but it was enough to send him off balance. I followed up with a right hook to his face. He recovered quickly and launched a sharp left hook to my cheek. It was like getting a kick from a mule. I stumbled backwards, dazed. He used the half-second to pull out a baseball bat underneath the counter, dart out from behind, and come at me. He took a swing. I managed to duck out of the way as he sent a fake Gibson Les Paul careering into a shelf stacked with crockery. Plates, cups and bowls shattered all around me. I squatted down and grabbed up a little china teacup.

Not ideal.

I spun around on my hunkers and tossed the little cup at his face like a frisbee. It landed square on his nose. Blood spurted. He staggered backwards, hands going to his busted snout. I threw myself at him. He barely moved. I sent a volley of punches into his big red face. He started to crumple. I snatched the bat from where it hung at his side and jabbed him hard in his stomach. He went down, pulling a rack of CDs on top of him. I kicked some of the debris away from my feet and loomed above him, the bat poised in a swing.

"Are you ready to have a conversation with me yet?"

Chapter 7

"Get your ass up off the floor," I said. "You're making the place look untidy."

I pulled over an ancient wooden chair and gestured with the bat for him to sit. With a weird expression on his face somewhere between anger, embarrassment and trying to still look tough, he somewhat awkwardly did as he was told.

"You're gonna be dead after this," he growled. "Ya know that?"

I whacked the bat down on the arm of the chair just beside his fingers. He flinched.

"Shut the hell up and do what you're told," I said evenly. "Right, you're going to give me every last bit of my stuff, asshole. I sincerely hope you reflect on your customer service skills after today."

"Take it. It's all crap anyways," he said sullenly.

"Is it?"

I took a half swing and cracked the bat off his right knee.

"Ow!" he shouted.

"What did I just say? The customer's always right."

"Just take your stuff and get outta my shop."

"So, it *is* my stuff then? That's progress. Now, were you going to mention what's in your front window?"

"What?"

I swung the bat back behind my shoulder.

"Alright, alright!" he said, raising a hand.

"My poster." I said, letting the bat swing gently at my side. "You bag all this stuff up and then I'll be on my way."

He licked his lips, looking like there was something he wanted to say.

"What?" I demanded.

"Take your stuff. I don't care. You say it's yours, then alright." His eyes took on a sly look. "The poster, though… I dunno if you know what it's worth, but I can sell it quick. Split the cash with you."

"Split it with *you*? You've a brass neck. I don't want to sell it. And if I did you could whistle for a split."

"I've got it up on eBay. You should see the amount of interest. Seriously."

eBay? It rang a bell. An online auction or something.

"What do you mean?"

Interest in it? My stomach gave a little flip. My hands felt sweaty as they clutched the bat tighter.

"Yeah. Bidders. I sell a lot there now. Especially weird old stuff. Lotta people have viewed it. It's gonna make some serious dollar."

"Show me," I said.

I let him get up and gave him a few yards of space to get himself sorted. He plugged in a couple of leads, booted up his computer screen again and a little box screamed like it was being strangled.

"Here, take a look," he said after a few minutes, clicking around on his cluttered desk with the mouse.

I stepped across, avoiding all the broken debris lying around under my feet. I leaned over and tried to make sense of what I was looking at. I spotted a small thumbnail of my poster and a bunch of figures and text around it.

"What am I looking at here? How many are interested in it?"

He squinted at the screen and made a few clicks with the mouse.

"So far there's thirty-five bids and over a hundred have viewed it."

Not good.

"Can you see where they're from. Where they live?" I said.

He made a few more clicks and let out a sigh. "From all over... er... some in the States, UK... a lot from Ireland."

Brilliant.

"Take it down. Take it the hell down from there."

He turned in his chair and looked up at me. "Yeah, but look at those bids..."

I swung and smacked the bat against a shelf behind him sending ornaments and assorted junk crashing all around. "I couldn't care less about what bids there are."

"Okay, okay!" He covered his head. "Stop! You're messing up my store."

25

"'The whole worl's in a state o' chasis."

I think the quotation was lost on him.

Just then the little bell rang, and an older couple began to walk in.

"We're closed," I shouted across. "Stock take."

They hastily retreated.

The shop-owner shot out a hand to the drawer underneath his keyboard. He flung it open. Grabbed for a black-gripped forty-five. I swivelled the bat and jabbed at the drawer with the end, trapping his fingers.

He squealed.

I gave his hand a light smack with the side of the bat for good measure, before letting him pull out his grazed and lobster-red knuckles.

It took him no time to take down the listing. I relieved him of his gun, discarded the bat and held the pistol on him while he went about bagging up my small stereo, my videos and CD's. I didn't bother with the knackered VHS player. Then he unhooked my framed poster and left it beside my pile of belongings.

He stood there panting a little. I kept the gun trained on him.

"That just leaves one thing. Tell me where you got this stuff from."

"Aww, come on, man...."

"I want a name."

His mouth tightened.

"Is this loaded?" I casually clicked the Glock's cartridge out and in again.

I pointed it at his left leg and closed one eye. He raised a protective hand. I rotated my arm and blasted a shot into the back of his computer screen. The bang was deafening and the small explosion following closely from the screen wasn't quiet either.

"Okay, okay! Jeeze. It's a guy called Lewis... Lewis Knight."

A plume drifted across from the destroyed computer in front of his eyes.

"Address?"

"I got it here," he said, gesturing to another table.

I let him go across and he began flicking furiously through a small green notebook.

He gave me the address. I gathered up my bags and tucked my poster under my arm.

"We'll make a good customer relations man out of you yet," I said, and dropped the gun into one of my bags. "Don't be telling anyone about this or I'll be back. Next time I'll crush your hand until your fingers all pop off, one by one. Then I'll shoot you in the face. Just try me."

I left. The bell did its *ting-a-ling* thing behind me as I headed quickly along the sidewalk with the hot afternoon sun on the back of my neck.

Chapter 8

I was dying for a drink. I went and dumped my stuff in the car on the other side of town and went off in search of a bar. I found somewhere dark and quiet. Their choices of libation were a little limited, but I was soon sitting with something claiming to be Irish stout and a clearly watered-down Jameson chaser.

Up on eBay. What the hell?

I wasn't particularly one for embracing the so-called modern age. I'd never owned a computer, but I had used one a couple of times. I didn't believe much that Y2K would cause all computers to crash, but I wished it would have happened right then. I'd no idea what risk was posed from my poster being up online, but the tiniest amount was too much. A hundred views was not a good start. There were people out there, intent on tracking me down. Intent on killing me at any cost. Those people would never stop. I know, because I used to be one of them.

I had joined the IRA in 1979. Neil Young had just put out *Rust Never Sleeps*. *The Empire Strikes Back* was about to be released into cinemas. The Troubles had been raging in my homeland for a decade already. I was twenty-five and had been on the fringes of the paramilitary movement but hadn't officially signed up.

British soldiers patrolled my streets. They beat and killed people from families that I knew. I wanted to be free. I wanted my people to be free. Joining seemed the right thing to do. Do I regret it now, knowing what I ended up doing on both sides of the conflict? If I'm honest, no. I can't imagine things happening any other way. How can you regret the path your life takes? It never seems there's all that much choice at the time. You're just a passenger in your own personal story. Do I regret the deaths I was involved in on both sides? If I'm really honest, also no. You can only be true to yourself. Whatever I've done, give or take, I've always done it for what I thought were the right reasons. I'm sure my former bosses in the IRA who were now fighting for peace don't regret what they did. No. They're just in a different place. Trying a different tack. It's only that I changed my own position about ten years earlier.

But what to do now? I at least had made progress in tracking down what had happened to my stuff. That didn't matter all that much. Maybe I would find the people who had my money too. The fact that I had potentially been exposed was all that really mattered. But if the IRA were now closer on my tail, that money sure would help. I couldn't let it go. It was the damn principle too. I necked the rest of my drinks and left the bar. Resolve was running through my bones again. Knowing what to do next was the only thing that ever calmed me at times like this. My life hadn't turned out all that great, maybe I was a fool to still trust myself.

As Beckett once said, "We all are born mad. Some remain so."

Ten minutes later I was back in my 1974 Hornet and sweeping along the freeway back towards Beaconsfield. The address I had been given for Lewis Knight was on the outskirts, a few miles outside of the town centre. It was late afternoon when I pulled up along the row of dilapidated bungalows on the West Side. I wound up my window, making the inside of the car instantly stuffy again. Humid doesn't begin to say it. A few kids played in the street outside, throwing a ball around. Further along the road a group of teens passed a joint back and forth, leaning against the fence of a boarded up house. The dandelion speckled lawn must have been near three feet high. I got out, careful to lock the car door, and patted the inside of my denim jacket where my new pistol rested snuggly. One for each hand if needs be. I swung open the rusted, half-attached gate and strode up the path, dodging the few cans and empty packets scattered about. The glass around the door was frosted and there was no bell. I peered over to what presumably was the living room window. A tattered net curtain hung behind the greasy glass, preventing any view of the interior. I gave the door my hardest Royal Ulster Constabulary-style knock.

It took about a minute before the door swung slowly backwards.

A stocky black guy in his early twenties looked back at me through hooded, heavy-set eyes.

"Hello, Lewis," I said, my voice even.

He shot me a questioning look and recognition flickered across his face.

"What you want?" he asked.

"You know what I want, you wee ballbag."

I pushed him hard backwards. I pushed him again, stepped inside and shut the door behind me. Suddenly he hurried away, limping as he did so. Beyond him, a dope haze hung in the air. A younger black kid was there, maybe nineteen, slumped on the worn sofa, honking on a doobie. He jumped up and I noted the roughly bound bandage around his left arm. I clocked a little snub-nosed pistol on the coffee table covered in empty bottles, rolling papers and an overflowing ashtray. I pulled out the Glock.

"Leave it," I said firmly to Lewis's retreating back.

"He's got a gun LJ," the kid on the sofa warned him.

Lewis stopped dead and turned his head. "Aww shit, man," he said to nobody in particular.

"Go and sit next to your buddy," I told him, gesturing the barrel towards the sofa.

Lewis sat beside his partner in crime. Both were wearing shorts and baseball caps. Lewis was in a tight black T-shirt and the other in a long grey vest. His knuckles were badly bruised. A hurley stick will do that to you. I sat down on the wooden stool on the other side of the table. I plucked the pistol from the table and dropping it into my jacket pocket.

"I'm starting quite the collection today."

Lewis eyeballed me with something approaching hatred.

On a small TV off to the side, a blurry pirated copy of *Fight Club* played silently.

"What d'ya want?" said the younger one, leaning forward in his seat. He looked very nervous.

"You know what I want. How's the arm?"

He looked down at his arm like he'd never seen it before.

"Don't tell him nothin'," Lewis said in a raspy voice.

"Shut up, if you value your knees" I said. Then looking at the younger guy, "What's your name? I've seen you about."

He looked at Lewis and Lewis shook his head.

Casually I got to my feet, grabbed the television set with one hand and flung it off its stand onto the ground with a crash. It lay there after a flash and a thin release of smoke.

"God-damn-it," Lewis said, his face all wrinkled up.

"Okay, okay," the other one said gesturing with his bandaged arm. "Brandon, I'm Brandon. I've delivered pizzas to your garage a couple times."

I nodded, placing him now.

"Shut up, man," Lewis hissed at him.

"No, *you* shut up." I pointed the gun in his general direction. He seethed. I went and sat back down.

"It's too late for that, Lewis," Brandon said, rolling his eyes. "He's in your crib, man."

Lewis tightened his jaw, then made a meal out of chewing on his lip.

"We took the guy's stuff, he's gonna be pissed," he said. Then he turned to me, "Listen... Mike, isn't it?"

"Michael."

"Listen, we thought you were away somewhere. Your car hadn't been out your place for a couple weeks."

"Oh, so sorry for the confusion," I said. Then, "How'd you know where I lived? You only delivered pizza to the garage I work at."

"We followed you a time or two."

"Shut up, man," Lewis said, punching him lightly on his good arm. "You two gonna start exchanging Christmas cards too?"

"I just want my money," I said.

Lewis blew out his cheeks sullenly and leaned back on the sofa. He reached for his half-smoked joint and lit it up.

"That'll be a bit of a problem," Brandon said.

"It wouldn't need to be. You two have already caused me enough problems."

Brandon sighed. "Listen, man. We ain't got it. Had to give most of it away."

"Shut up, Brandon," Lewis said, shoving him again.

"I'm not going to tell you to pipe down one more time," I said.

I got to my feet again. He cowered back, allowing a plume to escape from his mouth.

Brandon gave him a hard shove back, then turned to look at me.

"Give us a break, man. My cut ended up being like forty dollars."

"Forty dollars?" I half shouted. "Aside from what you pawned, there was already a ton of cash in my box."

31

"I know, I know," he said, looking fearful. Perhaps not just because of me.

"So, where's the rest?" I demanded.

They exchanged a look.

I pressed the gun against Lewis's right knee.

"What have you done with my money?"

Chapter 9

Less than half an hour later, Lewis was taped up to his chair with heavy gaffer roll. Brandon and I were about to leave. Both guns were in my pockets. After much reluctance, they had given me the name that would lead to my money. The threat of violence had been enough without needing to inflict any, which I was happy enough to have supplied if I had to. I think it might have been me telling them that I'd spotted an anthill outside and a bottle of maple syrup in their living room. Those two things plus a naked body could equal a lot of pain.

Once I had the name, I informed them that first I would be tying up Lewis, and second, Brandon would be accompanying me on my little trip. Neither had been very happy about that arrangement. But again, a few threats and waves of the gun had done the trick. Both were now scowling at me.

"Cheer up, fellas. It might never happen," I said and walked out the door.

I caught Brandon's expression change as he gave my gleaming beauty the once over.

"She's looking well, isn't she?" I opened the passenger door for him. "Get in."

Brandon shrugged and did as he was told.

"So, back out towards the big smoke, then? That's where this guy lives?"

Brandon didn't say anything, his face set hard.

"Is it where he lives?" I said.

He nodded.

"First stop, a drive through," I said, and gunned the engine.

"Why?"

"Because I'm half starved."

***

After I'd fuelled up on fast food, we carried on with our journey. We were headed to the home of one twenty-nine-year-old hood by the name of Isiah. Seemingly he was a local entrepreneur of sorts; drugs, theft, with a little prostitution on the side.

33

"So how come this guy has all my money?" I asked after stuffing the last of my fries into my mouth. Brandon took a slurp of the strawberry milkshake he had begrudgingly accepted after turning down something to eat. There's not many who offer to buy those who have robbed them a meal. Aside from the weathered look around his eyes, he almost looked like a child. His cap was pulled low over his brow, his mouth set.

"We owed him money. Well… mostly Lewis did," he said in between sips.

"He owed him the guts of a thousand dollars?" I shot him a look as we sped along the freeway.

Night was creeping in. A very yellowed moon was rising up behind us.

"Yeah. Well… I still got forty dollars and Lewis kept some back I guess… Expenses, or whatever. He lets me kip on his couch most nights," he added, almost apologetically.

"Forty bucks? I think you should think of getting yourself some new friends," I said.

Brandon looked out of the window, his face blank as he took another drink.

"Do you not have any family?" I asked.

"Nope," he said simply.

***

We ate up a few miles in silence.

If he wasn't up for talking, I sure as hell wasn't.

Eventually I asked, "So what kind of resistance am I looking at here?"

Lewis let out a muffled laugh. "What *resistance*?" He blew out his cheeks. "To Isiah being asked to hand over one large?" He shook his head and now returned to looking much older again.

"Okay if I smoke?" he asked.

I raised my hand with the Marlboro in it and shrugged. He pulled out a pre-rolled blunt and sparked it up.

I frowned and wound down the window. "Jesus, you sure you want that before going in here?"

He blew out a plume of grey smoke and offered his own shrug. "My tolerance is pretty good," he said.

I took a last draw of my own and ground the butt out in the overflowing built in plastic ashtray. I noticed Brandon rub at the bandage on his arm.

"That giving you much trouble?" I said.

"What? No, it's fine." He looked away.

I nodded.

"It's the next left off of the exit from the freeway," he said.

I slowed down and made the turn and he gave me a few more directions over the next couple of miles. Even with the window down, the car stank of weed.

"Seriously, though. How many guys you expect him to have in the place?"

Brandon momentarily closed his eyes and let out a little sigh. "I guess there's usually two or three others in there with him. Could be more." He shrugged again.

"Okay." I nodded.

I couldn't tell what he was thinking. He looked... kind of resigned. I respected that. You make your choices, you take what follows. At Lewis's place he had held up his hands, took responsibility. Didn't muck me around. Now he was trying to get me my money and I guess he imagined that one way or another, things weren't going to work out that well for him. And all this for forty dollars. Or maybe he was doing it because I had all the guns.

"These guys don't mess around, Michael," he said quietly. "They'll all be packin'."

It was the first time he'd used my first name and it made me side-eye him.

"It'll be fine," I said. "Just do what I tell you."

"Who you think you are? Rambo?"

"Yeah, something like that," I said.

There was the faint hint of a smile somewhere underneath that cap.

"I thought you were a mechanic?"

"Not even. I paint cars sometimes. But I can do other things too."

He told me where to stop further down the street and I pulled in and killed the lights.

The internal light flicked on in the Hornet and illuminated his face for a moment. He looked very nervous and began rubbing his hands along his legs. He turned to look at me.

"Even if this goes... I dunno... some ways good for you, which it probably won't, where does that leave me?" Brandon asked.

My stomach gave a little flip. I didn't want to put this kid in danger, but he brought the trouble to *my* door. I put on my game face. "I'm sorry, Brandon, but that's not my problem. But sure, it'll be grand. C'mon, let's go."

He got out slowly as I patted the pistol in my pocket. I pulled out my Colt M19 from the glove compartment and shoved it down the back of my jeans. There was Isiah's gun still in there too. The way I was going, The NRA would offer me free membership.

Isiah's place was on a similar looking street to where Lewis lived. But it was maybe two times the size and it had a newly built five-foot wall surrounding it. It was mid terrace, but on either side the houses were bricked up. I wondered if they had been asked to leave- politely or otherwise. We began to make our way along the sidewalk towards it. Two large black men blocked the front door, smoking and sharing some kind of a joke. Their faces hardened in unison as their hungry eyes watched us approach.

We were maybe ten yards from them now.

I gave Brandon a half-smile and quoted some Beckett, "I can't go on. I'll go on."

He gave me a quizzical look. I quickened my pace and Brandon fell into step alongside me.

"Lads, lads," I said jovially, stepping up to the pair of big black guys out front. "Is himself home?"

"What?" The guy on the left squinted at me.

"I need to speak with Isiah," I said, fixing him with a stare, lowering my voice.

"You got an appointment?" asked the heavy on the right, with a mean half smile.

"No, sorry. I guess I missed his clerical staff when I tried to book a slot."

"He's busy," said the first.

I shook my head and gave them a pained expression. "I'm afraid that just won't do, buddy. Me and my friend Brandon here need to have a word with him quite urgently."

I gestured to Brandon, and he looked down at the ground.

The first guy looked at Brandon, then at the other, then nodded his head back towards the door. Silently, the second guy pulled the storm door open and went inside.

"Glorious weather, ay?" I said, beaming at the first one.

He said nothing. He looked back at me like he thought I'd escaped from my carers. I noticed Brandon roll his eyes beside me.

After a minute or two of deafening silence, the second one came out again and nodded at his mate before looking straight at me. "You can both go in. But you leave any weapons with us. Got it?"

They both eyed us with even more suspicion.

"I ain't got nothin'," Brandon volunteered, raising his arms and allowing himself to be patted down.

"Now you," said the first guy.

"You're not putting your hands on me. Not until you buy me a cocktail or three first," I said. "I've got a gun, right here," I patted my pocket. "But if I give it to you, how do I know you won't go trying to take my bus money off me as well?"

The first one curled his large mouth into something resembling a smile. "I guess you'll just have to hope I don't."

"Well, I suppose you do have a trustworthy face."

I reached inside my pocket slowly and the second guy shot his own hand quickly into his inside pocket.

"Steady there quick-draw," I said.

I eased out the gun by its barrel and offered the grip.

The first guy snapped it from my hand. It disappeared into one of his deep pockets.

"After you, honky," he said, then flashed me a wide, mirthless smile.

***

We were led down a narrow corridor into a large room that had been knocked out of two smaller ones. The theme was something approaching *modern trendy* by way of *junkie chic*. It was an odd mix. The walls were painted a dark purple and were lit by four thin free-standing chrome lights. Some kind of low-bass rap music pumped from a large subwoofer speaker off to the side. I've no idea what it was, but it was terrible. There was a large bar built into one corner with a triangle of large mirrors behind it. The rest of the room contained several leather sofas, a coffee table and a huge TV screen. Seated in a reclining La-Z-Boy, was Isiah. He looked tough, confident. He was tall and athletic, closer to the build of a long-distance runner than a boxer. He wore black shorts and an LA Lakers vest, tying in with the huge Lakers poster framed on the wall behind him.

Brandon stood off to my left, trying not to fidget with his watch. Our two escorts took up their positions on either side of the door we had just entered through. I turned for a moment and gave them a closer inspection. The larger one looked to be carrying underneath his top. Incongruous with the rest of his attire, he wore bright red sneakers. His cohort, older but smaller, also looked to be packing. He simply worse a traditional pair of steel toe caps on his feet. I was the only one in the room that had any hair to speak of. And I was by far the oldest too.

Isiah held a blunt loosely in one hand, squinting at me. He wiped his other arm across his nose and sniffed. He got quickly to his feet, a ball of nervous, dangerous energy. He walked towards me. I saw beads of sweat on his forehead, some dripping down towards his bum-fluff stubble. He was on something, that was for sure. Something more than the weed. Coked to the eyeballs, I thought.

"Welcome..." he said theatrically.

He grinned widely. I wished he hadn't. His teeth were a worse set than you'd get at a bottle bank. Then he placed a thumb and forefinger together in the air like a conductor. Then he pointed at me.

"Michael," I said.

"Michael," he said, narrowing his eyes and then looking across at Brandon. "And you, nigga. I met you one time recently didn't I?"

"Yeah... with Lewis," Brandon said, his voice low and cracked.

"Yes," Isiah said serpent-like. He pulled hard on his blunt, then blew out a plume into the air. He took another step towards me, shook himself and let out a little, "Woo." It made me think of Rick Flair. Then he set his eyes on me again and was suddenly very still.

"So... What you doing here whitey? What you want? I don't know you, and I'm here wantin' to have me a sweet sherry or something and a chill, y'know?"

"I won't keep you too long, then," I said. "There's a *business* issue I need to make you aware of."

He took a slow pull on the number and raised an eyebrow. "A business issue you say. Go on, then."

I gave him a little nod and glanced behind me at the two goons before continuing.

"Young Brandon here got himself mixed up in a little trouble. Some trouble with your buddy, Lewis."

"Boys will be boys," Isiah said and chuckled to himself.

"That may be true. Thing is, they broke into my home. They stole a lot of my stuff. I'm not so worried about that. But they took a thousand dollars of mine, then they gave it to you."

Isiah had gradually broken into another smile, though his eyes remained cold. He shot a look at Brandon, chewed his lip and gave his head a little shake.

"Motherfucker," he said under his breath.

"So, you can see how I have a problem," I added.

Isiah took a final pull, then threw the butt at an ashtray on the table, it glanced off it and spilling ash as it skidded across the glass.

"Lemme get this straight," he said in a hushed voice, clasping his hands together, "These two niggas rob you, some of the money ends up with me, and you reckon that means I owe your ass?"

I stared back, arms at my sides, rigid. I towered over him. "Yeah, that's about the height of it."

He looked around me exaggeratedly at his guys, then broke into a fit of laughter. He shook his head, still laughing, doubled-up.

"Well, damn," he said under his breath.

He lashed out his right arm suddenly and landed a hook to my face. I took it as my head flipped back. My feet stayed planted where they were. Isiah looked disappointed.

"Do I take that as a no, then?" I said evenly.

"Yeah, you take that as a fucking no, nigga," he said jabbing a finger in the air at me.

"I want my money," I said again.

"I ain't no bank, man! You even change money at a bank, you don't go lookin' for your same notes back."

"I guess I'll just have to take it, then."

Beside me, Brandon looked sicker by the second.

"Take it, you say?" Isiah spat. "You believe this guy?" He said looking past me again at his sidekicks. Then he moved to sucker punch me. But I was quick. My left hand shot out and gripped his outstretched arm around his wrist. My other hand came around too. I braced his arm and with one quick movement, snapped his wrist bone. There was an audible crack. It even made me wince. He yelped. I let go and he jumped away howling. The two at the back immediately began moving toward me and fumbling in their pockets.

Brandon stared at me with his mouth hanging open. He moved further to the side. I nipped to the table at my left and grabbed the large glass ashtray. As I scooped it up, I flung it towards Red Sneakers. It caught him on the top of his head. He went down. Toe Caps made a move for his gun, but I pulled mine from behind my back and cocked it.

No better sound than that.

He stopped what he was doing. His hand came out again, empty.

"Never piss off an Irishman," I said.

Chapter 10

Five minutes later I had two guns in my pockets and my own in my right hand. Isiah and his two mates were now all seated on the sofa, looking like the worst chat show of all time. They emanated misery, Isiah worst of all. He clutched his bent arm, breathing heavily. His face had taken on a scarlet tinge. Red Sneakers had a huge, nasty-looking bump forming on the top of his forehead. Isiah glared at Brandon beside me. Brandon didn't look anywhere in particular, but I thought he was about to vomit.

"It's simple," I said to them. "Any one of you move and you're getting a bullet. Maybe two."

I took a step back, turned to Brandon, grabbed him by the arm and swung him around to speak to him quietly out of earshot.

"You alright?"

He looked at me open-mouthed, his nose flaring.

"Okay, stupid question," I said.

"You're gonna get me shot," Brandon said. "Maybe not tonight. But I'm dead."

He swallowed hard and his eyes moistened. I felt a tightening knot in my stomach.

"Listen, I'll work something out." I rubbed the handle of the gun across my sweating brow. "We just need to get my money and get out of here. That's first, okay?"

He chewed his lip.

"Okay?" I said again.

"Alright, damn."

"If I give you one of these guns, can I trust you to hold it on them?"

"I don't want it."

"Well, I need you to for a wee minute. I can't get my money and keep an eye on all three of them at the same time."

He sighed.

I pulled out the Glock and offered it to him.

He closed his eyes, then grabbed it from me. With apparent muscle memory he checked the rounds, flicked it closed and aimed it at an angle towards the ground. I nodded.

We turned together and held the guns on them.

I hoped Brandon wouldn't turn his on me.

"So now you're going to give me my thousand dollars," I said.

Isiah narrowed his eyes, hooded and bloodshot. Whatever he had taken had long since worn off.

"I don't owe you nothin', man," he said writhing a little where he sat, his voice high.

I strode up to him and pushed my gun against his temple.

"Yeah, you do, fella."

***

Minutes later and Isiah had instructed Red Sneakers on how to open his safe, which was concealed in the base of the bar. He came out with a large black tin, about two feet square. He retrieved the key from behind an optic, opened it and set it on the table next to me. He went and sat back down.

"Keep that on them," I said to Brandon.

I set my gun on the table and began pulling out huge stacks of bills. Twenties, fifties, hundreds.

"You know you're going to be a dead man," Isiah called across the room.

"Pipe down," I said.

"I got friends."

"Good for you," I said, going back to my counting. "Hopefully one of them's a doctor. Now shut your bake."

I had a pile of crumpled bills to the sum of one thousand dollars in a pile. It was a little under half of what was in the tin.

"I'm just taking my grand. That's about what you owe, never mind the inconvenience. You can keep the rest of your *hard-earned* cash from cake sales or whatever you gentlemen are into."

"You won't last the night," Isiah said.

I nodded to Brandon, and we moved towards the door as one.

"If I have to come over there again, you'll have no wrist left to jerk off with. The three of you stay put until you hear us drive away. Just give me a reason to shoot you. And don't think about coming after us later. I'll be ready. And I won't be as courteous next time."

I gave my hardest stare and turned on my heel.

Once we were up the hall, through the door and had slammed it behind us, we both broke into a sprint. There were a few groups of youths huddled about who all turned and eyed us with suspicion. We ran on towards the Hornet. Behind us the front door flew open. I turned to see the three sofa surfers run into the street, each with a pistol in their hand, even Isiah. His other hand was cradled against his body.

"Get in!" I yelled.

We scrambled into the car, I gunned the motor and threw it into drive. The tyres screeched. I heard sets of feet thundering towards us. Then there was the pop-pop of gunshots echoing in the street. Bullets whizzed past the car. My exquisitely maintained AMX Hornet faced our assailants. If it took one single hit, I'd be *really* furious. We took off, lurching towards them, twenty metres away. Isiah struggled with his busted arm on the sidewalk. The other two were now stood in the middle of the road aiming their guns at me. Thankfully nothing had hit my beauty as yet. If it did, none of them would be walking away. They both fired another round each as I swung the wheel hard to the left. Brandon near flew off his seat. I mounted the curb and sped up. One of the huddles broke up and all dived over a fence as I swept past them. Skidding near to the two gunmen, I swerved and put two wheels back on the blacktop. A huge smile split my face when I tore past them, inches away from Red Sneakers. He landed clumsily on his butt once again. He knocked down his buddy too as we raced away. I stomped the pedal to the floor. The mighty, finely tuned engine turned over and roared its approval. It paid sometimes to be mates with a mechanic.

"Yeah!" I shouted, elated. I banged a hand off the wheel. We accelerated off along the road.

"Brilliant," Brandon said dryly. He shook his head and strapped on his seat belt.

Chapter 11

"Pass us the red sauce there, young Brandon."

He set down his mug and passed the grease-stained bottle across the Formica tabletop. We were in an all-night diner, ten miles from home, a popular stop with truckers. The five other customers inside looked to all be of that profession. I forked up a rasher from my large portion of bacon and over easy eggs. It tasted good. It tasted flipping great in fact.

"You sure you don't want anything to eat?"

"I'm fine," Brandon said, sipping at his coffee, half-doused with cream.

"Suit yourself." I took a large slug of my cup of *Joe*.

The warmth felt good, sliding down my throat after the bacon and eggs.

"You never hungry?" I said between mouthfuls.

"You never *not* hungry?"

We sat in silence for a few minutes, an old track by The Meters playing quietly in the background. My eyes fell on the grill chef; sweaty and animated, flipping and prodding behind the counter.

"Good grub," I said.

Brandon stared out of the window into the darkness. I flicked through a newspaper left abandoned in the booth. Bill Clinton was waxing lyrical about some new liberal laws to be approved. His PR campaign had been on overdrive since his disastrous affair scandal. Shagging your secretary in the Oval Office and lying about it didn't play so well with the electorate. One of the main international news stories was from back home. Eamon Collins, the so-called IRA *supergrass*, had been tracked down and murdered. He was infamous for authoring the autobiographical *Killing Rage*, detailing his time working with the Brits against the IRA, much like I had done. That was the last thing I wanted to read about. I needed no reminding that the IRA did not let sleeping touts lie. I folded the paper back up.

Brandon still stared out the window as if I wasn't there. I supposed I'd leave him for a few more minutes. The kid would have plenty on his mind. It'd been an eventful night. I finished my food, took a sip of water to take the edge off my salt-infused tongue and returned to my coffee. Almost on cue, a waitress topped up my mug. I thanked her and returned to our silent reverie. The adrenalin and relief had long been dumped and it was gradually being replaced by anxiety.

I'd got my money back, but had it been worth it? I only had a few hundred dollars in my checking account, so I certainly needed it, particularly if things took a bad turn. But had I brought more trouble with it? Sure, but what else was I meant to do?

I took another slug of my fresh and piping coffee. It was pretty good, but I wished it was whiskey. I dug out my packet, offered one to Brandon, but he shook his head. I took a long drag. It felt good. Nicotine coursed through me, but it only made me feel more on edge. The point of this was to calm the nerves. I sneaked a glance at Brandon. He looked like a little boy again. A scared little boy, trying his best to hide it. I'd brought a lot of trouble to his door, but I hadn't asked for this. My eyes fell on his bandaged arm. God damn it. He was the one that robbed me! Why did I feel so guilty?

"I appreciate what you did tonight," I said in a low voice.

He met my stare and shrugged.

"You could have thrown in with them, but you didn't."

He shrugged again. "You were the one with the gun."

That was true. I took another few draws and checked out the window. All was quiet. Night was fully here now.

Brandon was looking at me. "You can handle yourself, man," Brandon said.

"Yeah."

Brandon looked out the window again.

"Still," I continued. "Your part in it didn't go unnoticed. You had no right breaking into my place, and God knows it's given me a hell of a lot of grief, but you went some way in making it right."

"Oh, well gee, I'm so glad," he said sullenly.

"C'mon now, Brandon. I didn't ask you to rip off my house."

He blew out his cheeks. "Well, we're both screwed now. I stay in this town and I'm dead."

"C'mon, catch yourself on. That's not true."

"Isn't it? You don't know Isiah."

"We'll go and let Lewis out and we'll all have a chat. I'll work something out."

"Whatever, I'm going outside for a smoke."

"You can do that in here."

"A *smoke*," he said, and got up and left.

I watched him walk out. He pulled out a number just beyond the glass and was soon puffing away.

He looked panicked.

I squirmed in the booth. This was ridiculous. I was the bloody victim here.

But telling myself that still didn't make me feel any better.

***

Ten minutes later and we were back in the warm comfort of my car and heading back towards town. It didn't look like conversation was on the cards, so I rifled in the side pocket for a CD to put on. I slotted in *Dirty Mind* by Prince. The scuzzy synths and trebly drums kicked in. I sped up to around eighty on the freeway, feeling a little better again. After a few minutes I noticed Brandon's body almost imperceptibly move to the music.

"Good, isn't it?"

"What?" He seemed to be miles away. "Oh, yeah, sure."

"Early Prince. So funky."

"Oh, so I'll dig it 'cause I'm black?"

"Aww shut up, I think you'll like it 'cause it's damn great."

"It's okay," Brandon said. He flicked both shoulders in a shrug, then cracked the window and began on another joint.

"Better than his new stuff, that's for sure." I said. I fumbled around in one of the dash compartments with one hand on the wheel, searching for a light. Brandon passed me his. "And what's with all that symbol nonsense he does now? God's sake."

Brandon nodded, holding in a mouthful of weed before expelling it through the window. He didn't seem in any mood for my musical small talk. We listened in silence through the rest of the record as highway turned to fields, then to the rural town.

When we were five minutes from Lewis's place, I could see Brandon noticeably tense up. I stopped Prince mid-sentence, in the process of commanding us to *Party Up*.

It wasn't really the right mood anyway.

"If I've got this right, then it's Lewis who owes all the money to Isiah in the first place," I said gently.

Brandon's eyes fell on me. This time his voice wasn't so much accusatory, just sad. "Yeah, but it was me who just held a gun on him and took *his* money."

There wasn't much I could say to that.

We drove on in more silence. I made a few turns, then swung into the road and parked up outside Lewis's place. I killed the engine and looked towards Brandon, the seat making a squelching sound as I did.

"We'll go inside, untie Lewis and talk this thing through. Work it all out, okay?"

Brandon shrugged once again. He was going to wear those shoulder joints out.

"Alrighty then," I said.

The problem was, I had absolutely no idea how to work things out for him.

I followed behind Brandon as he traipsed up the steps and unlocked the door with his key. We went inside. The single lamp was still burning in the corner of the living room. There was a foul smell of stale tobacco and weed in the air. But there was something else too.

Brandon uttered a little gasp and stopped stock still. I moved around him to see.

Lewis was dead.

Chapter 12

He had been beaten about the face and was still tied up. There was a bullet hole in his left knee. But those things hadn't killed him. It was the bullet that had entered his skull and blasted the top half of it against the wall behind him.

"Jesus," I said, turning around, hoping to shield Brandon from some of it.

He was staring past me, open mouthed, very pale.

"Don't look at him," I said.

Brandon continued to stare. His feet were rooted to the floor. I walked towards him, put an arm on his shoulder and tried to turn him around.

"Get the hell off me!" He pushed me away. "This is *your* fault."

I raised my hands and backed off, bumping into the coffee table.

Brandon walked to the wall, steadying himself with a hand against it. I think he was crying a little.

I pulled out my gun and went off to check the kitchen. Nothing. The backdoor was locked. Nobody was in the backyard. I went and did a sweep through the little house. Clear. I pocketed my gun and headed back into the living room. Brandon was now in the chair in the corner, his head down, smoking. His eyes were wide, red and filled with fear. I allowed my brain to shift through gears and try to make sense of what had happened. My exhaustion from the day needed set to the side. I needed it to be clear, I tried to think through everything properly. To zoom out and try and gain some perspective. After several years of relative calm, the last few days had been an assault on the senses. But at least I had previous experience to fall back on. A build-up of reserves.

I crossed over to Lewis and inspected the scene properly. It was grizzly. He'd been beaten badly. I pulled up his T-shirt. His torso was badly bruised too. I knelt down and examined the bullet hole in his knee. There wasn't a mass of blood. His heart hadn't been given much time to continue pumping blood around his body. The head shot must have come very soon afterwards. God.

"Why?" came Brandon's voice from behind me. "Lewis was tied up. He didn't take Isiah's money. They must have seen that. Why kill him?" His voice cracked.

I got back onto my feet and walked over to him.

"Come into the kitchen for a minute. Come on, you need to get out of here."

He absently allowed me to lead him to the kitchen next door. We sat down on two old wooden chairs. Brandon's blunt had developed a huge cliff edge of ash, which then disintegrated, fell and spread in a dark flurry across the tabletop.

"I'm not sure that this was Isiah's doing," I said quietly. "I don't think he'll try anything tonight, not in the shape they were in."

"Who did it, then?"

I met his stare.

"Somebody else." I looked past him at the grim scene next door.

"Wha'd'ya mean?"

I puffed away, then licked my lips. I made a decision.

"Okay, I'm going to level with you." My voice felt heavy. "Nobody knows about this. Okay?"

He looked quizzically at me. "So what? Who am I gonna tell anything to?"

"I don't know for sure. I might have this all wrong. But I think this is about something else. About *me*. Hold on a sec."

I took my gun back out, went next door and checked through the blinds.

All was quiet.

Not a creature was stirring, not even a mouse… nor a hitman.

I walked through, checked out the back window, sat back down and set my gun on the table by my right hand.

"There's people who have been after me for a long time."

"What? What people? From Ireland?"

"Yeah. That's why I came here. That poster you two stole, it was rare. Very rare. And it has a link to me. That ass-hat in the pawn shop already had it up on eBay. It'd been viewed all over the world."

"You think it got back to the people who are looking for you?"

"Yeah… maybe."

Brandon ground out his smoke and immediately hit up another one. His hand shook as he lit it, but there was more colour in his face now. "That's gotta be a stretch. It makes more sense if it was Isiah's crew, surely."

"It still might be. But I don't know."

Brandon blinked back a few tears and dabbed his face roughly with his sleeve. "Why did they have to kill him?" Brandon said. His voice sounded far away.

"If it was Isiah, I really don't know. Dead men don't earn money back that they owe you. Isiah's pride may well have been hurt, but he's a businessman after all. Lewis didn't really do anything to him. If it was the other guys, it would make more sense. The beating would be to get information from him. Maybe my address, anything he knew about me. Kneecappings are common back home. Not many people lie after you shoot out one of their knees."

Brandon winced, but I continued on, "It's all well and good threatening someone with a gun. It can *really* discourage a lie if you've already shot them once. I'm sorry. I don't want it to be this either. I didn't want for your friend to get hurt. But I didn't ask to be robbed."

"But why kill him?" Brandon said softly.

"Once they were sure, they didn't need him anymore. Didn't matter to them." That came out more glib than I meant it to.

"Hell," Brandon whispered, putting his head in his hands, "So, they just off him?"

"It's a loose end. These guys are professionals."

Brandon started breathing heavily. He was in shock.

"It's alright. It'll be alright Brandon. I'm a professional too. I'll handle it. If it's them, I know how they think. I know what to do." I gripped his shoulder. "But it might not be them."

The problem wasn't that I didn't know who had done this.

That was a problem, certainly, but that could wait until later.

The problem was I didn't actually know what to do either.

Brandon's face contorted and he swung his head back like he was going to wail or something. But instead, he spoke very quietly again.

"It don't change much, whoever they are. Lewis is dead and we're dead."

"We're still breathing, kid. The night is young. First thing's first. We gotta get away from here. Whoever they are, they might come back."

Lewis ran a hand over his sweating brow.

"Have you got one of those mobile phones?" I asked.

"No. I got a pager, though."

I shook my head. "No good. I don't want to use the phone here either. We need to get to a payphone. C'mon, let's get going," I stood. "You want to grab a few things?"

Brandon got up from the chair like an old man, went off for a couple of minutes, then filled a bag.

I stood where I was, inhaled, and tried to formulate our next steps.

"All set?" I asked when he came back along the corridor.

He nodded glumly. "Michael, who are they exactly?"

"If I'm right. It's the IRA."

"Like... the Irish terrorists?"

I nodded. "A hit squad."

Brandon bowed his head.

***

We cautiously made our way across to the car. The night was humid, the moon bright and bold. It was around one in the morning. Nobody was on the street. We hustled inside and I locked the doors. My pulse quickened as I switched on the lights and put the AMX into drive. I hadn't much of a plan. No idea where to go. Where would they look for us? I didn't know. So, I changed things up and headed east. If they had come for me, I wanted to at least put fifteen or twenty miles between us tonight. If I didn't know where I was going, they sure of hell wouldn't either. After about forty minutes, I turned off the highway and found a row of shops all closed up for the night. There were two payphones outside. One had the phone handset ripped out of it. Both were covered in graffiti. I hoped the second one was in service.

I killed the lights.

"You wait here and keep an eye out. I'll make a call, if this phone actually works."

"Who are you ringing?"

"Somebody I hope might help."

51

I got out and jogged across a patch of scorched grass and over to the booth. I closed myself inside. It stank of sweat and piss. I pulled out the receiver and wiped the earpiece on my sleeve. Thankfully there was a dial tone. I shoved in a clatter of quarters and dialled the number from memory. I listened to a series of pips and then a click.

"Hello, switchboard," said a male English voice.

"Hello. I need you to put me through to a department."

"Do you know the department you want?" the voice asked. The pre-arranged system didn't appear to have changed.

"Oxford Freight and Delivery."

"I'll try that number for you now."

The line went silent. I worried that it had been disconnected. Thirty seconds later there was another click and the sound of somebody clearing their throat.

"Hello? Oxford Freight."

"Hi, I need to speak with my er… my handler." I was unsure if there was another stage in the rigmarole that I was forgetting.

"Is there a reference number?" This accent hailed from the south of England, I surmised.

"A reference…? I haven't had to call in for quite a while."

"A reference *name* perhaps?" The polite tone became a little impatient.

"Oh." Now I understood. "Cortez."

I heard him clickety-click on a keyboard. His breathing sounded loud through the earpiece.

"You haven't called in for several years, is that correct?"

"Yeah."

He rattled out a few more clicks. "Are you on a secure line?"

"Yeah, I think so. It's a public payphone. A random one, I haven't used it before."

"Okay. Please confirm your name then. Your *original* name."

"It's… Michael Walker." It'd been so long since I had uttered my own name, it felt strange on my lips.

"Alright, Mr Walker. How can I help you?"

"I need to speak with somebody, urgently. Is Kate Greene still there?"

"Ms Greene is still with us, yes, but she has finished for the day."

"Yeah, maybe she has, but I need you to get her for me."

"I suggest you ring back in the morning, sir. Sometime after eight-thirty, Greenwich Mean Time," he said a little sourly.

"No. I need you to ger her *now*. She's my handler. And it's an emergency."

"I can put you through to the relevant duty officer…"

"No, get me Kate," I said.

I heard him sigh and go at his keyboard again. "It really has been quite a long time since we've heard from you. It would be most unusual to contact our officers out of hours to…"

"Aye, I know. And I've told you, this is an emergency. Just put in the flippin' call, would you?"

"I will try, *sir*. Hang up and stay by the phone," he said crisply.

"Thank you. Do you need the number here?"

"No, we've got your number." He hung up on me.

I slammed the receiver down.

"Wanker."

Brandon got out of the car with a joint in his mouth and slowly crossed towards me.

"Any luck?" he asked.

"Maybe. Hopefully they'll ring me back soon. Listen… is there anyone you need to phone?"

Brandon exhaled a long thin cloud of dope. He shook his head. "No."

I felt my eyes narrow, "You sure, nobody?"

Brandon cast his eyes to the ground. He looked a little defensive. "No. I lived mostly with Lewis. I still got a mom, but I 'ain't seen her since I was little."

I leaned back against the outside of the booth. "Who raised you?"

"My grandma."

"She's not around anymore?"

"No."

We sat in silence, each casting occasional gazes towards the box. A lorry trundled by nosily in the distance along the intersection. There was brief laughter and a few shouts from somewhere a few streets away. Other than that, nothing.

Brandon shuffled his feet. "Y'know, I got some money of my own. I got places I could crash at. I don't need to be hanging with you."

I looked up at him. He had regained his composure somewhat, but there was a new quiet sadness about him. Almost as if he'd resigned himself to his lot; his lot being hopelessness. I didn't really believe he had anywhere to go. It seemed to me he just needed to make like he did. A pride thing, maybe. I knew plenty about that. The truth was, I didn't mind having him around anyway.

He absently tugged at his bandage.

"I'm sure you got places you could be, Brandon. But we don't know what we're dealing with yet. It's best if we stay together while we work out what to do. Yeah?"

"Yeah, okay. Just a day or two maybe. I've... I've never been in a thing like this before."

"We don't have to get engaged or anything." I smiled at him.

He gave a little laugh. It was the first time I had heard one from him.

I took a step towards the booth and looked inside. Checked that the receiver was fully down.

"Who is it you called?"

"Huh?" I walked back towards him. Checked my watch. In five or six hours the sun would be up.

"The call, man. Who is it that might help us?"

I sighed and pulled out another cigarette. I needed to cut down. Now wasn't the time.

"It's complicated. There's a lot of history. A long story."

"Looks like I've got the time. C'mon. You know just 'bout everything there is to know about me already. Least you could tell me is why these guys are on your ass."

I closed my eyes momentarily and nodded.

"Okay then, but just the abridged version for now. I'm tired and the night's not through yet." I took a long drag, then exhaled slowly. "For a while I... I worked for the British government."

He cocked his head like a spaniel. "What... like a spy?"

I guffawed. "No... Well, in a way, I suppose... Yeah."

"Like James Bond?" A smile crept along the edges of his mouth.

"No, not like bloody James Bond. Can you see me sipping martinis and criss-crossing the globe?"

"No… not really. Though seems you've already gone half-way round the world."

That was true enough.

"I was what they call an *asset* for a time. I'm not now. That's why I'm thousands of miles away."

"You worked for the British, but you're Irish, right? How's that work?"

"That's where the issue lies."

"These guys want to nail you just because you worked for the British? Because you're Irish?"

"Listen son, the IRA killed a lot of people just for working for the Brits; cops, lawyers, even flippin' maintenance men."

"Damn."

"Yeah."

This was all very surreal. It felt stranger than anything Beckett might have come up with. I'd hidden all of this for so long. But here I was, telling all to some kid who had robbed me.

"But they don't usually go looking for them halfway 'round the world, do they?" he asked.

Brandon threw down the end and then popped a stick of gum in his mouth. I could see his mind working things out. He was young and he'd had a rubbish start in life, but he wasn't stupid.

"No, not so much. They don't usually do that. The problem is… I used to be one of them."

He stopped chewing abruptly. "You were in the IRA?"

I nodded.

A sharp, shrill ring cut through the quiet of the night, killing our conversation dead. We both turned towards the box. My heart instantly started to race again. I hurried over, pushed back the door and lifted the receiver.

"Hello?"

"Hello, Michael."

Chapter 13

"Hi, Kate."

"Long time, no hear. You don't phone, you don't write." She gave a throaty laugh.

Her voice sounded just as it always had. To me it was somewhere between Helen Mirren and Mary Poppins. But on the sexy side. She'd been my handler through all the years that I worked for them. We had spoken many, many times, but I had never once set eyes on her. I knew she was about my age, but little else. Even that might not have been true. I always pictured her as being an attractive brunette, slender, with blue eyes. For all I know she was blonde, thirty stone and had the face of a moose.

"Yeah, I'm sorry Kate. I'm not really one for social calls."

"I'm told it's important. Important enough to call me away from my supper. One at which I am hosting."

It was hard to tell if she was taking the piss or not.

Brandon gave me a look then ambled off back towards the car. There was something questioning in his look. Maybe it was because he now knew that I had once been a terrorist. Or maybe it was because I had betrayed them. Maybe it was all sorts of things.

"I'm sorry to interrupt your soiree, but some people are trying to kill me, Kate."

"Habit of a lifetime, Michael. What's happened?" she asked, unfazed.

I laid out the nuts and bolts of the last few days: the robbery, the poster, the pawn shop, Brandon, Isiah, Lewis. It was a lot.

There was a long pause. It sounded like she was swallowing something. Probably a mouthful of expensive Sauvignon.

"Well, you have been busy, haven't you, Michael?

"Yeah. So, what do you think?"

"I think it was unlucky you were burgled. I think it was bloody stupid you kept that poster. I think it was even more bloody stupid that you went looking for it."

She always had shot from the hip.

"Come on, what was I meant to do? Especially once I knew the poster was gone. I was trying to nip things in the bud. And I needed my money back."

"And how did that work out for you?"

I chewed my lip. There was no point in getting shirty with her. People don't usually do you favours after you tell them to go to hell.

"Well, I got my money back."

"Yes, but in the process, you exposed yourself more than you had to."

"If I hadn't done anything, then thousands more might be viewing that poster online right about now."

"Perhaps," she said.

"It is what it is. So, will you help me? I need pulled out of here, Kate."

"Help you how, Michael?" She spoke a little stiffly. "Pull you out?" There was the hint of an incredulous laugh. "There's been a burglary. There's been a gang murder. That murder might not have anything to do with you, necessarily. I would tell someone in your position to go to the local authorities."

"C'mon, Kate. You know I can't do that. And the kid sure as heck can't."

"I would also tell you to focus on your own problems and not those of the young man who robbed you and caused this shit show."

When she swore it always sounded wrong, like if the Queen herself were to call somebody a 'wee bollix.'

"I can't do that. I'm not going to leave this kid after his mate's been offed." I tutted. "Is that how you people work? You've got what you needed from *me*. Now there's almost peace in the North and I can go whistle? And I just shove this guy under a bus while I'm at it?" I struggled to keep my tone civil now.

I heard her swallow quietly again, then release a short sigh.

"I think we have looked after you very well in recent years." Her upper class voice sounded clipped. "We pay your rent every month. We set you up in America, even though it would have been much cheaper somewhere closer to home. I told you that at the

57

time, if you remember. But that's what you wanted, and we honoured our commitment to you. Yes, I do think that our arrangement has finished in a sense. However, I'm a reasonable person. *We* are reasonable. I'm willing to do reasonable things. You come to me out of the blue with a tale that Hans Christian Anderson would be proud of and what? I'm expected to send over the SAS to swoop you and your robber friend up in a Chinook? You're halfway around the world, Michael, for God's sake."

"I thought you might be interested in the IRA coming after me because I turned tout for you!" I tried to control my voice and failed. "*That's* what I thought."

"You haven't told me anything that leads me to believe it even is the IRA. If you followed the news, they're on a ceasefire. You appear to have got yourself mixed up with a lot of unsavoury gun-toting Americans. That's what I'm hearing. And what's more, you've brought a lot of it on yourself."

"It's more than that. C'mon now. The beating, the kneecapping, right after the poster thing. It's not a coincidence. It's them. And if you think they're completely on ceasefire, then you're off your head."

"No, it's not a coincidence. It's because you shot up some local drug dealer's house. And a pawn shop."

I blew out my cheeks and closed my eyes. I opened them again and saw my hand was burgundy from clutching the receiver.

"So, you're not going to help me at all?"

She exhaled loudly. "No, not right now. Not until I know more. These things are incredibly complex. Michael...listen..."

"Fan-fucking-tastic, thanks for nothing." I slammed the receiver down once again.

I turned as the car door opened and Brandon hustled across.

I was seething.

"It went well then?"

"Aye."

We got back in the car and continued west.

I didn't speak and Brandon appeared to have the good sense not to ask me anything.

I was exhausted. Exhausted and furious.

After eating up a few miles I said, "Let's find somewhere to get our heads down for the night. There's bound to be a motel sooner or later if we keep heading this way. I want get some things from my house and wait this thing out. But not tonight. Better to go in the daytime."

Brandon looked as wrecked as I was and simply nodded in agreement.

I drove on, gradually the tension trickling from me. The hum of the engine helped, and the dark fields all around, only illuminated by my headlights. Brandon passed me one of my smokes when he saw me eye the pack on the dash. Then he got a joint smouldering.

"I never said before, but y'know, you got a real sweet ride," Brandon said.

"Yeah, I know." I forced out a smile and gave the door of my Hornet a little pat.

"It's some *Dukes of Hazard* shit," he said.

"You know that show?"

"Yeah."

"It's better than a Dodge, though," I said.

Fifteen miles later and there was an old wooden sign telling us that Bateman's Motel and Grill was three miles from the next turn off.

"As long as it's not Bates's Motel, that'll do us," I said.

A few minutes later I pulled up along the gravel outside a row of seven single storey motel rooms. They looked a little tired and old fashioned, but it didn't matter any to me. If they had any kind of beds that would do just fine. There was a pick-up truck parked nearby and a couple of sedans further up. Attached to the row of rooms was a double storey building that looked like the office. Probably the owner's home and a small diner too. It was in darkness.

"Right, let's go wake up the guy. I'm sure he'll be pleased."

There was a bell attached to the frame of the glass-panelled front door.

I gave it a push and could hear a faint ring coming from somewhere inside. A light came on upstairs, followed by the noise of feet on stairs. Then more lights came on downstairs and floodlit a man walking towards the front door with a key. He was middle-aged, over-weight with greasy black hair, and his ruddy face was filled with sleep.

"Evening." He pulled the door back and squinting at us. He was dressed in a greying white vest and navy shorts.

"Hi. Sorry to get you up," I said. "We're too tired to keep going tonight so we're looking for a room."

He looked from me to Brandon and frowned slightly.

"Just the one room?" he asked gruffly.

"Well, yeah, if you have it… With two single beds. We'll take two rooms if you only have double beds."

"No, that's alright. We've got one. Number five." He looked happier. "You better come through. How many nights?"

We continued talking as he gestured for us to follow him in.

"Oh, I'm not sure. Can we pay for two and see how we go?"

"You fellas just passing through? On a vacation?"

"Yeah, something like that."

It only took a couple of minutes to pay him a few bills, write false names into the ledger and take the large metal key attached to a wooden plinth. The owner went back to bed. We crossed wearily to our motel room, ragged and fraying at the edges. We were too.

We went inside and I locked the door, pulled the yellowed blinds shut and turned on a little lamp with a tatty, beaded shade. I propped a wooden chair up against the doorhandle. Inside smelled musty, with the vague aroma mix of old tobacco, damp, and dirt. There were two single beds, a small, scuffed table and chairs and an old TV set on a dressing table. There was a door on the left leading to a tiny and very grotty bathroom. But it had a sink and a shower over the bath. There was everything we needed. It would do just fine. I flicked on a dim standard lamp beside the table, then we slumped down on the beds. Ten minutes later we were both out cold.

Chapter 14

Neither of us woke until after nine. Before I opened my eyes, I detected the sweet aroma of *Mary Jane* nipping at my nose.

"Jesus. That your breakfast?" I asked, opening one eye.

Brandon was still mostly under the covers, but smoking. He flicked ash into an old, stained plastic Budweiser ashtray.

"A doobie a day keeps the doctor away," he said.

"And what do a few dozen joints a day do?" I propped myself up on the bed.

"Are you my new Daddy?" His voice was low, but he smiled.

"I'm barely old enough, sonny."

"Bull. You could be my Grandpa."

"Yeah, if me and my da' had both been ten when we conceived, you wee eejit." I coughed and reached for my own. "Let's get dressed and see what kind of breakfast this hole can rustle us up."

The owner was working the tables in the little diner. I found out he went by the name of Bill. An older man worked the grill in the open kitchen, tossing about something greasy, but it smelled pretty good. There were only four tables inside. Everywhere was old, worn pine: the tables, the walls, even the ceiling. And that had a layer of grease on it. Hadn't they heard of extractor fans? The thought reminded me of a joke.

"What you call somebody who used to like tractors?" I said to Brandon.

Brandon raised an eyebrow. His eyes looked tired and bloodshot.

"Go on then."

"An ex-tractor fan."

"Man, you're corny."

We were the only customers remaining after a young couple nodded to us and left their table littered with plates, mugs and a smouldering ashtray. Early Fleetwood Mac played on an old hi-fi, which I approved of. We both got a pancake stack with a side of bacon and maple syrup. The pancakes were a little doughy and overdone, but the bacon was delicious. I thanked Bill earnestly as he set down a large pot of coffee between us. I needed that the most. Bill went back into the open kitchen, perched himself on a stool and flicked through a newspaper.

"Pretty good." I said and cut through my last pancake with considerable effort.

"Yeah, thanks, Michael. I'll pay you back."

"Don't worry about it."

Brandon slugged back some coffee and tilted his head. "Is Michael what most people call you? It feels kind of funny calling you that."

"Er… it's my name."

"Yeah, but can I call you Mike or something?"

"No, but you can call me Mick if you like."

"Okay, Mick," he said, trying it out for size.

"What will I call you? *Brands*?"

"Brandon is fine," he said, mopping up some syrup.

"Yeah, I think you're right.

Brandon gave me a sideways look. "Irish Mick, the former terrorist." He chuckled like he'd just told a dirty joke.

"Keep it down for flipsake." I glanced back towards the kitchen.

"Sorry. It's just hard to believe. But you were though, weren't you?"

"Yeah, I suppose. And maybe I'll terrorise you sometime."

"It's just, you don't really seem like the type."

I sighed. "The type?"

"Yeah. I mean, you seem *alright.*"

"Thanks, I guess? It's not like I was in ETA, or Baader-Meinhoff. I'm not some nut. I love Ireland and I was fighting for our freedom."

Brandon nodded. "I didn't mean any offence, man."

"I know." I allowed a smile. "It's okay. And I'm actually quite a badass you know. Didn't you see me causing all kinds of mayhem last night?"

"Yeah, sure" he said. Then his mood changed quickly. He stared out of the steamed up windows. I figured he was thinking about Lewis.

"It wasn't right what happened to him," I said.

"No. It wasn't"

"If it was people after me that did it, then I'm sorry."

Brandon shook his head. "It wasn't your fault."

"We'll find who did this, I promise you."

I meant it.

Brandon shrugged.

I looked out of the greasy window at the warm, dusty outside. It felt like the middle of nowhere, which I suppose it was.

"So, I think we should head over to mine after this. Check it out and see if it looks okay. I've rounds for the guns in there and I could do with some clothes to do me a few days. There's also a little more cash hidden away, that you thankfully didn't find."

I looked for another smile, but none came this time.

"Sure." He pushed his empty plate to the side.

I really needed some fresh clothes. My shirt was stuck to my back and the jeans could have walked off by themselves.

"Damn," I said. "I better ring into work first, I'm meant to be in there today."

"You think we definitely should go by your place?"

"Nothing's for definite. I don't want to do without any more of my gear." I set down my empty coffee mug and reached for the pot. "'Live every day as your last, because one of these days it will be.'"

"Who's this now?"

"You know *Gulliver's Travels*?"

He frowned, "That T.V show with Ted Danson?"

"Aye, I suppose. Jonathan Swift wrote the book that was based on. I'll have to educate you on some Irish Literature."

"Lucky me."

                                    ***

We called back to the room. I phoned the garage, then we started off on the forty-mile trip back to town. I chose an *Outcasts* Best Of album for the journey.

"Is this punk?" Brandon asked after a few tracks.

"Aye, Belfast punk. The Outcasts. Back in the day they were a beezer live act in the clubs."

"Beezer?"

"Yeah, like *class, great… very good.*"

"Okay."

"I suppose a few things get lost in translation."

"You speak pretty weird is all."

"Okay, cheers. Let this be the start of your Irish musical education. What sort of stuff are *you* into?"

He shrugged. "All kinds. Tupac, Biggie, all that. I like some older stuff too. Like LL."

"Older? Frig. To me older stuff is like Johnny Cash, Chuck Berry."

"I told you; you could be my Grandpops."

"I mean, it *was* before my time. Jeeze, I'm barely in my forties. I suppose that's still ancient to you, ay? So, mostly rap you're into?"

"I guess. I like other stuff. That Prince you played last night was pretty dope."

Scenery whizzed past us as the Hornet's stereo continued to blast out Greg Cowan and Co.

"Actually, Johnny Cash has done some very cool albums recently," I said. "Stripped back. But he did it with one of your hipper hopper guys. Rick Rubin."

"Hipper hopper." Brandon guffawed and shook his head again. "Rubin's done some cool stuff. I know all that Def Jam noise. Like Run-DMC. Now that's *really* old."

I tisked, turned up the stereo and pressed on.

As we got closer to home, my nerves began to set in. I had been trying to keep things calm and upbeat for the kid. My mind still fluctuated between two extremes. One second I was certain it was definitely the IRA, until I got back to thinking the notion was ridiculous. At best, there was still a murderer out there, and a nasty little gang I had royally peeved. There were plenty of reasons to be worried. It had gutted me that Kate had been no use. There was literally nobody else I could call. We were on our own.

One step at a time.

First, I needed to get in and out of my place with no fuss.

As I pulled into my street, I eased off the gas. My freshly tuned engine purred like a satisfied wild cat. I drove past my house at a walking pace. Nothing looked disturbed. Nobody was about except my neighbour three doors down, out mowing his grass. I pulled up near the end of the street and shut off the engine.

"Looks okay so far," I said. "Here's what we're going to do. I'll leave the car here, the motor idling. You wait inside with this." I pulled out one of the Glocks, checked the chamber, and handed it to Brandon fully loaded. I pulled out my Colt next. Twelve rounds in the clip and another in the chamber. "I'll go inside and grab my stuff, five minutes tops. Anything looks wrong and you start pumping the horn. Things get really bad; you start pumping some bullets. You okay with that?"

"Yeah."

Brandon put on a brave face.

"Okay, here we go, then."

***

I left Brandon out in the car as planned and hopped out. My right forefinger was wrapped around the trigger of the Colt inside my jeans pocket. I walked briskly along the footpath and up the path towards the door.

All quiet.

I slipped the key out with my left hand, turned the lock and tucked it back in my inside pocket. I glanced back towards the car, then pushed the door open with a creak. I looked back at the car once more and Brandon shot me a thumbs up. The living room looked normal. The same as I had left it, anyway. I took a step inside and drew my gun. Aimed it in front of me. It felt silly, walking through my room like I was in *Naked Gun* or something. I made my way around the furniture smoothly, paused at the foot of the stairs, looked up and listened. Then I moved on towards the kitchen. Just as I was about to step inside a voice stunned me.

"Stay where you are, Walker. Don't move a muscle."

I noted two things.

The voice was Northern Irish, and there was something metal pressed against the side of my head.

I moved my eye muscles a little but didn't get shot. A man came into view from behind me. His right hand held a six-shooter revolver to my head. He was about fifty. A little podgy and short, with mean eyes. I didn't recognise him.

Not a good situation. Not a lot of options.

"Speckren zee Doitch?" I said in what I thought was an excellent German inflection.

I wanted to draw his attention from his trigger finger for a moment. I didn't plan on going full-on reverse *Hans Gruber*. I was just desperate to put him off for even a second.

His eyebrows knitted almost imperceptibly, but that was enough. I swung my right arm, my own gun still clutched in my fist. I cracked him with it across his nose. Blood spattered across the wall. I dropped my Colt on impact and had to scramble after it. He regained his balance in no time. Aimed and fired just as I scooped up my gun from the floor. The shot rang out like morning mass in the small space. I dove to the ground, behind the sofa. A forty-five slug buried itself in the chair beside me.

Before I even heard his barrel rotate, I sprang back up, raised the Colt – only one of the best handguns ever made, its design deadly mechanical perfection, and aimed. I squeezed the trigger as I exhaled.

And I blew a hole right through his eye socket.

Chapter 15

I didn't stay to dwell at the puff of red mist above the man's falling corpse. Instead, I got to my feet and rushed back out the front door. I clambered through it in time to see Brandon jump out of my idling car, gun in hand.

He raised it and took aim.

For a split second I thought he was pointing it at me. Everything slowed down.

Then it sped up again, quick as a stretched elastic band returning to its normal form.

I saw another man running from the side of my house. Tall, with long, straggly red hair. He cocked a rifle on the move. Brandon pulled the trigger on the Glock. The bullet tore through the man's thigh. He crumbled to the ground. I almost ran right into him. He rolled and pointed the rifle towards Brandon. I skipped to the side, took aim, and shot him through the back of his head.

"I thought I told you to stay in the car!" I shouted as we ran towards the Hornet. The impatient hum of the engine beckoned us.

"You're welcome." He jumped and skidded across the finely waxed orange bonnet of my pride and joy.

I ripped open the door and got inside.

"Cheers, Brandon, but watch the paint work."

I slammed the pedal down, released the handbrake, and shot us away noisily in a shower of dust.

"Was it them?" Brandon was out of puff and his voice strained.

We screeched around the next bend.

"Two pasty white guys with Irish accents? Aye, I'd say so."

***

Nobody came after us. Not on the way through town. Not as we joined the freeway. As I pushed us up towards ninety, heading east, I began to ease my grip on the wheel.

"That was bloody close," I said.

"No shit." Brandon pulled out a joint. He seemed to have a magic bag of pre-rolled blunts stashed somewhere on his person. His hand shook as he raised the fresh happy stick to his lips.

"You did good. Very good," I said. "Good idea, aiming for the leg."

He gave little reaction.

"It's not nice having to shoot someone," I said.

"Yeah. But I tried to aim for his head."

I raised an eyebrow. "Well, it worked anyhow."

Brandon blinked a few times. He looked dazed.

"You ever shot somebody before?" I asked.

"Nope."

I didn't say anything.

We raced along. A finely crafted metallic-orange streak on the rural landscape.

"Now wadda we do?" Brandon asked after a few puffs.

"I make another phone call. This changes everything. Now I know for sure what I'm dealing with."

"And what is that, exactly?"

"An IRA hit squad."

"Oh cool, great."

"Sorry. But that's what it is. I don't know how many there'll be. There's probably a main guy, sent over from back home. He'll have brought a few men with him. They'll have met up with a few from over here I'd guess. Maybe a couple of the 'on the runs'."

"The what?"

"They're fellas who've fled the country and ended up here, or anywhere but the North of Ireland. Broke out of Long Kesh, or whatever. That's one of the big prisons back home. There was a big bust out a while back."

"Is that what you did?"

"No. I was never inside. I told you; I switched teams. I'm not that proud of it. I didn't *want* to. It's just what needed to be done."

I didn't feel like talking about it. I didn't like talking about it. It felt strange. Something I had kept hidden for so long. And a part of my life I didn't want to even think about. I certainly didn't enjoy trying to *explain* it.

"And now they have to find you and kill you?"

I shrugged. "That's how it works."

"And me too?"

"I'm sorry, Brandon. You've got mixed up in all this now. You don't have to stick with me, but I don't think you want to be on your own out there either."

"And take my chances with Isiah? Nice options I've got."

"I'm sorry." I looked over at him, conscious I'd apologised multiple times already.

He looked out the window. A cloud of ganja smoke drifted towards me.

"Well, I am sorry. You did a stupid thing, but you couldn't know any of this would happen."

Oscar Wilde popped into my head, but I kept it to myself; "No man is rich enough to buy back his past."

Brandon nodded, then looked thoughtful. "And was it worth it? Switching sides, I mean."

I finished my cigarette and threw it out of the window. It rushed away on the displaced air like a burning parachute.

"Is anything worth it? It's what I felt I had to do. You can't change what you feel at any one time."

"I guess not."

"'Truth is the cry of all, but the game of few.'"

"Who's this now?"

"A guy from back home- someone much smarter than me."

***

I dropped a few coins in the slot, then went through the same rigmarole with the passwords as before. We had driven thirty miles, this time to another small town I didn't even know the name of. We appeared to be in the centre of it, which constituted a few worn stores, a gas station and a bar. Brandon waited in the car while I stood in the single phone box that thankfully had offered me a dial tone. After a few minutes, Kate came on the line.

"You're like buses, Michael. Nothing for forever, then two calls within the same number of days."

"Yeah, or maybe I'm just a bad penny."

"And how can I be of service today?" She put on an exaggerated plummy voice.

"It's them. They were at my house. They tried to kill us."

69

"Seriously?"

"Serious as a heart attack."

"And apparently you survived." Her voice was low, considered.

"Apparently so."

"And the young man? Your travelling companion?"

"Yeah, he's okay too."

"You're absolutely certain it was paramilitaries?"

"Yeah. Two Irish, white guys who knew my real name. Oh, and they had guns and tried to kill me. Did I not mention that part?"

"Are you okay?" Her voice sounded concerned, it was a tone I had heard many times in the past. I could never work out how real it was.

"Yeah, we got away without getting hurt. Can't say the same for them."

"You... you killed them *both*?"

"Well, yeah, had to. They turned down my offer to make them a cup of tea to sit over while catching up on old times."

"Dear God, you're becoming a one-man crimewave, aren't you?"

"Not by choice."

"Okay, what do you need from me Michael?"

"I need to get the hell out of *dodge*, that's what. I need help getting set up somewhere else. *Anywhere* else for now."

She breathed out slowly. The receiver crackled in my ear.

"It's not as simple as all that, Michael. I will of course try. We have no jurisdiction there, if you had stayed in Britain..."

"Like Eamon Collins?"

"You heard about that?"

"Yeah. It didn't work out so well for him."

"No. Okay, let me think. Any police involvement yet?"

"No. Well, I guess they'll discover the bodies soon enough."

"Good," she said quickly. "So that's those two dead at your house, and then the thief... Lewis?"

"Yeah."

It felt like she was making out a shopping list.

"And you haven't quite managed to kill anybody else along the way?" She allowed a little humour into the lilt of her phrasing of "*anybody else*".

"Just a couple of close-run things."

"Well, that's something. And what's the likelihood that law enforcement will be looking for you?"

I breathed a long sigh myself.

"Well, I don't reckon so." I tried thinking it all through. "No, no. I think I'm okay. Apart from DNA and all that. I'd be screwed if I was on the system, but I shouldn't be. And the house isn't in my name, sure it's not? Not in either of my names?"

"No."

"And the car is off the books. If they talk to people, they'll have a fair idea of who I am. Who I've been recently, I mean. But that's not the end of the world, I suppose, if I get another new identity."

"That's fine. We can take care of that."

"They might come looking for Brandon, though. He'd been staying with Lewis. Brandon shot one of them in the leg, before I finished the job."

"Okay. For a start, are you ready to split up from him yet?"

"No, not going to happen. Not until I know he's safe." I surprised myself with the certainty in my voice.

She smacked her lips. "Alright, Michael. Like I said, we have no jurisdiction there. And I have my own bosses who I need to run all of this by. I won't leave you in the lurch, though. I can promise you that. I'll do everything I can."

"Thank you, Kate. I appreciate it."

"Our best bet is probably the FBI. I'll try and get someone to meet with you and get you somewhere safe. Then we can take it from there."

"Okay, okay, good." A warm feeling of relief flowed through my veins, "Thank you."

"Can you hole up some place and ring me again later? After I get the chance to make some calls?"

"Yeah, will do. Listen, Kate. I'm sorry about all this."

"I'll do what I can for you, Michael." Then more playfully she said, "Maybe you *are* that bad penny though."

"'Some cause happiness wherever they go; others whenever they go,'" I quoted.

"Oscar Wilde?"

"Very good. I'm impressed. Maybe you *were* listening to me all those years."

"Maybe I was. Take care, Michael."

Chapter 16

"It's brandy," I said in response to Brandon's pained expression.

"Never drank it." He took a cautious sniff.

"Good for shock. So my Granny always told me. I'll get us a few beers to chase it after."

After ending the call, I'd found a bar to help stiffen Brandon's nerves. And mine.

"Bit early, isn't it?" He checked his digital watch.

"Wasn't too early for a couple of joints," I said.

Brandon looked uncomfortable and adjusted his baseball cap. "Mick... I don't need you paying for everything all the time..."

"Shoosh, shoosh. Listen." I raised a hand. "You've more than made up for the robbery. God, you very well might have saved my life back at the house. Have a wee drink on me for flipsake."

His eyes met mine, then we clinked glasses, and both took a drink.

"Ahhh," I said.

Brandon coughed and grimaced.

"Powerful stuff, ay?"

"Can I have some ice in it?"

"Jaysus, you can't do that to good Cognac."

He took another small sip, this time avoiding a coughing fit.

"You get used to it. You alright?"

"I guess so."

"Good. Okay, so we'll go get some new duds. Sweat's drippin' off me."

Brandon choked a little on his drink, but also raised a smile.

"So, we'll get those, then some ammo for the guns. Best to stock up a bit. Then I'll ring Kate back, okay?"

"Okay."

I'd already filled him in on the conversation with Kate. It seemed to help a little. It was clear that the adrenalin was running out again, for both of us. I knew how that felt. But it wasn't the first time I had shot and been shot at. I gave myself a quick mental check. I was okay. It'd been a long time since my nerves had been properly tested, but I was holding up.

I pushed back against the old sun-bleached fabric backing of the booth. I'd been in some dives back in Ireland, but this place would have been up there. I turned to the window as the grey clouds that had been threatening all morning burst and a downpour started. Rain drops pelted off the glass and the sunlight all but disappeared.

"Good," I said. "It's been too frigging hot. That'll clear the cobwebs."

"You Irish are weird."

I shrugged. "I thought you knew that already. We're the great travellers. We travel all over the world, trying to find somewhere different, better. Then we open an Irish pub, get Guinness put in on draft and complain that the weather's too hot. Everyone pines for home."

I felt a small lump in my throat, an image of my family in my mind. I lifted my glass, raised it, before taking a large gulp to get rid of the image.

"So, Brandon, what do you usually do for fun? I mean, before all this crap rained down on you. What are you into?"

He looked at me as if I had six heads and shrugged.

"You into sports? Play cards?"

Brandon said nothing.

"You go to clubs?"

"I like bowling, I guess."

"Bowling?" I blurted out a guffaw.

Brandon's face dropped.

"I mean… yeah, why not? I like a game of pins myself."

"There's not much to do in town."

"That's the truth."

"I go sometimes… Went with Lewis now and then."

I nodded.

"And I used to go as a kid… it was… nice."

He shifted uncomfortably again and took a long sip. I could almost feel the pleasant burning sensation as it passed down his throat. It was obvious he didn't want to talk any more about any of that. Best keep things light. The kid was done in. He was holding up too. Michael Walker; *clinical psychologist*.

"What about you? What are *you* into?" He raised his voice a touch to compete with the pounding rain on the window.

I blew out my cheeks. "That's a question." Then I blew smoke out at the rain dancing on the window. "I used to be into lots of stuff. Going to gigs, darts club. Played a bit of football at one time. I was alright, too. Played for a while in our second division back home. I played for a few teams. Just amateur part-timers, really. I went to a lot of games too. My team was Glentoran."

"Soccer?"

"Yeah. *Football*. That rubbish over here isn't football."

He rolled his eyes. I was getting used to that.

"1882. That's when the club started. One of the oldest in Ireland. You didn't get a lot of Catholics supporting The Glens, but my uncle Jim had played for them, and our family always supported them. They were in the east of Belfast, you see. That's a working class proddy area."

"Proddy?"

"Protestant. And basically unionist, as in not wanting a united Ireland."

"That's some confusing shit."

"Yeah, try living there. Anyway, The Glens were class. I loved going to see them- nothing beats it. Actually, they came over here in the sixties, invited to get football going over here."

"Like a tour? Like the Globetrotters?"

"Aye, I suppose," I said with a laugh. "Not on that scale. Still, there was a competition. They played under a more American name. The Detroit Cougars."

"Cool."

"Aye. Anyway, good times. Then, I didn't do *any* of that stuff." I punctuated the statement with a rueful laugh.

"After you joined the IRA?" Brandon lowered his voice, only a whisper against the rain.

"Yeah, I suppose. I didn't have time for much else. It became who I was. A volunteer."

"A volunteer?"

"Yeah, it's what we called our soldiers. *Their* soldiers." I finished my drink and focused on the end of my burning cigarette. So much for keeping things light.

"What was it like at home? Belfast, wasn't it?"

"Yeah. In a word, it was a dump. Maybe that's not fair, but it wasn't good. It's hard to describe. Army were on the streets, peelers with them, looking for any excuse to pick up a Catholic and give him a good hiding. Where I lived, my estate, it was a ghetto. Hemmed in with barricades on all sides. A slum, really."

Brandon nodded, at once looking both sympathetic and empathetic.

"You grew up not having a fair shot," he said simply.

"Yeah, basically. I grew up in the sixties. Catholic areas didn't get the same number of votes. They didn't used to be able to vote at all. We couldn't get decent jobs and we couldn't get decent houses. The government was against us, the police were against us, then the damn army too. We were second class citizens. We had civil rights marches. Protesters were beaten, gunned down sometimes. It was like..." I paused and looked up at him.

"Being black?" he suggested.

"I didn't want to say that, but..."

"It's okay. It sounds like it was."

I nodded.

We both stared out the window at the rain, a fresh understanding passing between us.

Chapter 17

We drove out to Pilton. It was the only place I knew where we'd be able to buy ammo and cheap clothes. We were both tense as we walked along Main Street, checking all around us. The rain had stopped during the drive. It had washed away some of the heaviness and dirt, but we still held onto our own. We each got three sets of new clothes and a large holdall to put them in. Then we found a gun store. I used my fake ID and got us plenty of rounds and clips for whatever might be waiting around the corner for us. Neither of us wanted to spend any unnecessary time in the bustle of the town, feeling exposed and overwhelmed. Getting back in the car and slipping into drive, we both exhaled, shared a look and we took off back towards the motel.

"That shower was better than sex," I declared, padding out of the small bathroom in my boxers.

"Weird," Brandon said lying back on his bed.

"The only thing that's going to top that is putting on fresh duds. Thank frig we've got some new clothes."

I put on a pair of black jeans, loose fitting and shop-fresh smelling. I slipped on a new navy T-shirt and stretched out on the bed. It felt wonderful. The bed still wouldn't have passed a UV test and there didn't appear to be many springs still intact, but it was all good. Lewis had already showered. His face had a clean rosiness to it. His shortly cropped hair had dried quickly in the humidity. A new black baseball cap sat on his bedside table. He had on a pair of long khaki shorts and a white baggy vest. I noticed he had removed the bandage from his arm.

"Your arm feeling better?"

"Yeah," he said, closing his eyes.

"Good."

I put my hands behind my head and closed mine too.

"Mick," he said softly. "You've killed people before, haven't you? I mean before today?"

"Yeah, I have. I never wanted to," I said a little defensively. I glanced at him. His eyes were still closed. I closed my own again.

Silence for a moment.

"What did it feel like?"

"It doesn't feel great. I guess… as bad as it sounds, you kinda get used to it."

He made a hum. "Yeah. I shot that guy in the leg and I don't feel bad about it."

"You shouldn't. They would have shot and killed us and not lost a wink of sleep over it."

Brandon said nothing.

"Still," I stifled a yawn. "I hope you don't have to shoot anyone again."

Seconds later I was fast asleep.

***

We were both out cold until close to seven. Another shower of rain had come and gone, but outside remained grey. The room was almost pitch black. I switched on the lamp, and we roused ourselves. I went out and phoned Kate. It didn't take long to be patched through. She told me that unofficially somebody from the FBI would arrange to meet us the next day. They would help us, and we would discuss next steps. It was a huge relief. I hurried back to the cabin to tell Brandon. He broke into a wide smile. It was something to behold. He chatted excitedly. It's amazing what a little hope can do for you.

"Right, I asked the owner if there's anywhere near still serving food. We're in luck. There's a place about a mile up the road, through a little village. It's a pub so we're doubly in. We'll get a few jars, then kip down here another night. Tomorrow we'll be brand new. What do you reckon?"

"Sweet," Brandon said, rolling up a joint on the bedside table, his face animated. "As long as you're alright for money."

The funds were still looking good enough and now we had the FBI, or at or a least one of their agents anyways. Unofficially, but still. Things were looking up.

"'I spent a lot of money on booze, birds and fast cars. The rest I just squandered.'"

"Another one of your Irish writers?" Brandon asked.

"Nope. Geordie Best, the greatest footballer the world has ever seen. He'll be the first topic for your forthcoming Irish Sportsmen seminar."

HUNTED

"I can't wait."

***

Ten minutes later we were enjoying a pleasant walk along an old blacktop road running past fields and occasional stone houses. It was cool out now, which I was glad about. A breeze was rolling down the hill. I had on my black leather jacket and Brandon sported a half-zipped up black hoody. Evening had set in. If it got much darker, we'd need high vis jackets to even see each other.

It was nice. It felt good to stretch my legs, stretch out my muscles. The last few days had been the most intense workout I'd had in years. I could feel the aches. I wasn't as young and agile as I once had been. I'd never been a gym guy. Never really needed it. I'd never been bulky or ripped, but I'd always been strong. I'd been born that way and it hadn't deserted me yet. We chatted a little, but I think we both were just enjoying an evening walk through nature in each other's company.

In under half an hour, we could see an artificial illumination lighting up a small lump of pine trees from beyond. As we got closer there was the faint beat from a stereo system and the distant murmur of voices. We came up to a small gravel carpark out the front of an ancient red brick pub. There were five or six cars parked outside and a friendly hubbub was emanating from inside. There was a neon sign on the wall declaring the establishment to be 'Dulli's Bar'. This was the place.

"Let's go meet the natives," I said.

As we opened the door, the noise hit us. Thankfully it didn't stop abruptly with faces turning and tumble weed rolling past. It was a pretty nice pub. And nobody took any notice of us as we walked through. There were exposed brick walls with lots of mirrors, framed beer ads and a scattering of neon signs. Two pool tables were occupied by a few twenty-something men, mostly in T-shirts and shorts. There was a raised platform area with couples eating and a steady stream of busy looking waitresses. At the bar there were three or four barflys, most likely locals. Middle-aged men with bottles of beer and whiskeys, staring down at the polished wood top, working through their troubles. In all, there were around sixty people inside. The Rolling Stones played loudly on the jukebox, which I rather approved of. Mick sang about not wanting to be a burden. There was lots of baseball paraphernalia on the walls. The owner must have been a big Dodgers fan given the many framed pictures, logo signs and autographed baseballs.

"How are you fellas doing? Are you in for some food?" asked a young brunette with a tired, but warm smile.

"Good, thanks," I said.

"Yeah please," said Brandon.

We were shown to a table on the raised platform. I ordered us some drinks and we began examining the A3 laminated menu.

"Big Beefy burger?" Brandon said.

I scrolled down. *Big Beefy*. Two quarter pound patties, relish, onion rings, bacon and pepper sauce.

"Sounds like a plan. And a couple of large fries."

Brandon licked his lips and let out an excited laugh.

"Munchies?" I asked.

"No. I'm just hungry, man. Damn hungry."

The waitress came back with our drinks, and we placed our food order. Two finely poured pints of Guinness sat in front of us. I was pleasantly surprised.

"Another first for you Brandon?"

"Yeah. This my *Irish Drinking* education now is it?" he said.

"Now you're catching on young Jedi," I said smiling and clinking pints with him. A creamy splash of fine stout head ran down the side of the glass. I scooped it off with a finger, licked it, then took a long sup.

"Damn, that's good. Give it a try, Brandon."

He took a tentative sip and made a face.

"You gotta get used to it," I said.

Over the next twenty minutes, Brandon didn't get used to it. I ordered him a half pint of cider to turn it into a *Black Velvet Snake Bite*. That didn't seem to help either. I gave up and ordered him a bottle of Bud.

"That's better," he said. "Sorry, Mick."

"The youth of today," I said and rolled my eyes.

Our food arrived and Led Zeppelin came on blasting out *Communication Breakdown*. I was really quite enjoying myself. The food was delish. Maybe the burger was a wee touch overdone, but that's a mild criticism. It was really good grub. We had a cup of coffee afterwards. Brandon went outside for five minutes for a small one-skinner. When he came back, I suggested we have a few more beers up at the bar. There was a basketball game on the big screen beside it that I'd noticed Brandon glancing at anyway. I paid our bill, gave the waitress a good tip and a smile, then we walked down the steps to the lower section. There was a huddle of three large men below the screen and a few tired faced regulars along the rest of it. The whole bar section was maybe three or four meters long. The barman, probably the owner, was about fifty, burly, quite tall, with a shaggy beard and red cheeks. He was friendly enough as I placed our order for another Guinness and bottle of Bud. The closest and biggest of the huddle of three men turned to stare at us. Not just look, but *stare*. His eyes set on Brandon. I'm a pretty big guy, but he was huge. Arms like sides of beef, a head like a leather rugby ball. I looked at Brandon then back at him, not immediately comprehending. Brandon looked past him at the screen. Then I twigged onto the absence of any other black faces in the bar.

Ahh, a redneck.

"Evening, buddy. Want a picture?" I asked in a friendly voice, but my eyes had narrowed.

Brandon put a hand on my arm and shook his head.

The big guy said nothing. He just kept staring.

I shook my head too, lifted our drinks and found a spot on the far left of the bar, barely able to see the T.V.

"Prick," I said, fuming, taking a sip to quell the steam that was probably pouring out my ears.

"Leave it, Mick. He's just some asshole. I've had a lot worse than some inbred shooting me death stares."

I said nothing.

We sipped at our drinks.

We had another and began to relax again.

We watched the game.

I had a buzz on.

Then everything changed.

Right when three of the IRA hit squad walked in.

Chapter 18

The first to come in was Madden. I didn't know his first name. A few years older than me, but shorter and wider, with brown, messy hair. I had met him a few times at IRA joint cell sessions, but he mostly operated out of Derry. He'd been the same level as me. You might say *middle management*. Then a guy looking to be late twenties slipped in behind him. Wiry, with cropped hair and beady eyes. I didn't know him. I found out later that he was called Daly. Finally, swaggering in behind them was Marty Sullivan. Sullivan was a mean bastard. I'd met him many times and never once did I find something good in him. He was known to be a brutal enforcer of the volunteers, sometimes seeming to take a sick satisfaction in keeping men in line by whatever means. A bully. It was no surprise to find him heading up a hit squad. He was a couple of years older than me; lean, strong, with wide, intelligent green eyes. His shortish black hair had an unkempt fringe dangling above a constantly furrowed brow.

They each scanned the room as they took a few paces inside. Sullivan was the first to spot me and meet my eyes. His thick lips curled into an ugly smile.

I turned side on to Brandon. "It's them. Don't look, stay calm. We'll get out of this."

I felt sick. The booze sloshed around in my stomach like a 'Slush Puppy' machine.

Brandon's eyes bulged and I could see his Adam's apple bob up and down a few times inside his skinny neck. I straightened my jacket and leaned back against the bar, striking up a casual pose. I clocked Sullivan whispering instructions into his underlings' ears. Daly took up post by the door. Madden swiftly crossed the room and stood near the back exit and cast his eyes towards the match. Sullivan walked slowly towards us, his smile still in place. They were all wearing thick, dark jackets, and I assumed they'd all be packing.

That was a problem.

Our guns were back at the motel.

That was a bigger problem.

I pulled out my deck of Marlboro, all while keeping my eyes fixed on Sullivan's progress across the bar. He kept on. Then he walked right up to me, so close that I could smell his foul breath. He raised both of his bushy eyebrows.

"Ahh Mikey, sure what are the chances of bumpin' into you?" he said in his throaty Belfast accent.

"Yeah, what are the chances?"

He licked his lips, glanced at Brandon, gave a dramatic smirk, then set his cold eyes back on me.

"All the chickens come home to roost sooner or later," he said darkly.

"Do they? Go to hell, Marty."

"Now that's not very nice." He took a step closer. I straightened up. "That's no way to greet an old comrade, ay?"

"Old comrade may be about right, because the war's over, mate."

"Is it now?" He gave a rueful laugh. "There's still no United Ireland, last time I checked."

"No, but there is a ceasefire. Don't you watch the news? I know that reading a newspaper would be a bit beyond you."

"Cowards all sittin' 'round a table. Pah! don't make me laugh. This war is far from over."

I took a last draw and stubbed it out in an overflowing glass ashtray. "So, you're with the new crowd, then?" I said nodding at one of his goons.

"There's plenty who don't want to *bend over* for the British government," he said. His eyes twinkled with menace. "Some of us dropped their pants years ago," he said, his eyes narrowing. "But not me."

Brandon shifted uncomfortably beside me, furtively glancing across to the other two men, still in their positions.

"Brandon, get us a round in would you?" I said passing him a few bills. "These fellas will take a pint. The Guinness here's good." I turned back to Sullivan. "For old times?"

His eyes danced for a moment. "We're won't be here long," he said, patting his bulging inside pocket.

I patted my own pocket, though it only contained my wallet.

Sullivan rolled his eyes and poked his tongue around somewhere behind his cheek.

"Sure Mikey, I'll have a pint with you. Then we're all going to get going."

My mind raced. My brain clicking through options. Sullivan searched around in his trouser pockets for his deck and bit one out from the pack. He blew a hail towards the floor.

"We're going nowhere with you," I said.

"I says that you are," Sullivan replied, his face hard.

"We'll see who's right, then," I said. I tossed my half-smoked number into the tray as Brandon carefully set down three fine looking pints of the black stuff.

"I'll get the other two," I said and strode up to the far end where the owner was putting down another pint. I leaned half around the far end of the bar, pulled myself in and took a look under the counter. I smiled. Near to where the owner was standing was a black handled pump action shotgun.

"Hey," he shouted over, looking displeased.

"Sorry," I said, leaning back around. "Lost my balance there. I've had a few. Listen, I was just wondering. This the kind of place where fights break out much?"

He gave me a hard stare then said gruffly, "Not usually."

"And if they do?"

His eye flit down towards where the shotgun was for a moment, "Then I take care of it."

I nodded. "And call the cops if you need to?"

His eyes narrowed further, until they were just two black marbles. "Maybe."

"Cheers for the beers," I said chirpily, grabbing both glasses and turning away.

As I walked back towards Brandon and Sullivan, a heavy snare and hi-hats beat kicked in with a crunchy riff. Tom Petty sang out, "You don't know how it feels... to be me." That would do nicely for background music. I loosened up my body, focused my mind. Harmonica, guitar solo, the band played on.

I gave Sullivan a wide smile before lifting one of the pints, taking a slug, then wiping the creamy foam from my mouth with my sleeve. I set the glass down again.

"Your good health," I whispered in his ear, stepping past him.

I took two long paces, placing me beside the big guy who had glared at Brandon, balancing with one foot up on his tall bar stool. He turned. When he saw it was me, his gnarled face kind of scrunched up like it was made of rubber. His breath was vomit inducing.

"Hi again," I said jovially. He glared back. "I was wondering if I could have this dance?"

"What?" he said gruffly, looking genuinely confused.

"May I have this dance?" I asked with a grin, giving a little bow.

"Fuck you!" he growled, heaving his body down off the bar stool and squaring up to me. "Get the hell outta here, you queer."

"Now, that's not very nice," I said, taking a step backwards. Then quietly I said, "Why don't you make me fat boy?"

His buddies turned and eyeballed me in unison.

His own eyes glowed with rage. I saw his beefy right hook coming a mile off and sidestepped easily around him, firing my own right hook into the side of his face. Stunned, I grabbed him by his jacket and shoved him back against his friends. I looked over my shoulder and gestured with my head for Brandon to come over. He didn't know what was going on. I was heartened to see him push past a disgruntled Sullivan.

Turning back, I was too late to avoid a hard left to my jaw from the second guy. It was rather painful. I righted myself, hopped off my heels, ducked and sent a barrage of blows to his midsection. He dropped his arms to try and block them. I unleashed a heavy uppercut, sending him down on a heap on the floor. I looked back at Sullivan, seeing the panic now etched across in his face. His two commandries looked unsure of what to do as well. He raised a hand for them to stay where they were.

"Hey! Hey! Break it up!" shouted the barman from behind the taps.

At the same time, Brandon pounced up and swung at the third guy. Glanced the blow off his cheek. Brandon swivelled and

85

kicked the guy hard in the balls, making him double over. The big guy had now regained his composure. He set his eyes on Brandon and punched him hard in the stomach, winding him. Brandon began coughing and dry heaved. I felt enraged. I took two steps, hit the guy with a sharp left, then a right. Then I threw him against the bar. Pints, ashtrays and shot glasses flew everywhere. It was now a full-on brawl.

The third guy, a little green around the gills from his kick in the stones, came at me, swinging wildly. I caught an incoming right hook, twisted his arm up behind him and made him squeal. Then I sent two jabs into his face. Blood spurted from his nose. I let go of his arm and he hit the deck.

Click. Click. Boom!

It was the unmistakeable sound of a shotgun being cocked and then fired.

Everybody froze.

The diners and casual drinkers looked on in horror. This was clearly not the norm.

I turned around to see the owner with his shotgun pointed at the ceiling. Plaster dust fell to meet the drift of smoke rising from the gun.

"Stop what y'all are doing," he shouted in a whiskey-soaked roar. "Don't god-damned test me." He turned to one of the old guys at the far end of the bar. "Tom, go get the phone and call the cops."

I massaged my throbbing hand and looked at Sullivan with a smirk.

"'The whole worl's in a state o' chasis.'" I said.

His hand came out of the inside of his jacket, empty. He looked enraged.

I added a cheeky wink for good measure.

Chapter 19

"What about my phone call?" I asked.

The heavyset state trooper regarded me with disdain as he went to shut the cell door. It had only taken them fifteen minutes to get to the bar. Me, Brandon and two of the biker-types were taken in for disturbing the peace or whatever. Sullivan and his mates had all slipped away before their arrival.

We'd been in the station for about an hour. Brandon and I were separated almost immediately. I had been hopeful that we would have been released pretty sharpish, especially when, after a half-hour in the gloomy general holding area, I was brought out to talk with a trooper. I mean, it was only a wee scuffle.

Going over my name and address again, he checked sheets in front of him several times, his eyes narrowing. I knew that wouldn't be good. Then just like that, they marched me to a cell of my own again. That's when I decided to play my phone call card.

"Okay." He pulled the long metal key back out of the lock and gestured for me to come with him.

I was escorted to yet another part of the station, along a musty corridor that may have once been painted green. It was hard to tell with the layers of tobacco stains, the holes of bare plaster, and assorted blotches.

"You got three minutes." He swiped a phone card along a strip on the side of a payphone before handing me the receiver.

I stared down at the greasy receiver and gave it a quick wipe on my shirt. The trooper ambled a little way off down the hall and produced a pouch of tobacco and skins.

I dialled the number and listened to the little pips as the call tried to connect.

"C'mon, c'mon." I tapped the phone irritably. I really needed a hit myself.

"Hello, switchboard," said a male English voice, finally.

"I need you to put me through to Oxford freight and delivery department," I said quickly.

"I'll try that number for you now, sir."

The line went silent.

Hurry the hell up.

"Hello? Oxford Freight," came another voice.

"Yes, yes, please hurry. I'm in a payphone, Cortez."

"Cortez?" he repeated. I heard his keyboard rattle. His breathing echoed through the battered earpiece.

"Okay. Please confirm your name."

"It's Michael Walker," I said quietly, glancing furtively at the Trooper, nearly done with his cigarette.

"Alright, how can I help you?"

"Kate Greene. Please get her quickly."

"I'll try her now, sir…"

"I'm gonna get cut off, please hurry up."

The line went quiet. I thought it was dead. But seconds later I heard the crackle of someone breathing down the line.

"Michael?"

"Thank God. Kate, I've been arrested…"

"What?"

"Please, just listen. I'm at…"

Then the line did go dead.

Chapter 20

I paced my cell, anxious and thoroughly hacked off. I'd been brought back to my disgusting little cage that reeked of bleach, urine and bad choices. I'd been told I'd be interviewed in the morning, had a rough-fibred blanket thrown at me, and that was that. Nighty night.

I sat and stewed for an hour, maybe two. No chance of any sleep coming. Then the lights went out, and my tiredness took over. Against the odds, I fell into a deep sleep.

There was a phone box. It looked a little like The Tardis, and it was on the lawn of City Hall in Belfast. I felt cold. I looked down at my bare arms, then at my exposed chest and legs. I was wearing nothing but my boxers.

What the heck?

I started into a jog and headed around the side of the big war memorial. As I got around the corner, I had my clothes on again. Now I was in my old estate. My terraced house was just a few streets away. A bullet or a stone pinged beside me, but I didn't look back. I ran on, too scared to check behind me.

Then there was another, and another.

A cloud came over above me and the sky turned black.

I pushed myself on towards the corner, so close to my house. But I knew I wouldn't make it. Bang, bang, bang.

Something on my arm.

Had I been hit?

"C'mon, wake up."

I opened my eyes. Looking into the face of another burly trooper, I'm sure I looked a right eejit. My heart attempted to hammer its way out of my chest. I was sweating buckets.

"I'm awake." I sat up and ran a hand through my damp hair.

"They want to talk to you. You've got five minutes to get ready." He turned and left.

Jeeze, did I ever need a smoke.

***

Ten minutes later I was seated on a scuffed blue plastic chair. My hands were cuffed in front of me. There was a small, heavily scored table and a similar looking chair on the other side. There was a half-filled ashtray on the table and sheets plastered about on the faded cream walls regarding everything from testing for STD's to how to avoid being burgled.

The door shot open and in trod a short, stocky man of about fifty. He had greying hair, receding on top, and beady brown eyes. His face was ruddy, partly concealed by a smattering of uneven stubble.

"You want one?" he asked. His narrow eyes sized me up.

"Aye, cheers."

He offered me a full deck of Luckies, and I awkwardly pulled one out with my bound hands. He leaned across the table, a few folds of fat catching on the side, then he sparked me up. He pulled out his chair and wearily sat down. His brown shirt and black suit jacket could have used an iron. He tapped out a cigarette for himself with some apparent effort, lit it and leaned backwards.

He eyed the floor as he said, "My name is Lieutenant Marley and I have been tasked with carrying out a provisional interview."

He blinked a few times, then looked up at me.

I was too engrossed with the sweet toxic poison. I nodded at him.

"Your name is Michael Dempsey, is that correct?" He fixed his eyes on mine.

"Yeah, yeah. That's right. Listen, last night was just a misunderstanding…"

He raised a hand. "And this has always been your name?" he asked before sucking hard on his cigarette.

"Yeah, 'course," I said with a shrug.

"There just doesn't seem to be very much *paperwork* relating to you," he went on.

I said nothing.

Marley gave a brief eyeroll before thumbing through some sheets of paper.

"I've got a few questions to ask about a number of incidents that took place in the town of Beaconsfield." He blew a long plume of pale blue towards the ceiling.

90

"I want a solicitor."

Marley stubbed out his unfinished smoke and gestured with both hands dramatically. "Why now? Because I mention Beaconsfield? So, you *do* live there then?"

Crestfallen, I crushed out my own cigarette with my cuffed hands. I let out the last strands of smoke I hadn't managed to force into my lungs for keeps. Then I gave him my best hardest, yet calm stare.

"I... want... a... so-lici-tor." I enunciated.

He huffed air, frustration flushing his already scarlet cheeks.

"You shouldn't even be talking to me by myself right now. I haven't been read my rights or anything."

Crack!

His fist thudded on the table, bouncing the ashtray up and down, a few ciggy ends spilling out.

"This is my god-damned station and I'll do as I please. I'll keep you here for a week in irons with only bread and water if it takes my fancy." He leaned over the table, his eyes bulging and his spit spraying me. He lowered his voice. "I certainly won't be preached to by some ignorant, immigrant mick."

"My name *is* Mick. With a name like Marley, you haven't got much respect for the old country," I said quietly. "What's the matter? Did your ma get knocked up by her brother before she moved over here?"

He pulled himself out of his chair with considerable effort and began to navigate the tight route around towards me. I sat up and braced myself for the inevitable. Just then the door opened. A uniformed trooper with a Stetson hat peered around the door. He eyed Marley with some concern.

"You... uh got a minute, sir?" he asked.

Marley looked at him disapprovingly, shook his head, then followed him outside.

I breathed out and slumped back in my chair. I'd angered plenty of fuzz in my time, and I never grew tired of it. Maybe I just never learned. Suddenly I noticed he'd left his Luckies on the table. *Nice.* With a maximum of fuss, surely easily ridiculed if seen through the one-way mirror, I managed to extract another from his pack, light it and sit happily back down in my chair.

I enjoyed it. Really enjoyed it. I managed to hook out another. Five minutes passed and I stubbed it out too. Then a female trooper came in.

"Come with me, please," she said with something approaching deference.

I was rather confused. What was going on? I followed her out through the hallway and past the front desk. Somebody flicked my cuffs free and handed me my wallet and jacket. My eyes looked beyond them, fixed on the waiting area. In an uncomfortable-looking moulded plastic seat was Brandon. Beside him was an attractive black woman in her early thirties with poker straight, shoulder-length hair. She wore a perfectly fitted black pants suit and smiled widely while talking to him, displaying flawless white teeth.

"You're free to go," said a voice from behind me.

I shuffled forward, turned and gave them a quizzical look, then walked away.

"Mick," Brandon said with a sudden smile. He hopped up and over to me, and gave me a kind of half-hug mixed with a shoulder pat type of thing.

"Glad you're okay, mucker," I said and gave his arm a little squeeze.

My gaze hung over his shoulder as the woman with him got to her feet and flattened down her trousers with one hand.

"Hi," she said and made an awkward little wave. Her eyes furrowed. "Please come with me."

Well, I didn't have anything else to do.

We walked out together into the mid-morning assault from the sun. But it was good to be in the fresh air again. The outside. We stopped at the bottom of the steps, and I shaded my eyes. The red sun hung low in front of me.

"My name is Amy Landish," she said to me, offering a half nod.

"Good to meet you," I said offering a handshake. "I'm Michael, this is…"

"I know who you are." She clutched my hand for a second. "I'm with the FBI. Let's get going."

We followed her through the front carpark and over to a light blue Oldsmobile. Brandon and I shared a look behind her back. He gave an exaggerated shrug.

"You guys jump in. I'm sure you want to get your stuff from that motel. You can fill me in on everything along the way."

"Yeah, cheers." My eyes searched the surrounding area for threats.

It wouldn't be hard for Sullivan and his cronies to find out where we had been taken. There wasn't a hell of a lot of options.

Brandon jumped in the back. I got in the front. Amy put on a pair of large grey sunglasses. I buckled up. She peered over her lenses into the rear-view mirror at Brandon. He rolled his eyes and pulled his seatbelt across. Amy gave a little nod, gunned the motor and swung out in a wide arc, the speed taking me a little by surprise. I put a hand out to steady myself and clocked a smirk play at her mouth. Amy flew out of the carpark, sending loose pebbles flying, in search of the intersection.

"Okay then, Walker... or can I call you Michael?" she asked, her smooth mahogany forehead suddenly filled with lines.

"Yeah, of course. Or call me Mick if you'd."

She glanced at me and gave a little nod.

"Call me B if you like," Brandon said from behind.

I wasn't sure if he was being serious. I turned in my seat. "B?"

He looked awkward. "Yeah, man."

"Can *I* call you B?" I asked playfully.

"You can kiss my black ass, honky." He spoke softly, then leaned round and gave my arm a little punch.

I turned back in my seat, looked through the windscreen. Smiled. I was relieved that he was okay.

Things were finally looking up.

Then it happened.

Chapter 21

I had updated our new ally all the way to the part of my near-fight with a state trooper while handcuffed. She seemed to know most of it already but listened patiently just the same.

I'd just got to the part of me nicking his deck when it happened. Suddenly our car was shunted from the right, rear side.

Amy licked her lips, ducked her head and accelerated.

They *had* been waiting for us.

"Get your head down," I said to Brandon, turning around in my seat, ducking.

A black SUV was racing up behind us, a dent visible in its front grill. Amy checked her mirror and her lips pursed.

"These the same guys from last night?" she asked, her voice even, controlled.

"I never saw their car," I said. "Too far back to see inside this one."

"It sure ain't the Easter Bunny," Brandon said, peering through the back window.

The SUV accelerated past a Crown Vic and two Fords, now almost alongside us. There were two white men inside that I didn't recognise. The hit squad must have been bigger than I'd expected.

"Different guys," I said.

Amy nodded.

We all looked across as the guy in the passenger seat buzzed his window down. He raised a Berretta. Amy looked in the rear-view. She slammed hard on the breaks. Sent us into a skid. As we slowed and then drifted hard into an arc, I heard a shot ring out. It hit nothing. Amy was a good driver. She eased into the skid, fed the wheel, then took off in the wrong direction along the highway.

"Damn," mumbled Brandon, his hand on his belt buckle.

"I hope you know what you're doing," I said.

We began weaving between cars. Horns blared from every direction. The traffic was light enough, but still not ideal with us hurtling against it at sixty or seventy miles an hour. I checked back and saw the SUV swerve. It nearly took out a station wagon. Then it came speeding along in our wake. I watched as it began to chase us. The SUV had the easier job since we had cleared a path of angry drivers.

Amy's face was set. Her knuckles reddened as she gripped the wheel.

"Just a few more seconds," she said, perhaps to herself.

"Until what?" asked Brandon nervously.

Then Amy swung the wheel hard again. I hit up hard against the door with force. Brandon spilled around the backseat like an empty shopping bag. Amy just about managed to miss a Beamer as we tore off on an intersect, swung around again and sped off along a country road.

"Nice driving," I said.

I settled myself back into my seat. Amy nodded. She gave me a tight smile.

"We lose 'em?" Brandon asked.

The question was answered before Amy could speak. The big SUV tumbled out behind us. It looked more battered than it had a few minutes before. Amy put her foot down.

We sped along what was all but a dirt road. One narrow lane each way, old, crumbled blacktop, overhanging brush, nobody else around.

I checked over my shoulder and didn't like what I saw.

"Listen Amy, you're a damn fine driver, but the bottom line is they've got a better motor. A bigger engine. Simple physics. We can't outrun them."

Amy said nothing. She lifted a hand from the wheel to flick a stray hair away from her face.

As if to support my point, the SUV gained on us. An arm snaked out of the passenger window and squeezed off a few shots. The terrain was rough, and the shots went wide, but they wouldn't miss every time.

"Gimme your gun," I said. "I'll shoot for their tyres."

Her face crinkled. "I'm a federal agent, I can't just hand out my weap…"

"You know enough about me. I can handle a gun. And I'll try my best to not kill them."

Amy rolled her eyes. "I'm not worried about that."

She unbuckled her holster with one hand and slipped out a Glock. The steering remained ramrod straight.

"Just don't shoot yourself or some passer-by. I'm responsible for you."

This time I rolled *my* eyes. But I accepted the weapon and checked the chamber. The SUV tried to gain on my nearside. There was another volley of shots and then excruciating silence. My opponent was reloading. I hung myself out the window and pumped off some rounds. The first few shots acted as markers. I zeroed in.

Plumes of dirt exploded on the ground in front of the SUV. Shot four went home. So did five and six. Each one sank into their front left tyre.

There was a loud bang. The tyre exploded. The SUV swerved, slowed and almost ploughed into the forest beyond. It came to a halt. Dust swarmed around the car and steam rose from its hood.

Amy gave a little nod, slowed and pulled up on the hard shoulder. We were about three hundred yards in front of them. Amy bounced out and went around the side of the car towards the boot.

"Hey, careful," I said.

I still had her gun. I opened the door and shielded myself behind it. Aimed at the SUV. I had eleven rounds left if the clip had been full to start with. Just then the driver leaned out of his window and fired off a few shots from his Beretta. He may as well have been throwing rocks. There was no accuracy from that distance with a pistol. I returned a couple of shots to give Amy some covering fire for whatever the hell she was doing. Seemingly oblivious to what was going on around her, Amy had popped the boot, lifted something out and sat on the ground at the other side of the car.

"Holy hell," I heard Brandon say from inside.

I pulled myself across to see what had impressed Brandon so much. She had set up a black AR15 rifle and was down on one knee aiming it towards the SUV. There was an inconsequential click before the gun erupted into life. It sent a spray of bullets at the hood of the car. I ducked down instinctively. Ricochets pinged over the thunder of the semi-automatic plugging away. It took less than twenty seconds. I figured out her plan at the last tick. The gas tank couldn't hold out forever.

The explosion was huge. Flames shot up and out from the car. I thought the whole thing was going to take off. All the windows burst. Plumes of smoke flew out. Then it settled into a steady and unforgiving fire. Nobody could have survived that.

Amy stood up, ejected the magazine and smacked her lips.

"I'll get someone to clean this up. We best get going."

She walked back around to the rear of the car. I looked at Brandon and he raised both his eyebrows.

"Okay," I said.

Chapter 22

"Alright if I smoke?" I asked.

We were a few miles up the road, all settling down from the recent events. Amy had her shades off and eyed me with a frown. "Okay. But out the window."

"Thanks," I pulled out my half-crushed deck. "Those were some pretty cool moves."

I jutted my head out the window to light up. She shrugged.

"Hey Mick, one of those things are gonna have to do. Let me steal one, will ya?" said Brandon from the back.

"Aye, 'course." I passed one back to him.

Amy frowned again, pressing a button to shoot the window down in the back as well.

"We'll stop in a minute for some food." She briefly checked her appearance in the mirror. There was barely a hair out of place. "Then you boys can smoke your little brains out."

We drove on in a peaceful silence, the two of us smoking and Amy looking comfortable, hands lightly on the bottom of the wheel.

***

"Thank you," Amy said with a wide smile, handing our menus back to the waitress. Three coffees and three plates of bacon and waffles would soon be on their way to us. We were in a diner, just off the freeway. It was newer than some of the ones I'd been to recently. I suppose it was a little cleaner. But it wouldn't be long before it ended up just as tired looking as the rest.

"So," Amy said, her eyes wide, looking between us. "This'll give us a chance to tell each other a little about ourselves."

I was still trying to figure her out. It had been a weird couple of hours. Not the usual way you get to know someone. One second, she seemed a bit ditzy, verging on unsure. The next, she was as in control a person as I'd ever met. She was certainly very capable. Sweet and endearing, but also aloof, and maybe even ruthless.

"My name is Michael, and I'm an alcoholic," I said, giving a cheeky grin.

"My father was an alcoholic," she said pointedly.

"Oh frig… I'm sorry." I fumbled for the right words.

"I'm just messing with you." She threw a stick of chewing gum into her mouth.

"So… uh what about that car? And the bodies?" Brandon asked.

"That'll be cleaned up, don't worry about it," Amy said, leaning over and patting Brandon's hand.

"This kind of thing happen to you a lot?" I asked.

"Not a lot, but it happens."

"Well, thank you anyway."

"Just part of my job."

"Your job is blowing up cars?" I tried another grin.

"Yeah, sometimes. Anyway, tell me something about *you*," she said slowly. "I don't mean the stuff in your file. I've seen that already. If I'm going to be keeping an eye on you two, I want to see who I've got."

I blew out my cheeks. She sure was keeping me on my toes one way or another. "Okay… well I'm Irish, I uh, I've been here about…"

"I know all that, c'mon."

Alright, alright, lemme see. I'm a big music fan I suppose. I like loads of stuff- a lot of blues and rock: Neil Young, Tom Petty, some heavier stuff too," I said frowning. "That okay for you?"

"It's a start, I guess" she said smiling widely.

Her face was already beautiful. Hardly any makeup on. And when she smiled, Jesus, she was a knockout.

"What about you?" I asked.

"Me," she said, running a hand down her blouse. "Er…" she looked out the window. Then she turned to me looking serious, "I like fried chicken."

I winced. "Fried Chicken?" I looked at Brandon and he gave me a shrug and a grin.

"C'mon, you're messin' with me again. Surely that's racist or something?"

"That I like chicken? I hardly think so." She stared at me. I didn't know what way to take her.

The waitress brought us our drinks and we thanked her. We all set about turning the coffees into our specific tastes.

"I like fried chicken too," Brandon said, giving me a wink and ripping off the corner of a sugar sachet. They shared a mischievous look.

"Alright, alright. Sure." I held up my hands in mock defence. "I thought bowling was your *favourite* thing, Brandon."

"White boy's getting all worked up," Brandon said to Amy.

"Honky's getting pissed," she affected a deep Southern imitation.

They both guffawed. I just shook my head.

We chatted on and kept the conversation easy. Much steam needed to be let off, for all of us. I liked Amy. The food soon arrived, and the chat grew serious again.

"Listen… Amy, we both appreciate you coming out to help us, what you did was…"

"Badass," Brandon chimed in.

Amy blanched a little.

"It was. So, what happens next?" I said.

She cut a piece of bacon carefully, dabbed it in some syrup, then popped it in her mouth. She held up a finger.

"Sorry… my that's good. Sorry. Okay, so, the way this works is I'm not really *here*. Not officially anyhow. The United States Government isn't sanctioning anything as such. I'm supposedly on leave at the minute, so this is strictly off the books."

I exchanged a glance with Brandon.

"Okay, I get that I suppose," I said. "But there is a plan, right?"

Amy chewed on another soaked piece of pancake for a few extra seconds before swallowing.

"Kind of," she said.

Chapter 23

"So, it's just you?" Brandon asked, his brow furrowed.

Amy made a face filled with indignation, or mock indignation. I still wasn't sure how to take her most of the time. "Am I not enough for you Brandon?" She pouted her lips slightly.

Brandon said nothing. But he reddened ever so slightly.

"Okay, lemme get this all straight," I took a drag, rubbed the back of my hand over the top of my head. "So, you're on some kind of leave, some of your bosses know you're helping us, some of them don't. You're going to help us get some place safe, then take it from there? You can ask for some help, but not much and nothing official. Is that about the height of it?"

"Yes siree!" she said with a little salute.

She sure was unique. Back home she might have been called "a bit of a character" by some.

"Okay, cool. So, what do we do first?" I said with a shrug.

"Next, we go pick up your stuff. Your car and such. Sound good?"

"Sounds great."

"Thank you," said Brandon with a subtle little nod.

"Okay, good," she said. "I love this song! She added suddenly." Amy leaned back in her chair, her big eyes looking happily up at the ceiling.

I paused and strained my ears. "*Mr Postman* is it? Cool. I like a bit of Motown."

She smiled widely, "What amazing vocals. And the production is out of this world."

"The Supremes, isn't it? Diana Ross?"

Amy looked at me like I had left my flies undone.

"The Marvellettes." She enunciated each syllable slowly, as if talking to a small child. She leaned across the table and cocked her head at me, breaking into a smile.

I raised a hand. "Sorry, my mistake. The Supremes did *Dancing in the Street*, right?" I somehow kept my face straight. Now she looked at me with proper disdain. I raised a hand again. "I'm just messing with you."

Amy rolled her eyes.

"Guess I know something about you now too," I said.

***

Our next journey saw Amy behind the wheel again. It was much less eventful than the first trip. Within an hour we had pulled up outside our motel. Genuine relief flooded my entire body when I saw my baby parked there safely. Just to be sure, I got out and inspected her, checking for any sign of harm. I patted the bonnet, or the hood as they say over here, and told her she was a good girl. I hadn't realised that Amy was right behind me. She raised an eyebrow, then took out her pistol, inspected it and slotted it back into her shoulder holster.

"I'll wait for you fellas while you pack up, just in case," she said. "Ten minutes enough?"

"Yeah, fine," I said.

Brandon nodded.

We walked over towards our motel room, leaving Amy leaning casually against her Olds. The room looked untouched inside. The dirt and damp were where we'd left them, undisturbed. It didn't take me long to throw my things together. Brandon wasted no time either.

"Thank you, Jesus," I heard Brandon say under his breath. He had located his stash tin and got to skinning up. "Just two minutes, okay Mick?"

"Yeah, 'course. I get it. I plan on having a few whiskeys later myself. A few dozen maybe."

"You never toke?" Brandon asked, his head still down, concentrating.

"Aye, I had my fair share of dope as a kid, same as everyone."

He nodded.

"Ours was shite stuff though. All we could ever get was big blocks of grotty hash. There'd be cellophane and all kinds of garbage cooked into it. Even vinyl from old records I'd heard it said a few times."

"Damn, that don't sound good. Check this bud out."

He waved his tin in front of me. It was full of dark green cannabis buds. I took a sniff.

"Christ, that smells strong."

"It is," he said with a grin.

Five minutes later and we were walking across the gravel, our bags hanging at our sides. From the corner of my vision, I saw a car in the distance. It rolled slowly towards us. There was a small dirt cloud thrown up by the wheels. It was maybe five hundred yards off. My piece was in the Hornet. I made a break towards the car, grabbing Brandon by the arm. Amy squinted at the approaching vehicle, then slipped a hand in her pocket. I got to my car, unlocked it and scrambled around inside for my gun.

"It's alright," Amy shouted.

"What?" I paused and looked through the window while still on my hunkers.

"It's just the owner." She was standing up straight, her eyes fixed on the car. "I saw him yesterday. He drives a navy pickup. Stand down, soldier."

Brandon and I blew out our cheeks in unison and clambered back out of the car. We took the opportunity to go and check out and get ready to make a move. We came back out again, me putting a hand to my face to cut out some of the glare. Brandon stood with me, beside my favourite possession in the world. Amy went to lean against it. I shot her a look and she frowned, tutted, then stood back upright. She really did have a beautiful face. It didn't matter if she was scowling. I couldn't help but notice how well her trouser suit clung to her as well. Surely it wasn't just off the shelf. Not the way it looked on her.

"Can I trust you boys not to get yourselves in any kind of trouble for a couple hours?" she asked in an exaggerated drawl.

"There's a chance," I said.

Amy cocked her head and made a face at the plume that Brandon was exhaling. He shrugged and continued to grin like a goofball.

"You got a cell phone?" Amy asked me.

I shook my head. "I've been considering investing in a fax machine."

She ignored me and turned to Brandon, "You?"

"Nope," he said. "… sorry." His goofy expression morphed into one more like Pluto's. "I'd a pager, but I tossed it. Didn't wanna get tracked or anything. I watch NYPD Blue."

She tutted again, folded her arms in front of her. "Well, aren't you a couple of little Amish girls? Good grief."

"Sorry Charlie Brown," I said.

She ignored me, took out a notebook, tore a page, scribbled on it and handed it to me. "Here's my cell. I'll be a couple of hours. I need to talk to my boss about what exactly happens next." She checked her watch. "It's three now. Call me at seven? I won't be too far away."

"Okay, cool," I said.

Her jaw dropped a little. "And seriously, Walker, do stay out of trouble."

I gave a little flourish with my wrist. "To quote Joyce; 'Mistakes are the portals of discovery.'"

Chapter 24

It felt good, me and Brandon back speeding along the highway in the greatest ride of my life. I mean that most sincerely, in every way. I loved that damn car. We cruised for an hour or so; Sly and The Family Stone pumping on the stereo, me tapping the wheel and Brandon getting stoned off his behind.

"What album's this?" he asked, trying to awkwardly skin up on his knees.

"*There's a Riot Going On,*" I said. "Funky, but there's some pretty dark stuff on it."

Brandon nodded. "Heavy. I don't mean like heavy guitar... it's... sludgy."

I smiled at him, partly at his stoned expression, seemingly pleased that he had finished his last sentence. But he was right, it is a heavy record. It's dripping with dark synths and infectious, yet murky beats.

"Sly's all burned out these days. Living on the streets apparently. Drugs," I said, lifting a knowing eyebrow.

Brandon ignored the comment and held up his newly made joint. "It's just weed, man."

I shrugged. "Probably not a good time to quit anyway." I lifted up a deck of cigs and pulled one free with my teeth.

We drove around for a while. I wasn't really thinking about where I was going. We'd time to kill and nowhere to be. And we both seemed to feel safer when we were moving. That being said, it wasn't long until we needed something to eat. We weren't very creative and decided on finding a diner near the interstate.

"Hey, aren't we getting a little close to Pilton anyway?" Brandon asked.

"Balls," I said, as if awakening from a dream, taking in the fields and occasional scattering of ancient farmhouses. "Right enough. I'll turn off at this next one... 'bout a mile isn't it?"

"Yeah, cool. I'm just about starved," he said.

***

I'd been in this diner once or twice before. It was much like any other, though the prevailing colour was navy rather than red. The décor wasn't great, but the music was worse; Backstreet Boys segued into Simply Red. Nasty. But the food was okay. Brandon looked high as hell, and he sure did have the munchies. We each wolfed down the house burger with fries. I was stuffed but Brandon managed a slice of pie with cream afterwards. It was good to see him eating well. Then he looked really damn sleepy. I was just reaching for my second cup of coffee when his eyes suddenly grew wide and then he turned a little in his chair. I half rotated; Brandon was watching somebody walk away towards the doors. I faced the door, and watched the fella go out. I hadn't seen his face, but he was black, about five eight, wore a baseball cap, sweats and a white Nike T-shirt.

I looked at Brandon. "Somebody you know?"

He shook his head, didn't say anything.

"Pass me that... please." He gestured to the little pot of coffee.

I pushed it across.

"I don't know him, but I've seen him about the place. Y'know... here and there."

I nodded.

"You think he's friends with Isiah?"

His eyes narrowed. "Not sure. Maybe."

"It's probably fine, right?"

Brandon didn't say anything.

"We'll finish up, then head on, to be sure. Okay?"

"Sure." Brandon pushed his plate away, his mood now dark.

I swivelled and looked back again. The guy seemed to hover around the outside porch area and look back inside again before heading out. He was clutching a cell phone to his ear.

"I'll go settle up now, sure." I stood up and drew my wallet from my pocket.

Brandon nodded.

There was a queue for the counter. I felt myself begin to feel a little anxious too. One woman struggled to find the right change and some guy was being an asshole about how easy or not his eggs had been. Finally, I made it to the counter, paid and left a good tip. I could feel Brandon's eyes on me.

"You do the dishes as well?" He slid out of the booth.

"Big queue. Lots of dicking about. C'mon, let's go." I moved in front of him and led the way.

My eyes scanned over the single men, couples, families, women with babies, who all occupied the various booths.

Nothing unusual.

Nothing to worry about.

I pushed open the glass door to the porch and clocked the same guy, now texting on his phone. His eyes met mine, settled on Brandon behind me, and then he turned and hurried away.

"Shit," said Brandon.

"Yeah, doesn't look great. C'mon, let's get out of here."

We crossed the weathered blacktop outside that led to a strip of parking bays, half covered in weeds. My hand slid inside my jacket pocket. Then another car pulled through the gates of the carpark. It was an old Black Mercedes, but it had been souped up in most ways imaginable, none of them tasteful. Isiah was seated in the front passenger seat.

Chapter 25

"Run."

I shoved Brandon in the direction of my car. The Merc swerved through the entrance and sped up towards me.

Red Sneakers was driving, Toe Caps was in back. Isiah had a wide-eyed expression on him. One arm was in a sling and the other one held a semi-automatic above his head.

"Told you I'd find you niggas!" he screamed out of the window. The few people nearby all scrambled away.

I skipped off to one side. Pulled out my gun, braced my legs, aimed and fired. I pumped off two shots and then dived away, rolling painfully across the dusty ground. The car swerved again and pulled up in a cloud of dust. I'd broken the windshield and was pretty sure I'd sent one into Red Sneakers's right shoulder.

Brandon was ten yards to my left, crouching down behind my Hornet.

"Get her started!" I flung the keys towards him.

I shuffled along the ground on my hunkers, in an arc towards an old, rusted sign advertising Pepsi. I chanced a look. Sure enough, Red Sneakers was stemming the blood flow from his shoulder. I leaned over the top of the sign and sent a bullet into the front right tyre. Isiah and Toe Caps burst out from the car at once. Isiah had a horribly crooked smile on his face as he sent a spray of bullets towards me. I dove behind the sign, hearing the last of the burst ping off the well-worn metal. I'd glimpsed a great big Magnum in Toe Caps's hand and now I heard the unmistakable thud of bullets hitting off the sign.

It sure as hell hadn't been designed to withstand that.

I waited for a pause and fired around the side three times blind. I heard cursing and then the sound of feet on gravel. I bent around the sign, showing as little of me as possible. The two of them were hurrying back towards their car for cover. I plunged off a shot at Toe Caps and got him in the leg. He fell and dropped his gun with a whimper. Isiah looked startled, then swung his gun around and sent another few rounds towards me. I ran away from the savaged sign towards an old skip. Bullets flew everywhere. Then I heard the melodic sound of the Hornet's engine. The spray of bullets stopped. I peered around the side of the skip. Brandon gunned the engine and spun the wheels. Isiah turned towards the car, the gun loose at his side.

Don't even think about it.

I stepped out and began striding towards him, firing as I went. The first went wide, but the second got him in his good arm. Two arms for two. The gun dropped from his hand as I gave him another in the arm and he fell to the ground.

Brandon sped around towards me, tearing up the gravel as I jogged to Isiah and kicked away his gun.

He looked up at me, his eyes wild, and tried to put a hand to his newly injured arm, but the sling prevented him.

"You gone and messed me up good," he said.

I pointed the gun at his head.

"That us even now?" I asked.

His eyes became incredibly small, then widened again. His skin greyed.

I aimed the gun closer to his head.

"Okay, okay, nigga. Get the hell outta here, man. We're good. Damn."

"Good enough." I slipped the gun back in my pocket.

I hopped into the car and Brandon turned her loose.

"Jaysus, go easy," I said as we sped away.

Chapter 26

"You can pull over whenever you want," I said after a few miles. "I can take over."

Brandon looked okay. He still hadn't cracked. The kid had grit, I'd give him that. I thought that last episode might have pushed him over the edge. But he seemed fine. He might even have been amused at my concern for the car. I think I even saw a smirk when I winced as he ground the gears into fifth while we hared along the freeway.

We needed gas. So, we stopped a few miles later and swapped over, thank God.

"You alright?" I asked, once we were back on the freeway.

"Yeah, I guess." Brandon rolled up a fresh J. It hadn't taken long for his buzz to get well and truly killed from the last one. He was set on regaining it. He looked at me, "You think they all made it?"

"Those three? You mean *survived*?" I fumbled out one for myself.

"Yeah."

"I suppose so." I shrugged and sparked up. "They'll all be a little messed up, like." I blew out fresh, beautiful pale blue smoke. I cracked the window.

"They had it coming anyways, I guess," he said absently.

"Flippin' right they did." I reached into the door canal. I found the quarter bottle of Bush I'd left there, spun the lid and took a pull.

I changed CD and fired on *Headhunters* by Herbie Hancock. I flicked to track two: *Watermelon Man*. Brandon looked bemused as the weird synth and whistles intro began. Once the drums and bass kicked in, he was grooving a little in his seat, sucking hard on that fat spliff. I cranked it up and we sat like that for the full track, cruising onwards.

"That's a track," Brandon said with a wide smile.

"It really is. Here give us one wee draw of that." I motioned for the J.

"Really?"

"Aye, just a wee bit."

He passed it and I slowed down the car a little and focused on the upcoming road signs. I took a couple of draws, coughed and handed it back. I got a nice little hit off it. The buzz bouncing off the whiskey was outstanding. But I didn't want to get back in the habit of it. All good things in moderation.

He passed me it again and I took another pull off it. It was tasty stuff, I had to admit.

"What time is it?" I asked, checking out my reflection in the rear-view, tilting it down for a moment. I looked a wee bit high around my eyes, not that you could really tell with the bloody big crow's feet and blotchy face. I needed a good night's sleep. You wouldn't have called me fresh-faced.

"Couple hours to go 'til we call her yet," he said.

"Okay," I moved into the outside lane and turned off at the next intersect.

"Where we headed?"

"Just wait and see."

***

We passed through a town by the name of Newtonlig. I hadn't been there before, but it was big enough, and I was hopeful to find what I wanted. I circled the town centre a couple of times.

Brandon looked at me scornfully. "You don't know where you're going, do you?"

"Hold your horses."

"It's what I was told growing up."

"What was?"

"White folk is all crazy."

I rolled my eyes, then I smiled. "Gotcha!"

I took the next left onto somewhere named Bridge Street. I pulled up out the front and shot my finger at Brandon in a pretend gun.

"There you go."

"Really?" He said.

"Really."

"Now?"

"Why not?"

111

***

"Half-strike" I shouted triumphantly, sauntering back towards the booth in front of the little screen. "Suck it, kiddo!"

Brandon shook his head and stood. "Suck it, kiddo? Man could get himself arrested talkin' that way."

He pushed past me and picked up a couple of bowling balls, trying them out for size. I could tell he was pleased I'd remembered he liked to play. I was pleased to have found a place. We both needed to blow off a little steam anyways. It was quiet in the bowling hall. There were maybe twelve lanes, but less than half were occupied. Some dreadful country music played in the background and the old neon signs everywhere appeared to be dulled by time. But the staff had been friendly, and the lane was cheap to hire for an hour. I picked up our pitcher of beer and poured us both a glass. Brandon had now settled on a heavy looking purple ball.

"Right, Brandon, let's see what you've got. You want me to get the gutter bumpers on for you?"

He ignored me, already approaching the lane carefully, his legs set apart. He broke into a little skip, swung back and sent the ball spinning along the lane, right over those black arrows in the centre. It was straight as a die. Then it crashed into the middle of the pins, scuttled every last one, earning him a strike with his first roll.

He turned, nonchalant. I could see he was suppressing a smile. He winked at me, blew on his fingers like they were on fire and pointed at me, giving a little click with his tongue.

"You just got lucky," I said with mock annoyance. I knew it wasn't a fluke, though. The kid could play.

Brandon made a face, then ran a hand down his T-shirt and broke into a strut.

"I'll tell you one thing, son. You play better than Isiah could." I raised my hands limply with a grin.

We had a fun game. The hour passed by quickly. *Fun*, though I got totally thrashed by him. But it was nice. We didn't know where Amy would want to meet us later, nor if we'd have far to drive. Before booking the lane for any longer, I went over to the payphone and dropped in a few coins. It turned out that she was only a few miles away and said she'd meet us there. There'd be time for another game, then.

"Good news, *dude*," I affected what I thought was a surfer tone. "Amy's gonna meet us here."

"Dude? As in *The Dude*?"

"What?" I poured the end of the pitcher evenly into our two glasses.

"From *The Big Lebowski*. The stoner bowling movie out last year?"

"You lost me. Now I feel like I'm high."

"Never mind. And you must be high, considering the way you're playing." He shook his head. got up and reinspected the bowling balls.

We played on. Brandon continued to kick my ass.

***

"You throw like a girl," a familiar voice stated behind us, just after I'd thrown one of my better shots.

I turned to see Amy smiling at me. She peeled off her black jacket and I glimpsed her gun for a moment.

I raised a hand. "No sexism please. I'm a modern man."

She strode up to the reservoir and began weighing up a few of the balls. "You boys avoid getting into any trouble like I said to?"

I looked over to Brandon. He stifled a smile.

"What you reckon, Brandon? Did we keep our noses clean?"

"Sure did. Didn't even need to wipe a single booger."

Amy turned, made a disgusted face, and then turned back to the bowling balls.

We grinned at each other while her back was turned. Amy took a few more seconds to make her choice. She stood back up, the fingers of her right hand in the holes, her left hand cradling the ball. She moved in closer to us:

"So, it wasn't you two havin' a good old-fashioned shootout in broad daylight? Not you two mixed up in some cray-cray Wild West stuff?"

Her face gave nothing away, but I thought she was a little pissed at us.

"It wasn't our fault," Brandon said suddenly.

I offered a non-committal shrug.

Amy cut her eyes, flicked her hair, and began walking towards the lane.

"I sorted it," she said, and launched the ball.

At first it looked strong and headed through the centre arrows. Gradually, it spun into an arc, ending with it dropping into the gutter, just before the pins.

I heard her curse under her breath. I looked at the ground, trying not to smirk.

She looked at me as she hurried back for her second ball. "Shut up Walker."

"I never said anything. Surely we've been through enough already that you can call me Mick?"

"Yeah, but I like calling you Walker."

Then she hit a solid ten-pin spare.

Chapter 27

"I'll have a small one," Amy said. "Seeing as I'm driving. You're driving too and shouldn't risk another."

"Yeah, I know, but I've a high tolerance. Sure, aren't I Irish?"

We were chatting in a nearby saloon. She'd had two games with us, all of us gradually unwinding. Stretching our muscles, but not in battle for a change. I'd suggested having a drink afterwards to talk things through. Amy told us that she was still waiting on getting more information from her boss. Seemingly the wheels of justice turned slowly. That sure had been my experience before. We wouldn't be hearing anything until tomorrow apparently, so the only option was to bunk down in another motel for the night.

"I've a joke for y'all," Brandon announced.

"Okay," Amy said, a smile curling at the side of her mouth.

"A guy phones into work and says to his boss, 'Listen man, I'm in bed and real sick.'"

"Go on," I said.

Brandon continued, So the boss says, 'How sick are you...?"

"And he says, 'I'm in bed with my sister," I interrupted.

"Aww, you heard it already." Brandon sounded a wee bit annoyed.

Amy gave me a little dig on the arm.

"Ouch. Yeah, I heard it about thirty years ago."

Brandon looked crestfallen.

"You're an asshole," Amy said.

"I'm sorry, man," I said. "I'm just being a dick."

Brandon took a pull on his beer.

"Bacardi and Diet Coke?" I turned up my nose as Amy took a little sip of hers.

"Yeah, what of it? It's a good drink," she said a little too defensively.

I held up a hand. "Alright, settle down. It's alright. It ain't one of these, like." I held up my beautiful amber single malt to the light. She rolled her eyes.

I was in danger of annoying them both without meaning to. It's just how we bantered back home. Maybe I was tired, or maybe I was just being a pain.

"These Irish think they they're the only ones who can drink," Brandon said, taking a sip of his bottle of Bud. "He made me try stout the other day. It was like cream vomit."

Amy nodded and smirked, her lips parting into a grin.

"Some people got no taste," I said.

"You and me, we'll stick together." Amy raised her fist. Brandon gave it a little bop with his own.

"Whoah whoah," I said, then quieter, "what is this? A *Panther* meeting or something?" I gave a wink.

Amy offered me a playful glare.

"Alright, enough of this bull," said Brandon, "What's happenin' next? What do we do now?"

Amy set down her drink. "We hole up for the night. Simple as that. My boss phones me in the morning and we take it from there. You know what it's like. I gotta boss, my boss gotta boss, and so on. Nobody wants to make a decision in case somebody busts his ass."

I nodded. "Fair enough."

"We'll know better in the morning," Amy said.

"So we go find a motel after this?" Brandon asked.

Amy nodded. "Sure."

"Slumber party," I said.

***

We drove in a convoy of two. Amy wanted to put some more distance between us and recent events. After checking the dilation of my eyes and all but making me walk in a straight line, she figured I should be okay to drive for a bit. We drove for almost an hour, sitting at around seventy-five for most of the way. When she signalled off, I followed and did the same. Brandon had dozed off in a dope haze and I nudged him awake.

"Hey, Bob Marley, *we is dere mon,*" I said with an affectation.

He woke up quickly, shaking his head. "That's racist, man."

"Shut up," I said, worrying he was being serious. "Wait'll you hear my *Bruce Lee* impression."

We pulled up at a well-known mid-priced motel chain. At this one we found a little office, a dozen cabins, but no bar or restaurant. It would do us fine. It was only for the night anyway. Me and the kid got out of the car, having parked next to Amy. She got out too, dismissed us back inside our car, then went over to take care of the booking.

Half an hour later and we were comfortable. We were in one of the two identical rooms, halfway through a box of beer I'd picked up on route. There were two single beds inside. It was pretty clean and it didn't stink too much of sweat and bad decisions. We had a couple of lamps on, and Brandon had turned the TV on low to a music channel. Me and him were lounging on one bed. Amy was on the other one. It was the most relaxed I'd seen her. Her jacket was off, the top button on her blouse was open, and her hair was a little ruffled. Her legs were up on the bed as she leaned her back against the wall.

"Where you say you were from again, Amy?" I asked.

"Indiana."

"Cool. I mean, my Geography is wick, so I don't exactly know where that is." I shrugged

"It's an okay place," she said and gestured with one hand. "I mean, it was okay living there… for a time. I couldn't live there forever." When she said *forever*, it sounded like *For…Ev…Ah*. She gave a quick little laugh. "I was in a small town, surrounded by small towns. Just not right for me I guess."

"You still got family there?" Brandon asked, licking the paper on a fresh joint.

She nodded. "My Momma."

"You don't mind if I…?" Brandon said as an afterthought.

"Not really," Amy said, adjusting the pillow behind her back. "I'm not going to arrest you or anything if that's what you mean."

"Nobody else special back home?" I asked, wondering if I was pressing her too much. Amy was still very much an unknown quantity to me. I caught Brandon looking at me quizzically, which I ignored.

"My Daddy went when I was little. There's nobody else." She smiled fully with her eyes and took another sip of beer.

I nodded.

"Those guys earlier…" Amy looked at Brandon. "That Isiah guy the one who put you up to the robbery?"

"Yeah, it was." His eyes darting towards me, then away again.

Amy nodded. "They were in pretty bad shape.".

"Could have been worse. I let them off easy," I said.

"They came looking to off you both. I get it," she said simply.

Amy took another pull of beer, then wiped her mouth.

"So, Walker, you want to tell us about who's after you?"

I blew out some smoke. "You mean specifically? You're talking about Marty Sullivan?"

"Yeah." She leaned forward a little.

I squashed my cigarette in a miniature metal ashtray and blew out the last of the smoke off to one side.

"Okay," I said. "Martin Sullivan. Well, he's a bastard." I shrugged, with a half-smile. Amy cut her eyes at me. Brandon said nothing. "I knew him back in the day. Back when I was a *soldier* too. He was always a mean sort. He was a few years older than me. Led one of the teams. He got off on the power of it all."

"How d'you mean?" Amy asked, her eyes wide and full, staring at me, attentive.

I blew out my cheeks. "I'll give you an example. I was with him and his team one time- working on a joint mission. We were in a safehouse out in the country. Way out in the grasslands of Connemara. It was the day before the job, and we were running a simulation. It was a timed thing out in the hills. One of his team messed up. I mean I admit, the guy was being sloppy. But when we got back to the house, Sullivan singled him out. Bollocked him. When the guy gave some back, Sullivan beat him half to death. There right in front of us. Just laid into him. Brutal."

"What did you do?" asked Brandon.

"I didn't do anything," I said, a little sensitively. "Sullivan was senior to me at the time. If I had done, the day before a mission, I could have been shot for insubordination. Yes, we were illegal paramilitaries, but we were run the same as an army at war. A ruthless army. And we *were* at war."

Amy chewed on that for a moment. "You ever kill anyone?" she asked.

I nodded my head. She nodded back.

"It's what I believed in."

Amy shrugged. "I killed two people yesterday for what *I* believe in."

"And what's that?" I said.

"I serve my country. Whatever that happens to be."

"That's what I tried to do. Fighting seemed to be what that was. Until it wasn't."

Brandon cracked open a fresh beer and passed it to me.

"Cheers, B."

"What about your mission?" Brandon asked me.

"What? Oh, that. Yeah, it went fine. The young guy who got the beating, he couldn't be part of it. He was bedridden for a week after. But he took his punishment and went right back out again afterwards. About a year later he was placing a bomb in a shop in Belfast city centre. It went off early and blew him to pieces."

"Damn," said Brandon.

Amy nodded, her eyes sad, her face attentive. "Did you see this Sullivan guy again?"

I took a drink and nodded. "One more time." I took another sip, closed my eyes for a moment. "When I was pretty sure I was compromised. I mean, after I started spying for The Brits. This was a few years later. When I was pretty sure my cover was blown or close to it, I went to visit my folks." I forced a lump back down my throat and began fiddling with my lighter. "I wanted to look my Ma and Da in the face and explain why I'd done what I'd done. I arrived at their house outside Belfast and there he was. Sullivan. He was standing on their porch, like he was just leaving. My father had a look of thunder on his face, it was all blotchy and scarlet. Ma was crying."

"What did you do?" Brandon asked.

Amy shook her head in an understanding kind of gesture and placed her hand on my leg for a moment.

Tears pricked behind my eyes. "I drove away."

Part 2: Rust Never Sleeps

Chapter 28

We all slept well that night. Me and Brandon in there and Amy next door after leaving us at about one in the morning. The three of us had chatted for hours. It was nice. Really nice. It was strange. I'd been so disconnected by then for years. So bereft of company. People were trying to track me down and kill me, but at the same time, in a way, I was having a better time than I'd had in forever.

Amy knocked on our door about nine in the morning, her face ashen. Neither of us had showered yet and the room stank of tobacco, beer and weed. I cracked open a window and made a pointless effort to tidy a little before bringing her inside.

Amy ran her hand down her outer thigh, straightening already pressed trousers. She sat down on the single chair and gave a little sigh. Her hair was pulled back and she had on a simple white T-shirt with a short black jacket over the top. Her face was taut. She looked very different from the relaxed, chatty girl I had last seen a few hours before. Brandon propped himself up on the bed. He picked up his navy *Braves* cap, used his fist to unflatten it, then placed it on his head.

"What is it?" I desperately needed coffee. My throat was dry and tickly, but I took the first nicotine hit of the day too.

"I spoke with my boss for quite a while there." She slowly, deliberately, rolled her eyes. "It's not going to be as simple as we thought."

"What you mean?" asked Brandon.

I chewed on the filter.

"It means they aren't just going to set you guys up somewhere else. They won't do it. My boss, John McGoohan, says that won't necessarily solve anything anyway. The bottom line is they don't want to pay for it." She shook her head. "I'm sorry."

"Bollox," I said under my breath.

"Yeah, I know." Her tone was sympathetic. "I really am sorry."

"Ach, it's not your fault, Amy," I said. "So, what *are* we meant to do?"

She looked at me, then Brandon, then back to me. "That's the tricky part."

"The tricky part?" I repeated.

"Sooo…" She slowly crossed her legs. "The powers that be want to go down a diplomatic route."

"Wha?" Brandon scowled.

"They want you to meet with some of your former allies, Walker- try and negotiate a peace…"

I jumped up, feeling a wave of panic creep in, "What the hell? That's nuts. Sorry." I raised a hand. "I know it's not your idea, but what are they thinking?"

"Take a seat, Walker." She maintained a calm voice while offering me a hand. I took it for a second and sat back down. "I'll give it all to you, just hear it out anyway, okay?"

"Okay." I chomped harder on the fresh, comforting filter.

"McGoohan says that's want they want you to try. And when I say *they*," she raised a finely plucked eyebrow, "I mean my people, the higher ups, and your Brit friends too."

I sighed, but said nothing, allowing her to continue. Brandon started skinning up.

"*They* want you to meet one of the top guys. IRA, I mean. As you know better than I do, there are various factions over here. Some more active than others. Some just raising money for bombs and bullets to send back home. Some are even more active. Seemingly the hit squad that's after you is working closely with the team in Philly."

"As in Philadelphia?" I asked.

She snorted, then smiled at me like I was a toddler. "Where else?"

This was a lot to take in. Especially hungover.

Brandon lifted his cap off his head and ran a hand over his sweaty scalp.

I thought for a moment. "Joe Pierce?" I asked, meeting her eye. She nodded. "Yes."

"He's still the top guy there?"

"Yes."

I nodded and ran a hand through my own hair. "Joe Pierce," I repeated under my breath.

"You knew him?" It sounded more like a statement rather than a question.

"Aye, well I met him a couple of times, that's all. It'd be near ten years ago. Back when he was a local commander. I'd heard he'd snuck over here."

"Were you friendly with this dude?" Brandon asked.

I shrugged. "I didn't really know him. Like I said, I just met him a few times."

"But he was alright?" Brandon pressed.

I blew out my cheeks. "He was an IRA commander, so he wasn't exactly Mr Nice. He didn't seem massively impressed with me then. I imagine since turning tout I haven't risen any in his estimations."

Amy eyed me carefully. Her knee jiggled up and down.

I squinted at her. "So, what's the plan exactly?"

She closed her eyes for a moment then swept back a few strands of thick black hair that had come loose from her ponytail. "They want you to set up a meet with Pierce. Have a 'sit down'. There are foundations of peace back in your country. The IRA are meant to be putting down their weapons. We're on the road to reconciliation, is how your Brit friends put it."

"They're no friends of mine."

"They don't want the expense of moving you about for forever, I guess, and with young Brandon here too... They'd rather you thrash things out between y'all."

"Why in the heck would they even speak to me? What's in it for them?"

She scratched at her ear, then crossed her arms. "There are back channels. Nothing direct. Things are too delicate over the whole *Irish Question*. Nothing official. But the dialogue I'm hearing is that it would gain the Republican movement some good grace maybe. Some bargaining chips even. You dead won't gain them much. Surely they'd rather have movement on things back home: policing, Irish language, devolved government... all of that stuff."

I chewed on it.

Brandon looked from me to Amy. "I'm no expert on any if that. It confuses the hell outa me. But I do know most people don't like being betrayed none. Somebody's gone to a lot of trouble trying to kill you so far, Mick. You go show yourself to them, motherfuckers are gonna shoot you."

"Yeah, maybe," Amy said nodding. "But we'd take precautions."

"Bulletproof vest and a prayer circle?" I asked.

"Might be a start."

"Four leaf clover? Extra rosary beads?" I added.

Amy said nothing.

I sighed.

"Might as well be shot for a sheep as a lamb. You know how it's likely to go, though, don't you?"

"I'll come with you, Walker. I'm going to help you," she said.

"I appreciate that, but there's only so much you can do. I'd say I'm pretty screwed."

"Come on, that's not going to help," she said.

"I know." I was exasperated. "But it's the way it is."

I took a breath and gave a brief smile. I saw that Brandon looked worried and I shot him what I hoped was an encouraging wink.

Then I quoted Behan. "'It's not that the Irish are cynical. It's rather that they have a wonderful lack of respect for everything and everybody.'"

Chapter 29

We were close to a thousand miles from Philadelphia. Amy didn't seem to consider that much of a distance. I supposed the Feds were used to crisscrossing various state lines. Maybe just Americans were. Back home you could hardly drive a hundred miles in any direction without plunging into the sea. We studied her map in the cabin and she showed me the rough route, but said it was well sign posted anyway. I essentially had to drive straight for about a gazillion hours. Sixteen actually, she estimated. We agreed that we'd stop off somewhere around Pittsburgh to sleep in the early evening. We'd try and keep the stops to a minimum during the day to eat up as many miles as we could. Brandon travelled with me. Then we could regroup and plan things out in more detail.

In the car I played Brandon a couple more Prince albums and then we listened to some radio. I was in danger of running out of CDs. I'd never duplicated all that much of my vinyl and tape collections to digital. But it was 1999 after all, and I needed to get with the times. At least the drive gave me some distraction and purpose. I thought everything through, looked for the angles. But I was gutted by what few options we had.

It was tricky enough to stay in a two-car procession over such a long distance. It felt okay on the big freeways, but outside the cities the sheer amount of traffic and lanes were a head melt. Brandon's navigating skills also left much to be desired, which I told him. Several times. My baby was purring nicely and was more than a match for Amy's, though she was driving at quite a clip. As we bypassed Chicago, I got a little twang that I'd love to visit it. I'd never been. How preferable would it be to take out a wad of cash and disappear into some blues den or another for the rest of the day and night. But that wasn't to be. I had pressing concerns. Maybe another time.

After the double *Sign of The Times* CD ran out – which Brandon had nodded his head along in approval with – I switched on a local channel for the news. It was depressing listening. In this state alone there was more violence than the whole country back home, it seemed. It was enough to make Brandon begin to skin up a fresh joint. Maybe those things weren't connected.

"You never run out of that?" I asked.

"Nope. I'm frugal with it."

I allowed my eyes to widen dramatically. "*Frugal* indeed?"

"I did go to school, y'know."

"Yeah, but I'm not sure you learned much if you think the way you smoke is frugal."

"Probably not as bad as two packs of Marlboro reds a day and drinking like a fish."

He had me there.

Once the newsreader was done telling us the bad stuff going on in Pennsylvania, we got some general USA reports. Breaking news came through that John F Kennedy Jnr and his wife had been killed in a plane crash.

"That family can't catch a break," I said. "Unlucky buggers."

"Understatement."

"Bloody jinxed, them lot. But at least two of 'em got the ride off of Marilyn Monroe."

Brandon winced. "C'mon man."

"What?"

"Bit tasteless."

"Wind your neck in. I meant it. That their luck is terrible, like. And I'm only messing around with the Marilyn stuff. Still- good for them."

I passed across a packet of salted crisps. *Chips* as I should call them. Chips to me are thick strips of deep-fried potato, dripping with grease. Even better with cheese and beans, or a spot of gravy. These things were what we called crisps, and they weren't very good. What I'd have given for a packet of Tayto cheese and onion.

"I know, but they're kinda like our Royal Family." He pondered this with the large joint in his hand. "You'd be offended if people were talkin' loose about The Queen."

"Not me." I rolled my eyes. "Sod the Queen."

"I'm so confused, man. I can't work out who you're for or against." He finished rolling his latest creation, the last one still smouldering between his lips.

"Me neither, mucker," I said.

We drove on. The Hornet held up nicely. I like driving. I like driving long stretches. But I don't like feeling that I'm being hunted. I suppose that's a given.

Amy had held steady around eighty just in front of us. She slowed down in the lane beside and pointed to the next exit. It was past lunchtime, and I was half starved. We found a *services* station which looked beyond awful, so we continued on to a small town called Brostan Hills. It seemed a decent size, with a couple of main streets. We parked up near an empty baseball park, down a side street. The three of us walked towards the town centre, stretching out our aches and pains. Brandon and I sparked up at the same moment. I noticed Amy's look of disproval.

"You never been on the ole cancer sticks?" I asked her.

Her eyes narrowed. "No."

I shrugged. "Never, like?"

"Well, when I was a teenager or whatever."

"Ahh, you see." I waved my ciggy at her.

"But I grew out of it."

Ouch. I changed the subject in a hurry. "So, you know this town?"

"Never been here. Don't know if you noticed, but America's quite a big place."

Brandon smirked.

"Aye alright, Amy. You're some yoke, so you are."

We shared a smile. The three of us enjoyed stretching our legs and kicking our shoes through the dirt. My back ached. All the recent scuffles wouldn't have helped any. I felt like I'd just played a Boxing Day grudge derby for Glentoran against The Blues.

"Let's get us a feed. My stomach thinks my throat's been cut."

Brandon raised his eyes to Amy. "You get used to the way he talks." His voice dripped with mock reassurance.

We walked along Primrose Street, past a little fountain and a monument to some forgotten senator. The layout of the town centre probably hadn't changed much since the time of Cowboys and Indians. It was like the old blood splattered wooden shacks had just been built over with eighteenth century bricks. I supposed that *is* what had happened. We passed a drugstore, a butcher's, and a fruit and veg shop. Then we each locked eyes on a two-storey restaurant at the end of the square. It looked decent. Through the big glass windows we could see a smart little place a few rungs up from our recent greasy diners. As we waited for a crossing sign, a big burly guy of about my age walked towards us. His narrow brown eyes met mine beneath his worn navy baseball cap. He barely tried to avoid bumping into me as he passed by.

"Hey, watchit," I said.

I half turned, watching his large frame covered by a red lumberjack shirt moving away. Amy and Brandon both formed scowls. I heard the man mutter something while he walked away. It took me a little too long to compute what he had actually said.

"Nigger lover."

What the hell?

I went to go after him. Amy grabbed me by the arm.

"Don't," she said.

"No, man," Brandon said at the same moment.

"Seriously like!" I looked at them both, my eyes popping. "He can't get away with that."

"It don't matter," said Brandon.

"C'mon." Amy tugged my arm before releasing it again. "You get used to it."

They walked away and I reluctantly followed. They began chatting about something else and we went on through the doors of the café. I looked back a few times, but the scum-bag had disappeared.

It was even nicer inside than it had looked from outside. But I didn't care anymore. I pasted on a half-smile and chatted with them while we looked at the menu. Brandon and I ordered our now staple of cheeseburgers, and Amy asked for a plate of over easy eggs with sausages.

"Aww flip," I said after the waitress left, patting my shirt pocket. "I'm out of smokes. Be back in a sec." I got up to leave.

"Okay..." Brandon eyed me suspiciously.

I didn't look at Amy.

I came back ten minutes later with the same pack in my pocket and a bunch of bruised knuckles. I tried to hide my hands as I sat down. I didn't need to hide any other injuries because I hadn't taken any.

After a couple of false starts I had found him in one of the three bars at the end of the road. He'd been taking a leak. The bogs were empty. While his lad was still out, I grabbed him by the hair on the back of his head and slammed him into the urinal. He hit the stinking floor. I kicked him once in his exposed nuts and offered him a brief lesson on the dangers of racism.

Back in my seat, I placed my left hand over my right knuckles and said hello to them both. I caught Amy looking at me. She whipped a hand across to my jacket and slipped out my deck. She flipped it open and silently mouthed a quick count.

"So, if this is a fresh pack, you've already had nearly half of them in the last ten minutes?"

"What can I say? I'm addicted."

She shook her head with annoyance, but I thought I saw something else in her eyes. They both clocked my hand. Brandon gave me a discreet fist bump underneath the table. I saw the waitress moving towards us with a large tray.

"Here it comes," I said. "Right, I'm flippin' starving."

Chapter 30

On the next part of the journey, Brandon kept Amy company in her car. It felt weird without him, but I figured it was only right Amy wasn't by herself the whole time. Then I started worrying that they'd be talking about me. What would they say? It hadn't really entered my mind before. Maybe they blamed me for all the trouble they'd encountered. I rifled through my CDs, keeping one eye on the road. The knuckles on my right hand throbbed. I thought about the guy I'd decked. Only I hadn't just decked him, I'd given him a fairly good beating.

Why had I done that?

To stick up for Brandon and Amy? Or because I didn't like what he'd said about *me*?

I struggled to understand half of what I did at any one time, so I tried to put it out of my head. What did it matter now anyway? He'd had it coming.

I finished poking around the various piles of CDs and settled on the second Black Crowes album. *The Southern Harmony and Musical Companion.* Not a very catchy title. That didn't matter because the album was a monster. It captured that moment when a band as a group of musicians gelled so well that they lived up and exceeded the potential that had been brewing. When that happens in a band when the songs are good, is something to behold. It was a good distraction. The album was almost ten years old and I never tired of listening to it.

I ate up the miles, smoking while grooving a little, in time with the music. I almost pined for one of Brandon's spliffs. Our cars weaved in and out of lanes beside one another. At other times I lost track of them completely. A few times when I overtook them, I could see Brandon hunched over, knowing well that he was building a new blunt. Amy wouldn't be thrilled about that.

Just before 7p.m, we hit Pittsburgh. We passed by the outskirts and signs for the *Stealer's* home ground dotted our path. I'd caught a game on TV a few months before against The Washington Redskins. I'd tried paying attention for about a half hour, but I hadn't a clue what was going on. I'd not watched another game since. I'd given up on watching rugby about a decade earlier and at least I understood most of that. Football was where it was at. I still loved Man Utd and back home I'd watched The Glens as often as I could. As a young kid I'd pretty much gone to every game, home and away. Those were the days. In 1967, when I was thirteen, I joined forty thousand fellow Glen-men to welcome the mighty Benefica to The Oval. We were a wee part-time local team, and they were the kings of Europe, including World Cup legend Eusebio in their line-up. Somehow, we drew with them. The little local team matched these world class pros. When player/manager John Colrain launched in a penalty at the Sydenham end of our stadium the place went absolutely nuts. Two years later and Northern Ireland nearly destroyed itself in a plume of gelignite, gunfire and hate.

I followed Amy toward the west side of the city, a little beyond the centre proper. Her boss had organised a hotel for us there and at about twenty past seven, we pulled up on the gravel of the front car park. It was windy out and wet too. The light from the hotel was very inviting. It had only two storeys with maybe forty rooms, the bricks clad in a layer of rough wood. There were big windows downstairs where I guessed the bar and restaurant were. Once we got out of the cars there was also the aroma of something meaty and tasty.

Inside, we waited in a small queue, our rag-tag little group of three. There was a lot more pine inside and some questionable watercolours and ornaments. But it seemed clean, well maintained and the bar off to the left had a log fire, low music and good whiskey. Amy began talking with a dour-looking man behind the reception. I absently stared at a little tourist information sheet pinned to the far end of the long front desk. It had a nice black and white graphic all about Pittsburgh. Pity we were only passing through and wouldn't have any time for exploring. It informed me anyway that *The Steel City* had at one time three hundred steel businesses and was also known as *Bridge City* for its four hundred and forty-six bridges. Amy sidled back up to us just as I was starting on the potted history of the city.

"You guys go on into the bar. My boss is parked outside," she said in a low voice.

"He's here…now?" Brandon said.

She nodded. "I'll have a quick chat with him then bring him in to see you. Okay?"

"Sounds like a plan," I said. "What do you want to drink?"

She frowned. "I'd better stick with a bottle of Coke. But not the diet crap."

"Living dangerously." I gave her arm a little tap as Brandon and I walked on through to the bar.

Five minutes later and Brandon was seated opposite me taking a pull on his beer, as I had yet another smoke. Once this was all over, I'd have to think about getting nicotine patches or something. I was having a whiskey too. It was good.

"What are you puttin' in that?" Brandon asked.

Whiskey *with* lemonade and ice.

I almost blushed. It was a sore point. I'm Irish, but sometimes I like a little lemonade and ice in my dram. So what?

I shrugged. "It's nice like this sometimes. I'm thirsty."

Brandon let out a little laugh. "All this schoolin' you meant to be givin' me, and I gotta teach you how to drink *American*."

I rolled my eyes and took a sip, set it down and gave Brandon an ironic smile. "How good of you. Anyway- I don't reckon Jack and Coke is anymore sophisticated."

Just then, Amy walked in, looking both professional and still a million dollars. Beside her walked a tall, dapperly dressed man a little past his middle-age. He had a full white-grey beard and green horn-rimmed spectacles.

"Good evening." He spoke in a light American accent I couldn't quite place.

"Michael, Brandon, this is John McGoohan," Amy said, sounding more formal than usual.

It was the first time she had used my first name. As McGoohan bent down to shake Brandon's hand I raised my eyebrows to Amy behind his back and gave her a wink.

"How you doin'?" Brandon asked.

I stood, "Good to meet you." I shook his hand in turn, then pulled chairs out for them both.

"Please," he said, urging me sit down first.

We got settled. I offered him a drink, but he said he would perhaps get a glass of water in a few minutes.

There was a moment or two of silence. Brandon fidgeted with his lighter and Amy adjusted the crease in her suit trousers. McGoohan's beady eyes looked me up and down.

I didn't like him. My first impressions are usually pretty sound. He hadn't done anything wrong, but I already suspected that he was probably an unscrupulous and arrogant kind of sort. Hr just gave off that vibe. Maybe that was unfair, but it's what I thought. But I needed him. After the initial craziness of the break in and everything with the hit squad, I had been happy to somewhat go with the flow. I would follow their lead. As long as they could offer me and Brandon something, I would take whatever help they would give us. But I had a limit on what I would give in return. I already trusted Amy. I trusted she had our best interests in mind, to an extent anyway. After all, she had only known us a few days. For young, eager Feds, I knew that nothing would come above *The Homeland.* Still, I'd seen only good things from her so far. But as for the rest of them, and especially this guy, the jury was still out.

"Your rooms are ready upstairs," McGoohan began, clasping his hands together in a tent on the table. "There's one for each of you. Agent Landish has your keys."

"Great, cheers." I swirled my drink.

"Thanks," Brandon said in a low voice. He lifted his cap off for a moment and ran a hand over his short hair. "Er… Agent Landish has been awesome," he said a little shyly.

"Yeah, I second that," I said. "She's a credit to your organisation."

Amy looked mortified.

"Good, good," McGoohan said benevolently, like a preacher on his third service of the day.

"So, to the urgent matters in hand," he said soberly. I saw his lips purse behind the insulating layers of his beard. "Agent

Landish has informed you of the plan?" His voice quivered slightly on the last syllable.

My brow furrowed. "Roughly, yeah. I mean we haven't really talked in detail much yet."

He shot a school-teacher-like half glare towards Amy.

I saw her swallow and gather herself.

"Sir, as I informed you earlier, I have outlined the plan to both Michael and Brandon in broad strokes. We all agreed that at this time, with your assistance, we would develop the implementation further."

His expression softened and he almost smiled. "Yes, yes, that's fine." His voice was slightly clipped.

"Amy had explained that all to us, but I wanted to speak with yourself as well before finalising anything. Give you your place," I said a little clumsily, fearful I had accidentally dropped Amy in the turd.

"Please, Mr Walker, tell me your ideas for how we should *develop the implementation*," he said with a thin smile.

"'All the world's a stage and most of us are desperately unrehearsed.'" I said.

"Pardon?" He said a little haughtily.

"Sean O'Casey."

"Oh."

He fidgeted with his striped maroon and black tie.

I'd annoyed him a little. Good. I needed to play nice with these people, but I didn't have to be their whipping boy.

"Tell me first what exactly *you* want to get out of this," I said.

Amy shifted uncomfortably in her seat.

McGoohan smiled mirthlessly. "What *I* want to do, is to try and peacefully save your backsides."

Brandon nearly choked on a peanut.

"So, tell me about it," I said, unfazed.

He breathed out slowly and deliberately. He kept his eyes on me as he took off his glasses. Produced a handkerchief and began cleaning the lenses.

"Alright. We have made contact with Joe Pierce," he began, keeping his voice low. In the background the other patrons of the bar went on with their business as Mariah Carey sang some awful cheese on the stereo. "You are all of course aware that Mr Pierce is the top man in Philadelphia. The Irish Republican movement there is very active. There are several *on the runs* we know to be in hiding in Philadelphia. It is also a key cog for the fundraising wing of the IRA. AK47s from Libya are not cheap." He flashed a brief smile before returning his glasses to his substantial nose.

"But the war's over, right?" I asked.

"I think you know that that remains to be seen," he said. "Anyway, Pierce is also a key man when it comes to IRA movements throughout America."

"Like hit squads?" asked Brandon.

"Exactly," McGoohan said. A teacher pleased with a student this time.

"We hope that this all can be ironed out, peacefully," Amy cut in. "There are plenty of reasons why the IRA do not want to make waves at this delicate time. Our hope is that Pierce will see reason. That he'll call off the hunt. He has that power."

"And if he doesn't?" I asked.

Amy looked to McGoohan.

McGoohan's eyes bored into mine. "Then you are free to do something about him."

I leaned back in my chair. "And what does that mean exactly?"

McGoohan slipped out a stick of gum from his pocket and began chewing. "We have made first contact with Pierce through an intermediary. Pierce has agreed to meet with you."

"I'm sure he has." I blew out a grey haze and rolled my eyes. "Where exactly?"

"No time or place has been chosen yet," Amy said. "It will possibly be as soon as tomorrow evening. We don't want to give them too long to plan or to set a trap. We also can't be one hundred percent confident of the security of our internal communications."

McGoohan's mouth tightened again, and this time gave her his full glare. Amy looked away.

"And what if he doesn't want to let me go?" I said.

McGoohan composed himself and put both hands up. "Then you can do whatever you have to do."

"What... me by myself? Against God knows how many Provos?"

"We cannot afford to officially get involved in this, Mr Walker. Surely you comprehend that. We are assisting as a favour to your government."

"Not *my* government," I said tersely.

"We can offer you a certain amount of weaponry. And unofficially, Agent Landish will support you. Perhaps your young friend here too?" He gestured towards Brandon.

"You know I'm with you, Mick," Brandon said.

"Thanks, bud." Then I glared at McGoohan. "Three of us isn't exactly an infantry."

"Under the circumstances, it is the best you are going to get," McGoohan said crisply.

I held his cold stare, then turned to the others.

"Listen, I appreciate it, but I don't want either of you getting hurt. We'll have no idea what we're walking into. You don't know these guys like I do."

"That may be true, but we will work out a clear strategy how we can be successful," McGoohan said slowly. Then his eyes brightened, "'By failing to prepare, you are preparing to fail.'" He smiled at me. "Benjamin Franklin." The smile was sickeningly smug.

I looked towards the ceiling and shook my head.

McGoohan leaned back and fiddled with one of his cufflinks absently. "And what other choice do you have anyhow?"

Chapter 31

Not much of a damn choice, that's what.

Seeing as neither the Brits nor the Yanks were offering to whisk us away and hide us long-term, he was right. I'd no choice. Not really. We couldn't just run from motel to motel forever. They'd get us eventually. And my money would run out very soon. We spoke with McGoohan for another hour or so, thrashing out a rough plan, possible locations, possible scenarios. I didn't feel exactly prepared, but it was something. He slipped me a piece of folded paper with Pierce's number on it and I agreed to contact him the next day. Then McGoohan made his excuses and left. Once he was out through the door, it felt as if a weight had been lifted from all of us.

"Right, I'm going outside for a smoke." Brandon left us to chat.

Amy raised her eyebrows and shot me a look. "Well, that's my boss." She grimaced.

"What a peach."

"He's not as bad as… Well, he's not as bad as he comes across."

"He wouldn't need to be. I wouldn't trust him as far as I could throw him."

When Brandon returned, we ordered some food. Neil Young came over the speakers singing something off of *After the Goldrush* that I couldn't place. That irritated me slightly. I should have known what it was. But it was nice to hear it anyway. The food came and it was good. We had more drinks, and they went down easy. Amy kicked off her shoes. I drank more whiskey with less ice and lemonade. People in the bar became a notch livelier as they got more drunk, but it was a safe, good-natured kind of drunk. We stayed and soaked up the hubbub until just before midnight, then all beat and a little inebriated, we made our way upstairs. The stairs split off at the top into two wings. We were all on the left-hand side. Brandon and I were down one end in rooms twenty-six and twenty-seven. Amy was at the far end in number thirty-one. We said goodnight to Amy, all of us in good spirits, and speaking for myself, with a good little buzz on. Brandon came into my room for a few minutes and smoked a small one-skinner out my window. He was pretty chilled, considering it all. I gave him the Glock for under his pillow and locked my door behind him.

I switched off the main light and flicked on the lamp on my clean but tired looking pine bedside table. There was a lot of pine in the room, and a few more paintings of flowers and country landscapes. It was grand. The room smelled fresh and more than met my needs. It was a smoking room, which was the icing on the cake.

I took a leak in the small ensuite, then made a cup of coffee with the little percolator. I can drink coffee right before bed and it never gives me a problem. Sometimes I have bad nights like anybody else, but it isn't a cup of coffee at the root of it. I took off my jeans and top and sat on the bed just in my boxers. Jeeze, I was aching. I wasn't used to all the fisticuffs and raking all over the place all the time. I was feeling my age. I picked up the remote and flicked the telly on low.

Scrolling through, I couldn't believe it when I hit on a repeat of a snooker match between Jimmy White and the Northern Irish legend, Hurricane Higgins. Higgins had the same old swagger, though he was certainly frayed round the edges. I took a cautious sip of the hot coffee. I hadn't seen this match before. He wasn't as good as he had been but seeing him pull off some impossible shots; three sheets to the wind and chain-smoking throughout, was still something to behold.

I folded out that day's old newspaper on the writing desk and took out my Colt. I carefully took it apart, keeping an eye on the match, laying out the parts neatly on the paper. I was extra cautious with the recoil spring plug. It more than once had shot off towards the ceiling and disappeared from view. I went into the bathroom, got the glass and filled it with warm water and a tiny bit of soap. I snagged the complimentary toothbrush too. I produced the little vial of white vinegar that I always keep in one of my pockets, and set it all out neatly in front of me.

I paused and watched the last few frames while I finished my coffee. Cricket came on next which I definitely didn't want, so I flicked through the channels again, finding nothing, then through the radio options. I stopped when I came across BBC World

Service and the news that Nato had bombed Yugoslavia. I listened to the whole report while starting work on the cleaning. I didn't mind doing it. I had to stop myself from cleaning the gun *too* much. You can damage it like that. But I enjoyed doing it. It's a satisfying task. And it helps knowing that it can stop you from getting killed.

I was wiping the components down when a report came on about Northern Ireland. The violence had settled down, but it hadn't stopped. However, there was something new in the air, it seemed. There was hope. One big piece of good news was that the INLA had followed the IRA in agreeing to a temporary ceasefire. That was something better at least. When I leaned over and switched the T.V off, I turned off the light too. In the darkness I lifted up the gun, checked it was loaded correctly and set it back down on the side table, handle towards me. I wiped the rest of the grease from my hands on the bedspread.

I lay back, not minding the tart smell of vinegar in the room. I was sleepy. I actually felt pretty good. I had that feeling, that definite knowledge that you're going to have a great night's sleep. I let out a yawn and rolled over onto my side. The moon's rays crept through the blinds. Even with everything that was happening, I had the comforting sensation of approaching oblivion. I closed my eyes.

And I did have a great sleep.

Right until I woke up to someone trying to kill me.

Chapter 32

It was the footstep outside my room.

Just one creak.

I couldn't even be sure it wasn't part of the dream I'd been having. But that's what woke me. Then a second later, when I was fully awake, I heard it again.

I threw back the covers and grabbed my gun, noiselessly.

I stood in the room, only wearing my boxers, listening hard.

It could have been anything. There was no tangible reason to think anything was about to happen. Nothing except something on the air. Something that was making the defensive wiring in my brain kick in and the hairs on my arms stand up. I stepped back to the bed and grabbed a pillow. Then I shoved it under the covers to resemble a body. I padded silently into the ensuite and positioned myself behind the door, watching the room through the crack.

After about a minute of crouching and silent breathing, I began to feel a little foolish, hiding there in my boxers. A smile played at my lips for a second.

This is stupid.

No, this *was* something. I knew it was. Just as I had known at my house. My heart was now clenched like a fist trapped inside my chest, punching out. Adrenalin coursed through me. My mind played scenarios and solutions. I eased my grip on the gun, wriggled each finger a little, then held it tighter again. I was ready.

A minute passed by. Doubt crept in again.

I could make out the green illuminated face of the clock on my bedside table; 3.17 a.m.

Then I heard the quiet snick of the lock. With a whisper of air, the door opened, casting a dim semi-circle of shadow across a metre of the room. It disappeared as the door shut again and a figure slipped in, gun out. It was Madden. He was probably Sullivan's best man. It made sense. He took three quick steps, then plunged off two silenced rounds into my bed.

Pft, pft, went the dull bark from his revolver.

139

He took a step towards the bed, now about to pass the ensuite door.

It was too awkward to get a good draw on him. Twisting around the door would take a few milliseconds. Plenty of time for him to still get the drop on me. If I left it too long, he'd see I wasn't in the bed. Then he'd probably set his eyes straight on the ensuite door. Shoot first and ask questions later.

Instead, as he began to pass the door, I eased it fully open and launched myself at him. I managed to knock his gun away, but I lost my Colt in the process. Madden was a brute of a big fella. Only a few years older than me and fit as a butcher's dog. He tumbled half onto the bed, me grappling with him. We blocked each other's attempted punches. Somehow pure strength allowed him to spring back up again, shoving me off him. We separated for a second, then we were both on our feet, easing into fighting stances. Madden's looked to me like that of a 1950's heavyweight boxer. I didn't worry too much about style. I never had. All I worried about was having enough room to break into a low and solid stance. If you can swing your hips a little, there's a lot you can do in a fight. If you've room to swing fully, that's even better.

I had room to swing.

But I was too slow. The momentum was still with Madden. He feinted with a left, and I blocked a light right. Then he threw the real punch. The one he'd been stalling. It was a hard left to my cheek. It cut my lip as his huge fist scraped along my face.

I was dazed.

He hit me a second time. In the face again. Blackness crept around the edges of my vision.

Not a good start.

I shook my head, hopped backwards. Another punch glanced my jaw. I bent my knees, concentrated, instinctively felt what I needed to do. I slipped into the zone. I hadn't thrown a punch yet, but I already knew I was going to win.

Overconfidently, Madden went to grab me. I sidestepped a hundred and eighty around him, grabbing his arm with both my hands. I twisted, then bent his arm up his back in one sharp movement until I heard a crack. My eyes had adjusted enough to see the colour drain from his face. Then I let go, rotated and began a vicious barrage of jabs to his face. He was defenceless. He'd soon crumple. I hit out again with an uppercut. The door burst open behind me.

The young guy, Daly, appeared in the doorway. He also had a silenced pistol in his hand. I dove as it released a *pft, pft, pft*, the barrel flashed with light. It looked like one of the bullets may have caught Madden as he fell to the floor. I eyed my Colt just out of reach and scrambled across the floor towards it. There was noise from somewhere out in the hallway and I saw Daly look worriedly out towards it. I scooped up my gun. He turned back and started to take aim again. I plunged off two rounds. They soared into centre mass.

The roar of my gun ripped through the relative silence, a stark contrast to the silencers. I got him in the neck and chest. Daly yelped. He fell, blood spurting fast from his throat. The gunshots still resounded in my ears, but I rolled to my side, hearing another noise. The severely injured Madden crawled slowly across the floor, toward his gun. He was only a metre away. I aimed, closed one eye and blew the back of his head off. Blood and gristle splattered back at me. I raised a protective hand, but too late. I used the bed to haul myself up, stunned. I swam through the cordite fog. There was blood everywhere. Madden was most certainly dead. If Daly was alive, he wasn't going to be for very long. There was more noise from outside. Whispers. The shuffling of feet.

How many shots had I fired? Only three? More? I'd at least ten left, anyway. No time to change the clip. I inched towards the door, then used it for cover, peering round. Outside was only illuminated by dim security lights, but my night vision now was very good. Down the hall was a man in dark clothes. He inched along the hallway at the far end, pressing close to the wall, a gun in his hand. I heard Amy's door fling open and I turned. She burst out, with a Heckler and Koch pump action in her hands, held steady and low at her waist.

"Get out the way, Michael," she shouted.

She'd called me Michael again, I remember thinking, then I ducked back into my room. Then there was a boom, and another one. Smoke sifted in through my open doorway. The shotgun had spat twice. I gingerly peered out to see what was left of the attacker. Then I looked towards Amy. She jogged up to me, holding the gun soldier style.

"How many?" she asked.

"Two in my room."

"Dead?"

"By now…?" I said looking back. "Yeah."

There was a *click* somewhere and my heart gave a little palpitation.

Amy swung her gun toward Brandon's door.

It opened slowly. Brandon's sickly face looked out.

"You alright?" I asked.

He nodded. He seemed to stifle a dry heave.

Amy paced, watching the two exits, gun raised.

"At least they didn't come into your room," I said.

Brandon shook his head, then pulled the door back.

Me and Amy both took a step and looked inside. There was another man in black laid out on the floor, a blade rammed in his chest.

I looked at Brandon. "You did that?"

He nodded.

I smiled and patted him on the chest. "Well done, mate."

"We need to get moving," Amy said urgently. "There might be more."

"Yeah. Brandon, grab the Glock and we'll get out of here."

Chapter 33

We made our way carefully along the corridor. If any of the other rooms were occupied, they all had the good sense not to come out. There were a few empty bottles left outside rooms, ready for collection. Breakfast order signs were hung off a couple of doors. A number of 'do not disturb' signs too.

Well, that hadn't worked.

I led the way, with Brandon in the middle, and Amy taking up the rear. She pumped another round into the chamber of the shotgun. A few steps from the west end of the corridor, with the fire exit to the side, another man appeared from behind us. Amy shot off another big three-inch shell with a deafening boom. It missed the man. He ducked, and a chunk of plaster exploded from the wall beside him. I turned, just as Martin Sullivan appeared beside him. Martin's face twisted into a snarl. His eyes met mine for a moment. He had a shotgun too, but his was a sawn-off little number.

"Go! You two get out there. I'll hold them. Go on!" I grabbed Amy's arm before giving Brandon a shove towards the fire door. They looked like they were going to argue, before Sullivan launched off a noisy splatter from his sawn-off.

It missed. A chunk of wood snapped off from a windowsill as the widening spray of pellets flew wide.

My Colt sent a brace back, both missing their targets.

I hustled Amy and Brandon out of the door and skidded around the corner with them. A barrage of shots flew at us from behind.

"Go!" I said again as they each gave me a worried look. "I'll just be a sec."

Amy gave me a little nod with uncertain eyes before kicking the fire door open and grabbing Brandon by the arm. I checked my gun.

I looked down at myself, still only wearing my damn boxer shorts.

Jesus.

Boxer shorts splattered with other people's blood and guts.

143

I knelt at the corner and bent myself into the least uncomfortable position from which I could squat while intermittently firing around the bend. Another two shots flew into the back wall, sending plaster dust all around. I leaned into the bend, the dust and smoke giving me partial cover. I allowed myself a second to aim properly. They were both hunched down, maybe six metres away. It'd be easier to hit the other guy. I closed one eye and breathed out. I aimed and hit him in the stomach. He doubled over and I drilled round another into his head. I ducked back as Sullivan returned one from his sawn-off.

"Your mate lost his head there," I shouted towards the darkness, while checking my ammo.

Six bullets left.

Bollocks.

My spare rounds were in my room.

"Give it up, Michael," came the reply. His voice had everything I remembered about him in it. Arrogant, uncouth, reckless, but also strong and cunning. "We've you beat. There are loads of us."

I bent round and shot twice more. Both missed. He was too far away, and part shielded behind a large fire hose wheel.

Four bullets left.

"That's a load of shite, Marty. You're a bad liar, mate."

I began to bend around for another shot when he fired off a round. It took another chunk out of the corner of the wall.

"That was close Michael. I nearly had you there," he hollered.

He nearly did, too.

Then I had an idea.

I eased round and plunged off two more. I didn't think I hit anything. In the distance I could hear sirens call.

Two bullets left.

"Cops are comin' for ye," I shouted before grabbing up one of the almost empty bottles on the floor nearby. There was a little red wine in the bottom of it. I emptied that onto the carpet and poured some leftover liquor and martinis from cocktail glasses swiped off a couple of other trays. Someone had even left a fair shot or two of Scotch in a decanter. Must have been expensive stuff. What a disgrace.

"You must be nearly out of ammo, Michael," a shout came back. "I'll have you before they get here." Then his shotgun spat again. And again. I heard him reloading.

I carried on with my work, soaking a cotton napkin and stuffing it down the neck of the bottle. Then I prayed I'd found enough fuel.

A Molotov cocktail, Belfast style, usually contained petrol, but beggars can't be choosers.

I stood up, still protected by the wall.

I leaned around and shot my last two rounds, not caring much where they went.

No bullets left.

Then I quickly sidestepped around the corner, lighting the rag with a book of hotel matches. I could see Sullivan was a little closer, kneeling on the floor. I raised the bottle.

"Fuck you, Marty!" I flung the flaming bottle towards him.

He scrambled backwards.

I went back around the corner and bolted for the exit. The bottle exploded behind me. Should keep him busy for a minute anyway, I thought. I ran through the fire door and hurried down the metal steps, the cold steel pricking my bare feet. I arrived at the side of the building. Nobody was around, but the sirens were growing closer. I made a dash for the back of the building where there were bins and generators, and hopefully some cover. I skidded around the corner, almost bumping into the barrel of Amy's shotgun. Brandon raised his Glock at me too.

"Damn," he said, "I almost shot you."

"Just as well you didn't." I stuttered a little, catching my breath.

Amy looked me up and down and shook her head. At least she had a vest and jeggings on.

"That explosion… was that you?" she asked.

I nodded.

Then a bullet splintered a patch of wood in the little overhanging roof above us. We ducked down. Sullivan was running from the front of the building towards a dark sedan, trying a last shot on the way. Amy swivelled around and fired back, but it went wide. Sullivan hopped in the car, gunned the engine and sped away. Amy stepped out and fired a final round. His back window exploded, but the car kept on going.

I gave her a smile. "Not bad."

"You okay?" I asked Brandon, putting my hand on his arm.

"I'm okay," he said.

"Right well, I guess that's it for now," I said. "Cops'll be here in a minute."

"Get yourself some clothes, Walker, or you'll be done for public exposure on top of everything else," Amy said.

"I know you think I'm sexy," I said.

She rolled her eyes.

Chapter 34

It hadn't been the greatest start to the day. But a couple of hours later I was at least sitting with a cup of hot coffee. Unfortunately, it tasted like flavoured sweat. And I had been given a T-shirt and track bottoms. Not necessarily clean, but still preferable to *nada*. Seconds after Sullivan had made his hasty escape, the Troopers had arrived. It was all a mess. We were in some heap of trouble. Once they had allowed Amy to get her ID, it made things a little easier, but not great. We weren't exactly given the VIP treatment.

We were taken into custody, but after a series of phone calls and brief interviews, we'd been left in a dank interview room together, with less of an attitude from those keeping us there. I had my feet on the table, smoking. Amy had been given her mobile back and was furiously tapping away on the plastic buttons. Brandon simply gazed into space. I'm sure he was busting for a spliff. I'd chain smoked since they left us there. It helped. I offered one to Brandon and this time he took it. Then the door opened and McGoohan walked in, his lips tight, his eyes watchful. He closed the door behind him and pulled up a plastic chair.

"Hello, everyone."

"Sir," Amy said with a nod. She slipped her phone into her pocket.

"All okay?" He forced the smallest of smiles.

"Fan-fucking-tastic." I leaned forward. "Any thoughts on how they managed to track us down?"

McGoohan's expression dimmed. His cheeks flushed. Brandon hunched forward and looked away. I caught a slight grin.

"I understand your frustration, Michael. I'm sure you're all tired, but I don't appreciate your tone…"

"My tone?" I hadn't been consciously seething, but I guess it had bubbled under the surface unbeknownst to me, because I *was* seething. "Tired?"

I noticed Brandon sit up and take a long drag on his smoke. He looked pretty pissed too but seemed to enjoy McGoohan being on the spot.

147

"We're more than tired," I continued. "We get woken up by, like... five or six assassins. They found us *again*. That's after us travelling all day. America's a big bloody place and they miraculously find the place we're at? How?"

I pulled out a Malboro and flicked the pack away across the table.

McGoohan looked down at the dirty table passively, just a curl of general dissatisfaction on his thin, mottled face.

"And are you implying that this is in some way *my* fault?" He glared at me.

I gave a dramatic shrug. "You tell me. Apart from us, only you knew where we were. We haven't told anybody else." I looked from Amy to Brandon and back again. Amy looked uncomfortable.

McGoohan gave a snort and it really irritated me. He smiled mirthlessly, "Surely you do not think it is only I who knows anything about this... situation. Many people need to be informed in several departments in our organisation alone. And I too must report to my masters." He smirked with faux humility. "And let us also remember those friends of yours on the other side of the pond."

"I told you before, they're no friends of mine. I'm sorry to say I haven't made my mind up about you either. I can count on these two." I gave a nod to Amy and Brandon. "Somebody somewhere leaked it. And it meant we had to go all frigging *Great Escape* in the middle of the night."

"More like *Die Hard*," Brandon said. "But without the vest."

It made me smile. "True enough," I said.

"Listen," Amy stepped into the diplomat's role. "It's obvious that none of this is John's fault directly." She spoke slowly, looking between us all. McGoohan gave a thin smile. "What we need to focus on is what we do next," she continued. "But I do think we may have an internal problem somewhere."

She turned to McGoohan. His face fell a little, he shifted in his chair.

"Yes, well, Agent Landish... perhaps." He coughed and looked to be choosing his words carefully. "*We* can look into that. I appreciate that it's a potential risk we must address." He pushed his glasses up the shiny bridge of his nose and levelled his full stare on me. "Michael, how would you suggest that we proceed next?"

Well, I also didn't have a clue.

***

We talked on at length, briefly interrupted for some much-needed caffeine orders. I told McGoohan there wasn't much point in planning out anything much as it was likely to be leaked to our enemies. He didn't like that much. Tough. It was agreed that we would put off going right on to Philadelphia. We would lay low. The cops still had several homicides to account for and a ton of mess to clear up anyway. We couldn't just skip away from it all this time. They wouldn't let us off that easily. Even with help from the Feds and God-knows whatever other government agencies that were mixed up in it all with.

First thing first was to scrape this current mound of turd from our boots. We agreed that contact would be made with Pierce and the Republican movement there by the powers that be. We didn't have any proof that they were directly involved with any of the hit squads anyway. After all, by that time the IRA was scattering in all number of directions. It had once been a successful cell-structured organisation which often operated in isolation of one another. Now, who knew who the boss was of who now.

Whom.

But even taking into account all of that, I still thought Pierce probably sanctioned the failed hit directly himself. It would make more sense. We'd go somewhere safe for the next day and travel on the morning after if all was well.

It indeed turned out to be a very long day. Hell, as Ringo would say, it'd been a *Hard Day's Night*. We were another couple of hours with McGoohan and then a few more with the cops. Finally, we were let go. Then we'd driven for another bunch of hours in the vague direction of Philly. The less obvious, the better. Brandon came in the Hornet with me, and I put on one of my best comfort albums; Neil Young's *Harvest*. It seemed like a lifetime ago that I was in my house, with my busted CD player, listening to *Harvest*

Moon. So much had happened since then. It wasn't really Brandon's thing, but he gave it a chance. When *Alabama* was on and the band started really grooving, I noticed him moving a little in his chair, his foot tapping along.

I gave Brandon a wink. "You like this one 'cause you hate the white man."

He rolled his eyes. It was now my main communication device with both him and Amy. Maybe I am pretty annoying.

McGoohan had assured us that the location of our next hotel was on an extremely limited and strict need to know basis.

I'd said, "To hell with that." We'd find our own place and ring him in the morning.

I needed a good night's sleep. We found a cheap but clean hotel in a little town called Cyprus Creek. We all went off to our rooms in the early afternoon and slept the sleep of the righteous. I woke up, showered and gave my gun another quick clean. I hadn't expected to need to do it again so soon. I watched a little TV. There was a copy of The Washington Post pushed under my door in the late afternoon. Bill Clinton was on the cover, smiling widely, arm around Hilary. *Everything's rosy*. I don't buy it, Bill.

We met up for dinner in the restaurant downstairs. It was quiet. Midweek, off-season and off the beaten track. Suited me down to the ground. Then we went for drinks in the bar. Finally, I began to relax a little. I could feel a few muscles here and there untense. After a couple of beverages, we had all loosened up rightly. It felt nice, just the three of us again. Three soldiers back from another war.

I had no idea what was coming.

I'm glad I couldn't have known.

It would have ruined the moment.

Chapter 35

"Cheers, mucker," I said to Brandon after he got in another round.

McGoohan had given us each a rather generous envelope of walking around money. At least he was good for something.

"Mucker?" Amy made a face.

"I told you. Takes time to get used to this guy's funny talk. I barely even notice it no more. Give it a few more days, Amy."

"Mucker... ye know, like mate... pal, or buddy. I give up." I sighed. "Bloody Yanks."

I winked at Amy and lit up.

"So?" I wondered aloud.

"So," Amy said with a knowing smile.

"Yep," chimed in Brandon.

We all laughed and paid a little attention to our drinks.

"You want to know what I think our next play should be?" Amy asked, fixing a look on me.

"Well, yeah," I said and smiled at her. My big award-winning cheeser. I pushed back against the booth and crossed my legs.

"Do I have to do all the thinking?" Amy asked.

"You're the only one of us getting paid for it," I said.

She raised an eyebrow and creased her usually taut brow. "Yeah, tell me about it. I'm the one out here saving your asses."

I raised my arms in mock defence and looked at Brandon. "And we appreciate it, we really do."

"Yeah Ames, you're the best." Brandon looked a little embarrassed. He started fidgeting with his cap.

"You guys'll make me blush," she said, and rolled her eyes. "Okay, so here's my take. I'll have to run it by McGoohan, but..."

"Screw McGoohan," I said.

She rolled her eyes again and continued, "I *will* have to run it by him, but I reckon we ring Pierce in the morning. We could make it to Philly by teatime. Well, *you* should ring him. We'll find a hotel then meet up in the evening."

Brandon nodded, looking nervous.

"Right," I said slowly. "And if the meet goes badly, we can take him out?"

She shrugged. "Yeah, it seems so."

"I'm starting to feel like a hitman for your boss," I said.

Amy nodded thoughtfully. "It's not meant to be that way."

"Seems to me, with the peace process still in flux, that it would suit a lot of people if we keep cutting our way through what's left of the IRA."

"True enough," Brandon said.

"It's not what *I* want," Amy said. "But you're right, it would suit a lot of people, but it sure as hell would suit you too."

"I know, I know. It's just… I'm starting to feel like a pawn in a game of chess stretching across the Atlantic."

"Nobody could have known how things would have turned out. If we can agree a truce, then that's you done. The British will allow us to resettle you and it won't cost the earth. You'll be looked after. I've seen how it goes. You gotta understand, though, there are levels to this game. Different degrees of people who we hide and protect. Even the Russians who have changed sides. It gets darn expensive. And in the eyes of America, you really haven't done all that much to earn it yet."

"I get it." I ran my hand through my hair, avoiding spilling any ash. "They certainly owe me back home. I just want this all to be over."

That was true. Of course that's what I wanted. I didn't want to feel hunted. I knew I couldn't outrun them forever. But also, this was the most I'd felt truly alive in years. I'd been close to getting killed again, though I didn't have any kind of death wish. But I'd felt my blood pumping again. My pulse jackhammering. Adrenalin racing through me. And I'd connected with people.

Two people.

Against the odds, whatever they were, I felt close to these two people. Two people, both so very different from me and different from each other. But in that short space of time, we'd become a committed team. If I wasn't too mistaken, maybe even a weird kind of family. Or perhaps it was just like a holiday romance, something that felt important, but couldn't last.

"We'll give it our best shot. What else is there?" Amy gave me an open, fragile little smile. Then she seemed to sense this fragility. She took a sip of her drink and looked out the window at the dark carpark beyond.

The hotel bar was filling up. I like the mix of people you get in little chains like these. People doing their thing, all with varied wants and objectives. But it gelled. There was no feeling of any trouble on the horizon. Everyone was just going about their night, all seemingly in good spirits. It was obvious that there were a few on business trip folk in dark suits, with attaché cases. Middle management sorts. There were young holidaymakers from at least three European countries that I could make out: some with kids, some just couples. A man and woman sat at the bar. I was pretty sure they were an adulteress boss and his secretary, but don't quote me on it.

Thankfully there was no sign of real trouble anywhere. No other Irish voices for a start. Lenny Kravitz played on the stereo. His new single, *Fly Away*. It was okay. A bit cheesy for me. It was annoying that he was moving away from cooler stuff like *Are You Gonna Go My Way*? But hey. I got another round in.

The conversation moved on. The drinks disappeared faster. We began skating around more personal topics: exes, school, funny little things from our past. Then Brandon broke into a smile and said, "How 'bout we play Truth or Dare?"

I rolled my eyes.

It felt good. Maybe I could see why they both enjoyed doing it so much.

"I'm game," Amy said, raising her glass. She wobbled a little. The drink was kicking in alright.

"Okay, then. But I go first," I said.

"Just like the white man to push to the front," Brandon said.

"Goddamned Honky," Amy said. She gave a little giggle.

"Okay, okay. Enough of that nonsense. Right, my question is for Brandon. Truth or dare?"

"Aww damn. I've just been thinking 'bout what I'd ask you guys. Alright... er... I'll go dare."

"You sure?" I stretched my lips into a wide grin.

"Aww shit, no. Truth then."

"Make up your mind."

I laughed. Amy smiled and swigged the last of her glass before starting on her fresh one.

"Right, Brandon buddy. My question is – and I'm going easy on you to start with – what is the most embarrassing thing you've ever done?"

"Well, heck," Brandon smiled and scratching at the thin smattering of day-old stubble on his boyish chin. "Oh, I got it. Now this goes no further." He pointed at us.

"Cross my heart," I said, tracing a little cross with my finger across my chest.

"And hope to die," Amy said.

"Not the best choice of words given our present circumstances, Amy."

She rolled her eyes. Her turn again.

"Okay, so I was maybe sixteen," Brandon began. "Me and a few classmates were cutting school. Wasn't that uncommon," he said with a shrug.

"Go on," I leaned in.

"Well, we was in the mall, over at the big town, and I was in the changing rooms, trying on some Levi's. I didn't even have any money. Dunno why I bothered trying 'em. Suppose if I'm honest, I was probably gonna just take them. Then my bud pulls the curtain back and hisses to me that the headteacher is in the end cubicle."

"Crap." Amy stifled a giggle with a hand to her lips.

Brandon smirked, clearly enjoying getting to what he wanted to tell us. "I damn well forget I'm standing in my underpants. My shorts were on the floor beside the Levi's. My guy says to come with him and without thinking I bolt out of there. Just as I realise, looking out to the shop full of people, the curtain starts to open from the end cubicle. I scramble past my boy, put my head down and sprint through the mall. I'm on the damn third floor and gotta go down escalators and all sorts, just in a vest and briefs, man."

It made me laugh.

"God, Brandon," I shook my head.

Amy broke into a full-on wrinkle of laughter and clapped her hands together.

"That's amazing, Brandon."

"Hold on a second," I said, just thinking on it. "Still not as bad as me last night, lobbing petrol bombs at assassins, only in my cacks."

"True enough," Brandon said, smiling widely. "But I didn't tell you the best bit. It was a damn prank. The teacher wasn't there at all."

That made us all laugh again.

"I guess it's your turn next." I turned to Amy with a cheeky look. "Wonder what yours will be. Getting caught out in just your undies maybe?" I hoped she wouldn't take it thick.

"You'd love that, wouldn't you?" She gave me an ambiguous look.

***

We played the game for another while and chatted on merrily. It was fun. We all got drunker. Last orders were called for at midnight, and the by time we got our last round in, we were all pretty hammered. But it was a nice kind of drunk. Yeah, we'd all arrived at the more sedate stage, but nobody was feeling sick, nobody was sad, nobody was out of control. Hell, after what we'd been through, we were due a small blow out. Still, it then became a lot more serious, a little more reflective.

"Michael, don't answer this if you don't want to," Amy said, having trouble focusing on me fully. "I just wanted to know how you... you know, left one side and joined the other one." She raised a hand. "Don't talk about it if you don't want to," she said again.

Amy looked at me so earnestly, that it almost made me snicker. She was clearly worried about upsetting me and it was endearing.

"Well, that's a hard question for sure. But I don't mind. Hold on." I got a fresh Marlboro going. It felt like an effort. I leaned back in my chair, puffed and then flicked the burning end into the tray.

"You don't have to, Michael," she said again. Calling me *Walker* appeared to be a thing of the past. I was happy about that.

155

"I really don't mind," I said, waving it away. Dark tobacco smoke made a small swirl in the air between us. "You sure as heck deserve to know. We're all connected to it now. It was a long time coming. I mean, it wasn't any kind of overnight thing. I've already said why I joined in the first place. I mean, it's hard to describe what it was like. A sectarian police force breaking down doors on my street. Giving my family beatings. Then the army coming in too. We were second class citizens, like, if even that. Equality was not something on any Unionist agendas. It certainly wasn't on Thatcher's. At least now you have Blair who's making an effort. Seems to be anyhow. But back then, we were all just frigged."

I took another drag, then a sip of my Bush, ice and lemonade. It tasted really good. Nice and extra cold too. My head swam, the drink lubricating my muddled memories. "So, I joined in my twenties, in 1979. Belfast was a full-scale war zone by then. I played my part. Played my part for Ireland. As O'Casey would put it...*the worl' was in a state of chasis*," I gave Brandon a wink. "Seriously though, it was a no-brainer. So many young men wanted to sign up that they started turning people away."

"And you had to kill for them?" Amy asked.

"Yeah," I said simply. "Just like you had to the other night. I did what was expected of me. And those two you killed, they knew what they had signed up for."

Brandon swallowed hard and nodded. Amy stared at me, transfixed, her eyes like deep caves.

"I killed, because I felt I had to," I added, "Men with guns were everywhere. They wanted to kill my friends, my family. Seemed fair game to me. But I had problems with the other things. Bombing innocent people? Killing men because they delivered bread to the Brits? Children killed in crossfire? To hell with that. That wasn't for me. I carried on until about 1990 and my enthusiasm was on the wane, not that I ever told anyone that. But I was already thinking of getting out. My mind had already turned to ceasefire. To taking up the fight with the pen, violence being the stick if the carrot still didn't work. There was nobody I felt I could talk to about it on the inside. It seemed I was in the minority. Even my family wouldn't have wanted to hear it. I started to read more, about our history. I mean I'd been spoon fed Irish history all my life, but I went in deep. I'd always had my heroes: Michael Collins, James Connolly. Then I started reading a lot about Daniel O'Connell. You've heard of him?"

They both shook their heads.

"O'Connell was a member of parliament and the leader of the Irish Republican movement- in the 1800s, like. He was a massive figure, and crucially, he was anti-violence. One quote in particular I remember kept ringing in my ears; "...*the freedom of a nation is not worth the shedding of one drop of human blood*."

Amy nodded and bit her lip.

"So that's the frame of mind I was in when it happened. I was in London. I was in charge of a small cell at the time, running guns. My heart wasn't really in it. The campaign had focused more and more on targets in England. I mean, we even attacked the Cabinet. Victoria Train Station too, things like that. Again, I wasn't sure about the sense in all of it. Then one night the safe house I was in by myself was infiltrated by MI6. I'm sitting there with all the guns, on my tod, and suddenly surrounded by angry Brits with guns."

"Damn," said Brandon.

"Yep." I allowed myself a brief smile. "So, they gave me the choice. Prison and a big coup for them. Or... I could turn tout. Only it wasn't as simple as all that. They'd been following me for a long time. Targeting me apparently. I certainly wasn't the only one in their sights. The worst was they had pictures of my family." Something lodged in my throat. I downed the rest of my whiskey. "The real kicker was the pictures they had of my sister. She was never involved in the fight as such. She'd a fair idea of what I was up to, she was a Republican politically, but wasn't a volunteer. Only, they had these photos of her. Her with various known IRA men. The problem was that I'd also taken out the short lease for the safehouse in her name. My commander had ordered me to do it. I hadn't been happy, but they'd said nothing would come of it. Just another layer of cover. Well, it did come back on me, didn't it? The Brits told me in no uncertain terms that my sister would go down too, and that prison would be hard on her. I mean, they were right. She wasn't cut out for it. A stint would have destroyed her future. She'd just started college. She'd her whole life ahead. I didn't even need any time to think about it. I just said yes."

I felt a little choked up and busied myself with my lighter. Brandon and Amy said nothing for a few moments. Then Brandon gave me a gentle little punch on the arm.

"I'm sorry, Mick. I really am."

Then Amy got out of her seat, a little unsteady, walked around the table and threw her arms around me. Her perfume was strong and smelled like fields of poppies. She gave me a gentle kiss on the cheek, then stood up again and returned to her seat.

"Well shit, I know how to bring the mood down, don't I?" I wiped away the couple of tears pricking at my eyes.

"Thanks for telling us about it," Amy said.

I shrugged. "Now you know."

Chapter 36

I dropped a few quarters into the slot, then went through the whole rigmarole of keywords and passwords. It was the next morning. We'd had a good breakfast, with plenty of strong coffee, and I was now at the payphone out the front of the hotel. She took a few minutes to answer. I shoved fifty more cents in.

"Hello, Michael."

"Kate."

She'd only uttered four syllables, yet I could detect she was in some kind of uptight form.

"How are you?" Kate asked rather flatly.

"Well, I'm alive. Just about."

"I heard. You were lucky to all make it out. Are you alright?"

"Yeah, you know me. I'm an old, battered war horse."

"Yes," she said crisply. "What can I do for you Michael?"

"Well, I guessed I should speak to you before I go off on what might well be a suicide mission."

"You don't want to meet with Pierce?"

"No, not especially. I'd rather just get the hell out of dodge."

The slow exhaling of breath reverberated down the line. "We've gone over this, Michael" she said, as if speaking to an insolent child. "I can't just insist that the Americans do whatever I ask them and for them to look after you into old age."

"I don't think any of us are making it to old age."

"But we *have* gone over this," she repeated.

"Yeah, but I wanted to check you're okay with this new plan. I mean, I don't much trust this McGoohan, for a start."

"Oh, don't worry about him. He's a glorified shopkeeper. There are many rungs above *him*. I'm sorry, Michael. I don't mean to sound abrupt. This whole thing has turned into quite the mess. I mean, how many bodies do we have already?"

"Quite a few. Remember though, Kate, I didn't go looking for any of this."

"I know, Michael. Things weren't meant to go this way."

I didn't like the way that sounded.

"What do you mean by that?"

I listened to her inhale and exhale a few times. "I didn't mean anything." Her voice was almost shrill. "I mean, it all shouldn't have gone like this. It's all gone rather badly on the whole, wouldn't you say?"

"Yeah, yeah I would," I said absently.

It was probably nothing, but I just hadn't liked the way she had said it.

Why had she phrased it that way?

I put it to one side. We talked on about the plan until the pips came a few minutes later. It was all business by then anyhow. There was no sign of stress in her voice. No sign of anything. She wished me well, tried some reassuring words, and that was it. I hung up the phone and stepped into the morning sunlight. I felt unsettled. I felt all off kilter. It was getting warm. I hoked out my cigarettes and lit the second of the day. It tasted better than the first had. My eyes fell on the little bench next to the small side lawn where the hotel sign was attached to a plinth. I went and sat down. I didn't feel good. Jesus. I was hungover and filled with worry. Last night I hadn't felt like this. We had had some pretty heavy conversations, but it all had been just fine. Maybe I should have a drink. No, that wouldn't be the way. At least wait until lunchtime. It was bad enough I was going through so many ciggies. I needed to let my head clear for a while.

The last couple of days, I had felt more and more that I was being *used* in some way. Was it just the *powers that be* exploiting a series of events to their advantage? Of course, it suited both the Brits and the Yanks to get rid of militant and increasingly politically dangerous Republican terrorists. Bill Clinton was the sax-playing, secretary-shagging president, supporting peace in Northern Ireland. Blair was already intent on creating his political legacy, particularly relating to *The Troubles*. But I knew that *they* hadn't planned any of this. Nobody had. That would be crazy. It was Brandon and his stupid mate who caused this particular bout of mayhem. Still, I didn't like it. Things didn't feel right. My Spidey-senses were tingling. And I still didn't like how there had most certainly been a leak in the FBI, or CIA, or whoever was ultimately in charge. Surely those agencies wouldn't want to have tipped off my former *Ra* buddies. Whjy would they? So maybe somebody in there wasn't after peace. Somebody in the chain. They were after something else, and whatever it was included wanting me dead.

I don't know.

I stood up and willed the pounding in my chest to cease.

Some acid bubbled up into my throat, making me cough a few times.

I lit another, knowing it wouldn't help any.

What options did I have? Worse case scenario, I'd been set up some way, I still needed their help.

There was no choice. We wouldn't make it on our own. If there was a leak, we just had to be really damn careful. I wasn't going to work it all out right now anyway. I had to focus on the next thing in front of me.

Do the next thing.

Then do the thing after it.

It's all I had. I needed to focus. If I had any chance of coming out of this alive, I needed to be sharp.

I crossed back to the payphone and threw in the rest of my change.

"Yeah?" The voice on the other end was deep, the accent an Irish-tinged, mid-American mixture.

"I want to speak to Pierce."

Chapter 37

"Hello?" he said gruffly. His own broad Belfast accent had been slightly Americanised too.

"Hey Joe," I said in a sing-song voice

He sighed. "You always were a cocky wee shite."

"Well, thanks. So, how does coffee and a catch-up sound, Joseph?" I asked breezily.

He sighed again. I didn't imagine there were many who would talk to him like this and not receive a hiding, or worse, for their trouble.

"I can meet you tonight, if you like, aye."

He coughed a wet, phlegmy sputter. I wondered if he was still a heavy smoker. I think he favoured Henri Winterman cigars from memory. He may have upgraded to Cubans since then.

"It's a date, Joe. By the way, almost all your men got themselves killed last night. Did you know that?"

There was a pause, more heavy breathing. A little wheeze. Sounded more like a dirty call.

"I have no idea what you're talking about."

"Sure, you don't."

***

I spoke to him for no longer than two minutes. And I quite enjoyed talking to him like I didn't have a care in the world. To be honest, it was a hard act to pull off. But it was nice to flip him the metaphorical middle finger. Maybe I just had no idea what I really felt. My head was up my arse. But if you don't have humour, what have you? It's an Irish thing. O'Casey said it best: "That's the Irish all over – they treat a joke as a serious thing and a serious thing as a joke."

***

Half an hour later and we were on the road again. Amy was driving herself and Brandon was with me in my *lean, green, mean machine*. Well, it's an orange machine, but nothing rhymes with orange.

"I'd take some of your old man music over this any day. What is this rubbish?"

The radio was playing. Some dreadful boy band had come on. I'd no idea which one.

"Time for some more of your Irish musical education, then." I put on the "Best Of" from Northern Irish rockers, Sidewinder. Brandon didn't care much for it, and I didn't care much that he didn't.

We took the US-22E and drove for a few hours straight. Brandon was in good spirits. I was too, proven by allowing Brandon to choose a few radio stations to listen to for a while. We stopped at a diner near Harrisburg, got a feed, then Brandon travelled with Amy for the last two hours of the trip.

We made it to Philadelphia in the late afternoon. I felt a surge of anticipation as I swept around the city outskirts, taking in the many skyscrapers towering beyond. Where I had been living in the States for the previous few years, there was nothing like this. Nothing close. Back home in Ireland, seven or eight storeys seemed like a skyscraper.

I had the local radio station on as I headed to our meeting point. Will Smith was rapping away, which I supposed was quite appropriate since he was Philly royalty, though I would have preferred Bill Hayley. I got a bit lost a few times and the traffic was fierce. But the road signs were generally useful. I followed the postings towards Spring Garden, a residential district just outside the city centre. I passed by the former home and present museum dedicated to Edgar Allan Poe. I stopped at traffic lights just outside, looking at the huge statue of *The Raven* outside it. Tourists were gathered around, taking their turn to pose for photographs. Some of them even had brand new analogue camcorders. I'd have liked a visit too, but we weren't there for sightseeing. Still, I knew I was generally in the right place as we were meeting at *The Black Cat Tavern*, which Amy had told me was only a block from the museum.

I pulled off the blacktop and onto the gravel car park. Thankfully, I spotted Amy's car right away. I hopped out and set my hand on the bonnet. It was roasting.

163

"You did well, girl. Take a wee break."

I headed on in the door beneath the neon sign written in gothic script, complete with both a black cat and a raven outlined in white lighting. The interior was done in a mock-nineteenth century style with wooden beams, low lighting and framed posters of old book covers everywhere. It looked kind of cool, though I thought it was all a little kitsch and Disneyland-ish. The waiting staff were all in period dress too. A self-proclaimed 'buxom wench' took me over to a table where Amy and Brandon were already seated. I was surprised to find them each with a glass of cognac in front of them.

"You guys are straight onto the hard stuff? I've been a terrible influence on you, Brandon." I slipped in beside them.

"They're *Poe Toasters*," Brandon said with a shrug.

"We ordered you one too," Amy nodded at something behind me, just as a waiter came over and set a glass down in front of me.

"Thanks!" I took a sip. It was good stuff. "So, what the heck is a *Poe Toaster* when it's at home?"

"Well," Amy said conspiratorially, leaning over the Formica-topped wooden table. "A waitress was just telling us about it before you came in. So, you know Poe, right?"

"Yes," I said slowly. "Have you not noticed my occasional literary quotations?"

"Occasional?" Brandon smirked and took an enthusiastic sip of his brandy. I gave him a punch on the arm.

"Ow."

"Well, don't disrespect your elders, Brandon."

"Well, you sure is an elder," he replied.

"May I continue?" Amy asked.

"'I became insane, with long intervals of horrible sanity.'" I grinned at them.

Amy scrunched her face. "What?"

"It's Poe," I said.

Amy and Brandon rolled their eyes in unison.

Impressive.

"Anyway, apparently there was a secretive fella known as *The Poe Toaster*. Still is, according to the waitress. Every year this person creeps into Poe's graveyard in the early hours of his birthday. He's dressed in black with a wide-brimmed hat and a white scarf."

I raised an eyebrow and flicked off some ash. I took another drink. Very tasty, I might switch from whiskey for a while, I thought to myself.

Amy carried on: "He pours himself a glass of cognac," she said with a flourish, indicating the drinks. "And then he leaves three red roses on the grave and disappears into the night."

"How long's he been doing this? Like, is it just one guy?" I asked.

"Seems they think the same guy did it since the 1930s. The rumour is that he passed the role on to his son a year or two back."

"Well, that's commitment," I said.

"Good health," Amy said.

"To The Poe Toaster." Brandon raised his glass.

"Sláinte," I said, and we clinked glasses.

Chapter 38

We drove on afterwards to another small hotel in the same district. Another similar reception, another similar lift, another similar room. I remembered that the Irish Cup Final had been on the day before. The Glens against The Blues. I struggled with the TV for five minutes and finally managed to get the teletext up. It took me nearly another ten and a fair amount of cursing to find the results. Then there was more cursing. Beaten two bloody one, for dear sake. I switched the box off and had a shower. I dried off, put on fresh boxers and lay back on the bed, looking for a distraction.

I rifled through the couple of books I had in my bag. I settled on Philip Larkin's *The Less Deceived*. It's a fantastic collection of poetry. You see, I don't only exclusively read Irish literature. Though in saying that, Larkin did release this after living in Belfast for the prior five years. There are some great poems in it, and they helped provide some nice downtime for me then: reading, smoking and trying to give my head a break from thinking about what was to come.

After a few hours, we went to a bar across the street to meet McGoohan. It was just after six. The meeting with Pierce was scheduled for 9pm and we'd want to be in position at least an hour earlier than that. As we crossed the road together, a black Ford Crown Victoria pulled up at the sidewalk outside the bar. A thin man in his thirties with tightly cropped hair was driving. He turned to look at me. As the car slowed, the passenger door opened. My hand crept into my pocket and found the handle of my Colt.

McGoohan got out, straightened down his coat, and made his way crisply around the side of the car. He dismissed his driver and the car sped away. I relaxed my fingers and crossed to the other side of the street. We followed McGoohan into the bar.

At first the meeting was all business. Tempers were in check, everything was civil. We went over the plan, exploring the various scenarios. What we could and couldn't do. Brandon chain-smoked from my pack of Marlboros, looking sick at times; either due to the harsh nicotine hit or the intense conversation. But he was still clinging onto control. McGoohan then rambled on about this and that in monotonous and convoluted detail. Then he wished us well, but not before reminding us once again that officially they could have nothing to do with this. If it went wrong this time, they wouldn't be there to help at all. I told him that that was just wonderful. I think my exact words were "marvellous." I then said we'd be just fine without them anyway. Not that I believed that. And just for the craic, I quoted Behan to him: "If you accept your limitations, you go beyond them."

And that was that.

We went back to the hotel and got ready.
***

We were in position an hour and twenty minutes before time. It mightn't have been enough, but it was all we had. Sometimes you just had to roll with the punches and see how thinly your luck could stretch. There was a lot riding on it. If it got screwed up with no discernible result, we were done for. There'd be no lifeline from either side of the Atlantic for me or Brandon. If it went particularly badly, we were dead. So, it was just as well that I am generally somewhat of an optimistic kind of fella.

The meeting point was the carpark of the Holycross 7th Methodist church on Bethany Avenue, out on the west side of the city. It was a quiet, rundown area. A quarter of the commercial buildings were boarded up. There were many former homes in the same state. The old brick church was in semi-darkness. We parked a block away and Amy went first to take up her position. Brandon and I waited a few minutes, then locked up the car and headed into the night. We pushed open the squeaky metal gate to the church yard and crossed the gravel carpark. The main gates were padlocked shut, so people could only enter the grounds on foot. To the rear of the church was a patch of grass and a six or seven-foot metal fence that surrounded the entire plot. There were a couple of dim security lights casting more shadows than light. A half-moon hung in the black, starless sky doing its best to provide some further illumination. A black hearse was parked to the left of the church on another patch of browned grass. There was little else to be seen, save for some rubbish that had blown around: newspaper, chocolate wrappers and a few empty cans of beer.

"You okay?" I asked Brandon quietly.

"Guess so."

Brandon dug his hands into his pockets. I knew he had the Glock in the right one.

"Alright, let's do a wee *recce* around."

We set off anti-clockwise, walking the perimeter of the church. We didn't find anything. Back at the front, we stared off towards the rusty gates and the world beyond. It was very quiet.

"C'mon, let's have another look, Brandon."

I lit us both a cigarette. Brandon accepted his eagerly and we set off on another walk around. There's nothing worse than standing still, waiting for something to happen. We peered in through the church windows, checked the locks, climbed up and down the small fire escape at the rear.

Nothing.

Then we checked the perimeter. It was all secure, no gaps in the fencing. We found nothing. I almost said a little prayer of thanks. Maybe it would buy me some mileage when I asked for help with what would surely come.

"Okay, let's get ourselves ready," I said.

My own stomach was churning. God knows how Brandon was feeling. I patted him once on the back and we stopped at the front of the yard again. We stood in silence for a minute or so. I checked my watch. Jesus, this was the worst part. There was no telling when they would arrive. We had to be ready for when it did come. We had to stay alert. But at least I was fairly confident that the grounds were clear and that the front gate was the only way in. Just like we'd been told.

"Okay, bud?" I asked.

"Stop asking me that, will ya? Don't matter much if I ain't."

"You'll be fine, Brandon. You've already proven yourself more than once."

He nodded momentarily and pulled out a joint.

"I hope that's a mild one," I said.

"I damn well packed it," he said.

Chapter 39

They made us wait until ten after. They didn't even try and get there before us. Confidence? It might be that. Or it might have been a tactical decision to look strong and try to psyche us out. Or maybe they'd already been there much earlier.

A blacked-out sedan had stopped outside the gates. We were still standing out the front, away from the areas directly in line with the security lights. But they'd be able to see us just the same. We just wouldn't be illuminated like two damned Christmas trees. The headlights of the car stayed on as the engine purred and a faint trail of smoke drifted out from the passenger window. Then their lights went out and the engine quietened. The doors opened on the near side and five men got out.

"This is it," I said to Brandon.

"Don't get scared now." He attempted a little smile.

The five men gathered themselves in front of their car. All were dressed in dark, long coats. I clocked Pierce right away. He looked a little older than before. And he had considerable seniority to the rest. His more salt than pepper short hair glistened under a streetlight. The other four looked like clones of one another: tall, reasonably thin, and generally non-descript. As they approached their faces were set; world-weary and ready for whatever might come their way. In his fifties, Pierce was fairly plump and shorter than the others too. They advanced; two in front of him and two behind. The gate wheezed open as they made their way through it towards us.

I nodded to Brandon and we walked forward a few paces together, our hands in our pockets. The church was behind us, the hearse off to the side. Two of the men held back near the gate while the other two moved to flank Pierce as they came closer. They stopped ten paces away. Pierce had an odd haughty expression, liked he'd sniffed a fart, but realising it was one of his own, quite liked it. The rest of them wore blank expressions, but their eyes were furtive.

I looked him up and down and tried to project cockiness. That was alright, because I can come across as a bit cocky even when I don't mean to be.

"You all look like you're off to a funeral, right place for it I suppose," I said.

"Maybe we are," Pierce said, raising a bushy eyebrow. Up close, his face had got much craggier. And his voice had a transatlantic ring like John Drake in that old spy series, *Danger Man.*

"So, how's things?" I asked with a broad smile.

He smiled back wryly. "I don't think we need any small talk, do you?" His voice boomed. "What do you want from me, Michael?"

"Fair enough. Okay, basically I want you to stop sending people to kill me. And Brandon here too," I said gesturing beside me.

Pierce's eye fell onto Brandon as if only noticing him for the first time. His lips turned down and he looked back at me, "You don't have any proof that I'm doing any such thing."

"Cut the crap, Joe. You're not on the phone now. Nobody's listening in, nobody's watching you. I know you're the one's been sending them. And I'm asking you to stop. Only this once. Because I'll just go on killing them all and who wants that, eh?"

Pierce smiled for real this time. His eyes creased up like a cracked windowpane. "You always were a right wee bollix, Walker." Then his eyes hardened. His voice turned to marbled glass. "And now you're a traitor too." He spat on the ground, then lifted a handkerchief from his breast pocket and dabbed at his mouth. "A fuckin' tout. A fella who's gone and got his mates killed."

"The war's over, you dumb prick," I said. "You can't see past your blood-vessel covered nose. People want something different. *I* wanted something different."

"I'll tell people what they want," he rasped.

I glanced at Brandon. He was holding up okay. But I knew his tells by now and he was on tilt. I made a decision. They hadn't come to chat. There was no diplomatic way out of this. But where was Sullivan? It didn't matter. I had to force a play.

"So, I guess we're not coming to any kind of agreement here, then?" I asked.

"No, looks like we're not," said Pierce.

"Okay." I spat on the ground. "Frig away off then."

I stared at him, feeling warm blood gush around my veins. My eyeballs bulged. My face reddened.

His eyes widened and he looked about ready to pop. I could feel Brandon tense beside me.

"And take your pound-shop gangsters with you, you stupid old wanker you," I added.

At this I knew I'd forced Pierce's hand. He was going to do something, but this way I got to maintain control while forcing a reaction. He went clumsily inside his pocket for a weapon. I got my Colt out smoothly, just as the goon beside him also went for his own. I plugged the guy twice in his torso. He went down as the shots rang out like fireworks.

Then came the real show.

A hail of bullets wisped through the night air with a rapid and angry bark. The man at Pierce's right went down, bleeding from at least four or five machine gun slugs on target. They had come from the hearse. Pierce finally got his big showy Magnum free. Too slow. I aimed my Colt again and shot him in his left leg. He yelped, then crumpled down unceremoniously. The two men at the back ran towards us, guns out.

Brandon had his Glock drawn and began squeezing off rounds at them. He got one in the shoulder. Another spray of bullets blazed from the open window of the hearse. Both men hit the dirt, but they were still alive. Amy flew out of the car, a large SIG Sauer machine gun in hand. She strolled towards the two flailing men and finished them with two high frequency bursts. Smoke and cordite filled the formerly cool and light night air. I looked Amy and Brandon up and down and nodded. We were each unhurt and so far, four out of five of our opponents were dead.

The three of us surrounded the now kneeling Pierce. He panted, blood flowing freely from the wound in his leg. Amy looked around. No sign of anybody else about. But someone would surely report all the gunfire soon.

Pierce held a hand over the bullet hole, not making much of a difference. He looked up at me, his eyes wide, his face pale.

"C'mon now, Michael. It doesn't have to be this way."

"And what way should it be?" I asked.

"I'm sorry, alright? I wasn't looking for things to play out like this."

"You went to draw you gun on me. Your men were all armed to the teeth."

I checked my gun's chamber.

Pierce's eyes grew glassy.

"C'mon Brandon, we'll get moving, Michael can catch us up."

Amy rested her gaze on me as she ushered Brandon away. She understood what needed to be done and her eyes told me that she didn't disapprove.

"Listen… Michael," Pierce said, close to pleading. "It wasn't all me. I was just doing what I was told. It's New York. Them 'uns up there…"

"That's enough," I said firmly.

He stopped talking for a second.

"Jesus," he spat and dug a bulky fist into the ground.

I waited until the gate had squeaked shut after Amy and Brandon's exit from the church yard.

"Is it true… about New York?" I asked.

He nodded.

"What about Sullivan? Where the hell's he?"

"I told him not to come," he said gruffly. "He's made it too personal."

I said nothing.

I lit us both a cigarette and went to pass one to him.

"I quit," he said.

I rolled my eyes and gave it to him anyway. He took a slow, smooth drag. He looked up at the moon and blew out a luxurious lungful of smoke.

Then I shot him in the head.

Part 3: After The Goldrush

Chapter 40

In less than half an hour, we were back at the hotel. We took my car. Amy spoke to McGoohan on her cell phone for much of the ride back. He was satisfied with the outcome apparently. *Yippee*, I thought. He told Amy to tell me that our services to the United States had been duly noted. Brandon and I would be looked after well. That was something anyway. My eyes kept darting to Brandon in the rear mirror. He seemed okay. Chain-smoking weed, but okay.

We went straight to the hotel bar. I got a round in.

"So," I said.

"So," Amy said.

"Yep." Brandon shrugged.

I took a second, not sure what to say next.

"I guess it was gonna go something like that," Brandon said.

"We were ready for them," Amy agreed.

"You're a dangerous woman." I gave her a wink.

"I'm well trained," Amy said.

"*I'm* well trained," I said. "You're bloomin' deadly."

That raised a smile.

"Badass," Brandon agreed.

We nursed our drinks and stared off into space for a few moments, each of us trying to process all that had taken place.

"What happens now?" Brandon asked.

Amy blew out her cheeks. "Well, I'll meet with McGoohan again in the morning and we'll try to work out what kind of package they're willing to offer you guys."

"Sounds good," I said. "We should probably get out of the area again as soon as we can."

"Yeah, agreed," she said. "Get an early night sure and we'll check out in the morning. I'd expect they'll get you a proper safe house now that you'll be a little less *unofficial*. That all should get put in motion tomorrow."

I nodded.

We tried to unwind with a few more drinks. It felt weird. It seemed like everything had been building to this moment, but what would happen after exactly was still unclear. We had three rooms on the top floor of the three storeys and we headed into the lift at about eleven. We were beat.

"I'm goin' to sleep like a monster." Brandon yawned and took his baseball cap off before rubbing a hand over his close-cropped hair.

"Too right," I said.

"I hope so." Amy stifled a yawn of her own with both hands.

The lift dinged and we made our way along the dimly lit corridor. It was very quiet, save for a TV someplace playing an episode of *Fraiser*. The canned laughter echoed along the hall. The only other noise was the steady pulse of a generator on ground level beneath the window. I hunted for my key as we approached my room first.

Then everything went to hell.

A figure appeared at the end of the hall. I recognised him right away. It was the driver from McGoohan's car. He had a gun in his hand. Then Sullivan stepped around the corner beside him with his own gun drawn.

"Get down!" I let my key fall from my hands and went for my gun.

Silenced shots buzzed around us as we scrambled for cover. Amy got her revolver out first and fired back, sending the two men ducking down. I got my Colt in my hand, shot but missed. Brandon didn't have the Glock on him. He crouched down behind us, panicked.

What the hell was the driver doing with Sullivan? My brain sought answwers as I shot back a few more times, sending them both scuttling around the corner.

He was the mole then. The bastard.

All at once, the driver swooped around again and fired off two rounds. I looked on in horror as they both plunged into Amy's torso. As she fell, dropping her gun, I aimed and shot the driver in the face. His blood sprayed across the wall. Brandon was instantly on his knees beside Amy, putting pressure on her wounds with his hands. Amy hadn't made a noise. Not a peep. The only sound now was her rasping, sharp breath. I knelt by her side to help. Out of the corner of my eye, I saw Sullivan appear again. He ducked low and fired. The bullet sank into the floorboards beside Brandon. I aimed and emptied my clip, one round after another.

Crack, crack, crack.

I hopped up, then I started to run at him, still firing.

He shot one back at me. It went wide.

One of mine glanced his cheek and left a bleeding gash.

Then we were too close for gunfire. I was on him. I struck him across the face with the butt of my gun. He went to raise his gun arm. I smashed the barrel of the Colt down onto his knuckles. Both weapons spilled onto the floor.

There was noise in the background. Doors opened and closed. All the while Brandon shouted in the background for an ambulance.

Sullivan regained his footing, then launched a huge left into my face. Then a right. I ducked the next punch. Lights flared across my vision. We wrestled on the floor. I got on top of him, but he earned himself breathing room with a push-kick. I scrambled to my knees. We were both on our way to our feet again. He bared his teeth. I bared mine. I came up with an almighty uppercut to his jaw, which surely did some damage. I heard the crack. Then I swept his leg and threw myself on top of him, onto the ground again. I released a few jabs to his face, leaving cuts and scrapes.

I thought I had him.

A door crashed open somewhere around the corner. I heard a hard, Philly accent cut through our commotion.

"Put your hands in the air. State Police."

I gave Sullivan a few more digs.

Then my side felt damp. I looked down. He pulled a knife back out of me. His eyes were wild. He glanced towards the demands to surrender from the police officer. Then Sullivan scrambled off me and fled away down the hall. I looked at the blood seeping through my shirt.

He stabbed me?

I hadn't even reacted to it.

I pressed a weak hand to the wound.

I felt woozy.

Amy. What about Amy?

I knew I was going under, there was no stopping it now.

But we had won. Hadn't we?

Then I remember my head flopping back on the carpet. I was looking up at some dusty, yellowed cornicing.

We had been so close.

Then there was nothing.

Chapter 41

It was like trying to swim to the surface of a pool, upside down with floats attached to your feet. That's the only way I can think to describe it to you. I don't know how long I was like that. I remember the vague notion of being moved several times, snatches of hands on me, voices in the mirky distance. I remember having the strangest of dreams, but I couldn't tell you what they were about.

I never heard any choirs of angels, but I do remember being in what I felt was semi-consciousness and something that sounded like Donald Byrd's *A New Perspective* played somewhere. Presumably inside my head. I heard the spiritual-like voices in unison, with the acoustic jazz swelling behind it. My Dad had liked that album in the sixties. I remember it playing a lot at home. I had never really got it. I did now. Then I drifted away again. That's about the height of what I do remember from that time, and it could have been hours, days or weeks for all that I knew.

My eyes seemed to open all by themselves. It was blurry. The face of a young woman hovered above me. I noticed her nurse's uniform, then she was gone. I struggled to keep my eyes open. I only could blink them open long enough to see I was in a hospital room. I didn't have the cognitive ability yet to even remember why.

Where am I... where...?

I must have gone under again.

The next thing I remember was feeling a warmth and vibrations on my face. I must have been closer to *compos mentis*, because I remember worrying that I was having a stroke.

More time passed by. I opened my eyes. The room was dark. Was it a new day? When I opened them again it was night. The same night?

I forced my eyelids to shutter open again and saw McGoohan standing over me, lightly slapping my cheek. He looked down at me like a specimen in a petri dish. Then sun was up and shining through the blinds behind him.

My mind felt a little clearer. I thought to myself, *Get the hell off me*, while imagining grabbing his wrist.

Then I realised I *was* saying it and I *was* grabbing his wrist.

His eyes widened behind those big glasses of his. I let go, the strength leaving me as soon as it had arrived. He backed off, cleared his throat and adjusted his tie. Everything flooded back to me. Back together again. Mind and body. I fell back against the pillow. Everywhere hurt.

"How long have I been out?" My voice croaked.

"A couple of days. You're in Fortwilliam Hospital." He eased down into the chair alongside the bed with a slight groan.

"How's Amy? Is Brandon okay?"

I tried to sit up a little. I gave up when the pain in my side flared up and settled for just angling my head towards him on the pillow.

"We'll get to that. You've had quite a nasty incident. The knife just missed your liver."

"Lucky me," I said hoarsely. "Can you pass me some water?" My tongue was dryer than Ghandhi's sandals.

McGoohan ran his tongue over his teeth before lifting a water jug and filling a plastic beaker with a straw dangling out of it. He held it out so I could suck in a few mouthfuls. It was delicious. Best drink I ever had. Only thing better would have been a smoke and a single malt to go with it.

He placed the cup carefully back on the table that was attached by a long hinge to my bed.

"I need you to tell me exactly what happened that night."

"Tell me about Amy and Brandon."

"Afterwards, Michael."

I sighed. Exhaustion was nipping around the sides again and I knew if I closed my eyes that I'd be straight out again. All I wanted to talk about was how my friends were doing. I felt weak, nauseous. There was a dull ache in my abdomen, but at least it was only that. Presumably I was pretty drugged up. I certainly felt a little *floaty*. It'd be easier just to tell him what he wanted to know.

"Alright. We were going to our rooms... then they came 'round the corner. Sullivan and *your* god-damn driver. I guess we know where the leak came from now." I broke into a fit of coughing.

His jaw stiffened. "Indeed. Please continue."

I cleared my throat. I rolled my eyes. I seemed to have picked up the habit.

"They started shooting. Your driver hit Amy, then I shot him in the head. I rushed Sullivan and gave him a bit of a hiding until he stabbed me. After that, he ran away like the little coward that he is."

"There was nobody else there? Just the two of them?"

"No. Nobody. Nobody until the cops showed up. Now tell me how Amy and Brandon are doing."

He stood and ran a hand across his face. He was sweating and deathly pale. That's coming from somebody in a hospital bed after being stabbed. I hadn't seen him look like that before. Hospitals tend to be hot, but this was something else. Despite the drugs and my injuries, I felt my stomach tighten. It hurt.

"Brandon is fine. He's waiting outside to see you."

"Good, good. What about Amy?"

He looked away, blinked.

I didn't like that.

He shook his head.

"I'm sorry… she didn't make it."

I felt my eyes blaze. "What the fuck? What are you talking about? Of course she's *made it*."

He shook his head again. "I'm afraid not, Michael. The damage done was too great."

I couldn't believe it. This couldn't be true. Amy was too… *good*. Good at what she did and just… good. We had been through so much together. She couldn't have been killed just like that.

"No," I shook my head. Tears formed quickly and began to run down my face.

"I'm sorry."

McGoohan coughed awkwardly again and padded towards the door. "I'll see you again, Michael… You need your rest… I'll tell Brandon he can come in."

Then he hurried away. I didn't say anything. I listened to the clip clop of his heels along the corridor, mixing with the low hum of conversations somewhere beyond. I stared up at the ceiling and at the glare of the strip lights, trying to process it all.

Brandon slipped in quietly, his baseball cap in one hand. His T-shirt was crumpled and dirty, sweat patches under his arms. And he was crying too. He bit his lip as he walked towards me.

"She's gone, Mick."

I stared at him. No, stared through him.

I closed my eyes for a moment, then raised a hand to beckon him over.

He leaned down and hugged me and we wept.

Chapter 42

I don't remember the order of things too well over the following days. I experienced two lots of surgery. There seemed to be endless reapplying of bandages to my side. And I slept a hell of a lot. Most of my awake time seemed to involve seeing a nurse coming towards me with a long needle, then me going back under again. The days slipped by with snatches of consciousness. Sullivan never came to finish me off, but he came for me in my dreams.

Brandon seemed to be there a lot of the time. Certainly, more often than not, he was beside me when I opened my eyes. He'd be dozing in a chair or had just walked in, reeking of weed. But he'd be there. Days turned into weeks. We cried together sometimes. We talked about her a lot. We even laughed about some of the things she'd say. Then we'd cry some more. We hadn't known her long. But what did that matter? The things we had experienced together you probably wouldn't have with a best buddy of thirty-plus years.

McGoohan didn't visit again, but he had set Brandon up with a temporary flat nearby and a guard who slept on the floor. At least it comforted me some that Brandon was safe. For now, anyway. I didn't have to worry about him when he went back at night.

There was a little TV in my very sterile and depressing room. We watched a few games together sometimes. Baseball and American football. I had no idea what the hell was going on, but Brandon seemed to enjoy them well enough. And I enjoyed his company. The kid had done right by me while I was sick. Much more than alright.

By the fourth week I'd made enough progress to be told I would soon be released. To what exactly, I didn't know. One morning when I was alone, reading a pulpy Robert B Parker novel, McGoohan appeared at my open doorway with a punnet of grapes. This was only the second time he had graced me with his presence at the hospital.

"May I come in?" His tone was oddly formal.

181

"*Mi casa,*" I swept a hand towards the blue plastic chair.

He walked in stiffly, set the grapes down beside my water jug and took a seat.

"And, uh, how are you feeling, Michael?"

"Just dandy." I sat up a little in the bed, wearing a pair of fetching, red-striped pyjamas.

He forced a smile, but it looked more like a grimace.

There followed a few minutes of toe-curling small talk.

"I'm glad to see you're doing better,"

"Yeah... thanks."

"Nice you have your own room."

"Yeah."

Then he thankfully cut to the chase.

"Listen, Michael. There's something I need to raise with you."

"Is there?" I allowed my voice to harden, just a little.

"It seems that the claim by Pierce was true. I mean about his remarks that all this IRA action is dictated by New York. As in the people who came or you. The people who killed Amy."

"So?"

"Well... I thought you'd be interested to know that."

"Why would I? I don't care. I already killed the scum who killed Amy. I'm out of it. I haven't been on a mission to take down the whole flippin' IRA in America. I was just minding my own business, living the quiet life. Then I got pulled into all this shit."

"I know, but still." He removed his thick glasses and began to give them a polish with his hanky. "We also hear that Sullivan is there with them."

I didn't answer that. I lifted the water jug and poured myself some. I wished it was water from the river Bush, triple distilled over about ten years. McGoohan replaced his glasses, looking a little too pleased with himself.

"It would appear that Sullivan has been thick with New York and unfortunately with our former employee as well." He gave another sharp cough and then took a breath. His eyes darted furtively about the room as he spoke. "Pierce was most certainly involved in things, but he was a bit player... a middleman. The primary conspirators were those two and the team in New York."

"What do you want, McGoohan?"

He blinked a few times. "It's a little delicate." He squirmed like a politician on TV being grilled by David Frost. "You must understand that I too have my masters…"

"We had a deal."

"Yes, I am aware of that," he said crispy. "But things have changed…"

"What things?"

"Well, this new information about New York for a start. And also, Agent Landish's death."

"What has *Amy's* death got to do with anything? It was your screw up. Your man working for the other side."

"Please calm down. I'm sure it isn't good for you. Whether you like it or not, things are different now… more complex."

"Say what you've come to say."

His eyes met mine and I saw his nostrils flare. He coughed and lowered his voice.

"We are looking after Brandon as you and I speak. Paying his bills. Paying for a guard. We will do the same for you when you get out, for a time."

"For a time?"

"Yes. But… if you want our support long term… we need you to do one last thing."

"Fuckin' Nora," I muttered.

"We want you to take New York out of the equation."

"Get the hell out."

I pulled back my sheets. Despite my weakened state, he looked like he nearly shat his pants.

"Really, Michael, we need to discuss this properly…"

I swung my legs over the side of the bed. He got up and backed away.

"Get out of here before I shove every one of those grapes up your tight arse."

He huffed and puffed indignantly, then hurried to the door. He stopped, once he was a safe distance, with nurses nearby.

"You both have until the end of the month, then," he announced before scuttling away.

What a gobshite.

***

That was a blow. Another addition to my already troubled mind. Just when I could glimpse this all coming to some kind of an end, it was snatched away from me yet again. I had to break it to Brandon and the kid was pretty crushed. He'd been through the ringer too. We carried on hanging out together much of the days left in the hospital. He even did some exercises along with me as I got on with my rehab. I'd been trying to reread *Dubliners* for the first time in years, but shamefully I never got that far into it. The days dragged, until finally, I could feel some strength returning to my body. We missed Amy like one side of a triangle, but at least we still had each other.

A few days later, I stood with Brandon out on the hospital fire escape, smoking. I'd been told that morning that I should be discharged any day. The clock was ticking down and I didn't have much of a plan. I passed Brandon one.

"Thanks Mick. Hey, check this out... Know what I saw in the paper this morning?"

"Bill Clinton boned another secretary? Tony Blair finally admitted to being the antichrist?"

"Nope, though both are probably true." He got his glowing and then carried on. "It was just a little piece in the local news section. Isiah's been killed. Him and the rest of his crew."

"Isiah? Really?"

"Yeah. Over at his crib. They all got slugs to the back of the head. Game over."

"Damn."

"Yeah."

"Did they get anyone for it?"

"Don't seem to."

I looked past him, out towards the noisy cityscape beyond. My mind whirred. I'd already wanted to talk to Brandon about something. I wanted to sound him out. There was nobody else I could talk about it to. If nothing else, saying it out loud would surely help get my thoughts straight.

"Brandon, I've been thinking a lot about things. This might sound crazy, but hear me out, okay?"

"Okay," he said slowly.

I scratched at my head. I'd a thumping headache. My side ached too, but at least I'd been getting slowly weaned off my meds and the pain was at a manageable level. They told me I was healing well.

"Think about all that we've done so far, B. We've knocked off a ton of IRA men. We've wiped out a local chapter. Now we've been asked to cut the head off the snake itself. Who benefits?"

He thought for a moment. "Well, McGoohan and his crew, I guess. And that Kate lady in England too. Both lots want it done."

"Yeah, they do. So, is it just a coincidence that I have to take care of it all for them?"

"How you mean?"

"Well, it's very *convenient,* isn't it? Did this situation just happen to fall in their lap? They're not even officially involved we keep being told. Both ends want the IRA threat to go away and they get me to do it for them. All it costs them is a little bit of money and time. Not a big ask for a couple of superpowers."

Brandon narrowed his eyes, "Well, yeah, I guess. But Mick, they couldn't have known it would all happen. How could they?" His brow furrowed.

"That's just it. They could if they planned it."

I let that hang in the air for a few moments along with our drifting plumes of smoke.

Brandon looked at me side on. "They couldn't have known *we* were gonna rob you," he said in a quiet voice.

"You said before that Isiah had me in his sights. He came to you with it. You'd only done that kind of thing, what three, four times?"

"Twice."

"Including mine?"

"Yeah."

"Anyway, why did Isiah target me? To the outside world I was just a single old Irish guy with next to no money, working part time as a mechanic. Not exactly plum pickings for a robbery."

Brandon thought about it. "I dunno, Mick. I guess he thought it'd be an easy score. It all seems crazy talk to think it was planned. Look how many have died. And Amy." He let the last two words hang there for a couple of beats. "They couldn't have known that your poster going on eBay would have kicked things off either."

"No, I don't think they did." I paused to get my lighter out again. The nurses didn't let me come out very often, so I tried getting as much nicotine into my veins as possible when they did. Maybe it was said nicotine, but vocalising all that I had been dwelling on, the hours alone in my hospital bed; it didn't sound as crazy out loud as I thought it might. "You see, I reckon they didn't mean to get the hit squad involved at all. I think they just wanted to give me a scare. They needed the threat of being discovered to hang over me. Maybe they'd even have faked something to think that I really needed their help. I think it all got away from them. Kate said something to me that didn't sound right. That it wasn't meant to turn out like this."

"What about Amy?" His eyes had gotten glassy.

I shook my head. "I think McGoohan is a two-faced little runt, but I don't think he wanted that to happen. That inside-man wasn't part of the plan. That was another thing that mucked things up for them a little. Something they hadn't counted on."

Brandon's face fell. "You don't think Amy knew about it all though, do you?"

I shook my head again. "No, I really don't." I put a hand on his shoulder. "Amy was good people."

Brandon closed his eyes and nodded; his Adam's apple bobbed as he swallowed hard.

"So, do you think I'm crazy?" I stood up stiffly.

"Oh, for sure, but maybe not about this."

Chapter 43

Right enough, I was discharged a few days later. We had about a week in the apartment until we were quite possibly thrown out on our ear. Maybe we could just squat there afterwards? The protection of a guard on the floor had already been removed and we were pretty much now on our own. Apparently, we weren't at risk the guy had told us. He'd presumably been *told* to tell us that. McGoohan had stayed away himself, perhaps too afraid of grapes being forcibly stuck up his rectum. It was Tuesday afternoon, and we were both in the little sitting room, each with our feet up on matching leather sofas. Brandon was laughing at an episode of *Jerry Springer,* and we were making our way through a sixpack of Bud. It tasted like pish, but our money was already running low. Beggars can't be choosers.

We'd made our decision.

What choice had we?

What else were we to do?

Neither of us liked it, but one more job and that was us supposedly set up for life. We'd been told that before, but there weren't any other offers on the table.

"You gonna call Kate soon?"

Brandon started a fresh joint and sent a plume towards me. I lit up in defence.

I looked over at the little clock on the sideboard; 1.07pm.

"Yeah, why not? It'll be about six there. She's usually around into the early evening."

I straightened up and flicked ash off my Tom Petty T-shirt and green cargo pants. Pizza boxes sat in the corner beside the overflowing bin. The bin was filled with empty bottles and a few gauzes I'd changed from my wound. Yes, we'd been living like a couple of university students, but it had been good. It's what I needed after being cooped up in pain for all that time in hospital. We were like old war buddies now. Buddies who were dealing with a lot of traumas, grief for our friends, and a hole in my side. But we were doing alright.

187

Brandon sat up too and muted the telly, just as a pair of burly security men broke up a fight between two angry rednecks. We had a phone in the little apartment which was handy for calling in takeaways and now for making my overseas call. At least it hadn't been disconnected yet. I'd get whatever I could out of the buggers while I could.

Number plugged in, ash flicked again, a plummy English voice, security codes, patched through, waiting, draw from my cigarette, and finally:

"Good evening, Michael."

"Hello, Kate," I said evenly.

"I've been meaning to call…" Her voice raised in pitch.

"Have you?"

"Of course… How *are* you? It was awful what happened."

"Well Kate, I've pretty much only been in two places; a hospital bed, trying not to die, and now in this apartment, still trying not to die. And to your question, yes, I'm doing alright, considering." I kept my voice low, but I'm sure she could hear that I wasn't in the mood for any mucking around.

"I'm glad you're doing alright. It was terrible what happened to you. I was worried." She chose her words carefully. "And… I'm very sorry about what happened to the girl. Amy, wasn't it?"

"Yes, Amy Landish. And she died because of the likes of you and McGoohan messing us all around. Playing your damned war games in your fancy houses, far away from all of the action."

There was a pause and sharp intake of breath

"Whatever do you mean, Michael?"

"You know what I mean. You set me up. You made me your hitman. I know you and McGoohan planned out the robbery at my home. You probably paid local law enforcement to recommend some clueless local hoods to do over my place."

I mouthed a *sorry* to Brandon. He gave me a thumbs up. We were both enjoying ourselves. Brandon was animated and I'm sure I was even more so. It really feels pretty great to find someone out and shove it in their face that you know exactly what they've done.

"That's ridiculous," she said.

I continued. "You never wanted to get the actual IRA involved. Just to give me a scare. Put the wind up me. But it got pretty messed up, didn't it?" I paused, listened to her heavy breath on the line for a moment. "Then Isiah turns up dead. I guess he was a loose end that needed tied. That could have been you ordered it. Or McGoohan. Pretty ruthless, Kate. Things were bad enough, and then there was a guy on the inside screwing everything up too. Jesus, you wouldn't have been expecting that one. And then an agent gets killed because of all the balls ups. One of your own and…"

"…Michael, this really is absolute rubbish…" she almost shouted.

"I haven't finished," I snarled. Amy's beautiful, intelligent face filled my mind's eye. "So, now there's really pressure on everybody from both sides of the ocean to get a big result. Pierce and the rest aren't enough anymore. You need rid of the whole lot now, don't you?"

"Including Sullivan," she said, her voice suddenly very low and clipped.

That stopped me in my tracks for a second.

So, she'd given up on trying to convince me of her innocence. I must have been very close to the mark, if not pricking the bullseye.

"Yes, I'm sure he's there too," I said slowly. "And I don't expect you or McGoohan to ever admit to any of this. That ship has long sailed, and I don't care anyways. *I* know. But I'll still do your last job for you. Just like I always have. But this is it. This is the last of it."

Brandon gave me a double thumbs up.

Kate cleared her throat and then said formally, "I can guarantee that if you do this last thing, you have my personal guarantee and that of the British Secret Service."

"Well, I don't put much stock in any of that, but I'll do it all the same. And Kate, if I don't get it, if Brandon isn't looked after right, I'm coming for both of you. And you know that I'll find you."

"You don't need to threaten me, Michael. I am a good to my word."

"Your word is nothing. After this you won't be hearing from me again."

"I understand," she said quietly. I thought there may be a trace of real emotion, perhaps even regret. "When will you do it?" she asked.

"Soon," I said. Then, "To quote Mr Yeats, 'Do not wait to strike till the iron is hot; but make the iron hot by striking.'"

Chapter 44

New York City is only a two-hour drive from Philadelphia. We left our apartment for The Big Apple three days later. This time Kate took care of all the details. I had a few awkward conversations with her; formal and cold. We both managed to pass ourselves, working out the play. McGoohan wanted to see us before we did anything. That was okay. I wanted to have a word with him too. There would be an apartment waiting for us in New York, down in the old meatpacking district. I was almost out of cash, so I was happy for them to pay for it. Neither me nor Brandon had been to New York before. We'd decided that we would at least enjoy one night in the city before we went after Sullivan and his associates. You never knew when it might be your last. Eamonn Boyle was the top man. I didn't care much who he was. He was now my meal ticket out of all of it. We'd take them all out-whoever else was left in town.

We found ourselves on the outskirts of the city after lunchtime. The drive had been easy and uneventful. We were both a little buzzing as the iconic landscape first came into view. We had a power station full of nervous energy too. It took us nearly another hour just to make our way around the edge of the city and into the right district. We were due to meet McGoohan there at five. He would give us the keys and a final briefing. After that, we'd be on our own. We found the place easily enough, and even more fortunately, a parking space nearby. I patted the hood as we got out. I told the Hornet she'd done well again, and to look after herself out on the mean streets. The area needed serious regeneration: all boarded up houses and closed, graffiti-shuttered businesses. We then found a bar that looked post-apocalyptic in its upkeep and waited out the couple of hours with a few drinks. We were both quite sedate. There was something missing. *Somebody* missing. I guessed he was thinking about her, I knew I was. After finishing our drinks, we walked back around the corner and waited for McGoohan. I wondered if he'd be driving himself around these days.

He was.

He sat outside the bar, this time in a recently valeted green Olds. "Gentlemen," he said as he got out.

I gave him a nod. No smile, no greeting. Brandon turned on his heel and began walking up the steps to the little three-story apartment block. We entered in silence, taking the lift up to the second floor. The whole place smelled a little damp and uncared for, but it wasn't the worst. McGoohan let us into apartment thirty-six and closed the door behind us. It had two bedrooms, a bathroom and a dining room with an ample kitchenette. It looked clean enough and smelled like there'd been a mini chemical warfare attack. I decided to prefer not to think about what smells it had attempted to mask.

"Please take a seat, men." McGoohan raised both hands and gestured to the two adjoining cream sofas.

I stretched my back, no longer needing to hold myself in. I allowed my face to harden. I stayed stood where I was.

I glared at him.

The prick looked more and more like a George Smiley wannabe. But without enough class.

"Take off your glasses," I said.

"What?"

"Take off your glasses. I don't want to hit you with your glasses on."

"That's outrageous, I mean…"

He was interrupted by me launching my fist towards his right cheek. I stopped at the last moment, opened my fist and backhanded him hard across his face.

H almost spun around a full three-sixty, his cheek inflamed and spittle flying from his mouth. He breathed hard, coughed, then blinked a few hundred times.

"Next time it'll be a proper punch. You screwed us. Then you got Amy killed in the crossfire because of it all. Shame on you."

I took a step towards him. He stumbled away, a hand pressed against his glowing cheek.

For once he appeared to have nothing to say.

I waited.

McGoohan just stared at me, open-mouthed. It was hard to tell if it was fear or indignation. Probably both.

HUNTED

Brandon appeared from behind us. "Get the hell outta here, dick-nose." His voice was harsh and his expression hard and mean.

McGoohan swallowed, tried to keep his voice steady. "But I must brief you, I..."

I took a step closer to him before he scurried backwards, fumbled with the lock and fled back out through the door. We listened to the comical clip-clop of his heels as he hurried off down the hallway.

"Dick-nose?" I said to Brandon with a grin.

"I dunno." He shrugged then belly laughed. It was the first genuine laugh I'd heard from him since Amy.

***

That evening we headed into the city. We walked around in the humid, night air, taking in the familiar sites: Time Square, The Empire State Building, the many skyscrapers that we'd seen in everything from *Ghostbusters* to *Friends*. We walked around smoking, stopping in a couple of bars for a libation or two along the way. We heard some live music: a folk singer, a very good Blue Note style jazz band, all sorts. It was the little lift that we needed. The drinks helped too.

Then we happened on a poster for the reformed sixties band; The Yardbirds. They were playing in a little club, just beyond where had been formerly the down and out *Deuce*. I'd seen it featured in more than one film or two. The area had begun cleaning up its act and wasn't just a bunch of porno theatres and scuzz shops anymore. It still had those, but less of them.

We found the venue about an hour before the show, bought tickets on the door and picked a table. Class. We sat and waited, listening to the jukebox playing out some 50s blues, drinking beer and smoking. Brandon popped out for a joint and when he came back in the lights went down almost on cue. The place was cool. Old-time New York. A proper little club that only could have held a few hundred people.

The band came on. All five of them. *Five, live Yardbirds.* I'd been a fan for years. Now there was no Clapton, Page or Beck, but they were still red hot. Of the originals there only remained the drummer and rhythm guitarist, but the band was well oiled and still dripped with a primal love of the blues. They went through

193

one familiar song after another, though Brandon didn't know any of them. Not even the hits, like *Heartful of Soul, The Train Kept a Rollin', Shapes of Things*. But he enjoyed it anyway. He said he'd never been to see much live music and he was grooving to it. They even played a version of *Dazed and Confused*. That was a treat. The guitarist was on fire. It'd been their song before Zeppelin's anyways. Jimmy's new band was going to be named Yardbirds 2 by Page when Keith Moon allegedly told him that it would go down like a Lead Zeppelin. And history was made. They just dropped the 'A'.

We opted for a big yellow taxi afterwards, neither of us having the inclination to walk the long distance back or to try and navigate the more complex transport systems. Joni sang in my ear all the ride home. We were both pretty relaxed and had made the best from our one night in the city. But we mostly kept quiet. Brandon had had about a half dozen joints, so he was on a higher plane. In saying that, I did take a draw or two. We let the cab driver chat away, ninety to the dozen, and made minimal noises in reply.

The lack of chat was kind of out of character for me and Brandon. We each had slipped into our own, separate worlds for a time.

Perhaps it was the anxiety about what the next day would bring. Sure, there was that. But there was something else too. We both missed Amy and wished she was with us. We wished she could be with us for what would happen the next day too.

We wished she'd be around every day.

But neither one of us wanted to say it.

I couldn't even ask myself the question of how exactly I had felt about her.

The driver didn't seem to take the piss out of us ignorant tourists and we were back at the apartment in just twenty minutes. It was only a quarter of midnight. I poured us each a generous measure of whiskey. We eased back onto our separate sofas and put our feet up.

Then there was a loud rap on the door.

Chapter 45

'Who is that rapping at my chamber door?' popped into my head. I almost laughed. I must have been more buzzed that I thought. Then I tensed.

We shared a look before I set my Marlboro onto the edge of the ashtray beside my drink. I padded across the floor, picked up the Colt and moved silently to the door. There was a little fisheye lens, so I slowly moved my head closer to look through it. I didn't want a bullet exploding through it at me.

"Who is it?" Brandon whispered, the question coming out more like a hiss.

I looked through the peephole.

My mouth literally fell open.

"It's a ghost." My voice caught in my throat.

"What?" Brandon whispered back.

I said nothing.

I just stared.

The room seemed to spin. Was I suddenly incredibly drunk? Was I high?

It was Amy, or it was a girl who looked just like Amy.

It couldn't be Amy.

It *is* Amy.

No.

It's Amy.

I wiped my eyes, looked away, then looked again.

"What the hell, Mick? What's going on?" Brandon got up and hurried across.

I looked again.

It *was* Amy.

***

I threw the door open. We almost dragged her off her feet. She kept her balance somehow and we clung around her. She smiled widely.

It's really her.

195

Then Amy winced at a pain in her side. We eased our grip. We hurried her into the little sitting area and down onto a couch like she was a beloved elderly relative. My heart pounded and I felt nauseous and elated all at once. I saw that Brandon was crying. Hell, I was crying.

"I'm alright, I'm alright," Amy smiled again and crossed her legs. She slipped off a pink anorak, revealing blue jeans and a purple top.

I'd never seen her dress casual.

I thought I'd never set eyes on her again.

"What the hell, Amy? It can't be you." My voice sounding really weird in my ears.

"What the... fucking...Amy?" Brandon added. He grinned from ear to ear.

We all laughed.

"I'm so sorry. I know this must be a lot to take in."

We nodded, which didn't seem sufficient in describing just how we were feeling.

"What happened?" I fumbled for a Marlboro, noticing the shake in my hand as I did.

"Well, I got shot... as you know." she flashed a little goofy smile. "I almost died, I guess. Then I had a lot of surgery."

"Snap!" I pulled up my shirt to show my bandage.

"I'm not showing you mine," she said.

"Then what happened?" Brandon asked, while balancing a half-made joint he was constructing on his lap.

"Then it got weird. McGoohan came to see me one day while I was recovering from one of the surgeries."

"Okay," I said, nodding.

"He tells me that he had thought I wouldn't make it and had prematurely told you I was dead."

"The hell?" Brandon screwed his face up.

"Yeah, I know. He said he thought it'd be better that way anyway. That things were done with you guys. He's telling me all this, standing over my hospital bed. We wouldn't be helping you, he said. I said the hell they weren't, and he didn't like that much. Then I was in and out of consciousness again for a few days. But

196

I started getting better and I knew I'd come and find you both when I was well. To hell with McGoohan."

"Why do you think he lied to us?" I asked.

"Manipulation? I don't know. There's always a damn angle with him. His thinking is messed up. He's unscrupulous."

"He's a dick," I offered.

"Yeah, he's a dick."

"Brandon actually called him *dick-nose*."

Amy loosened a little laugh. "Then he comes to see me a few days ago and tells me about this thing you're meant to do tomorrow. He seemed to be sounding me out about it. I'm still in the hospital for goodness sake. I played along like I didn't think anything much about any of it. He had a cup of coffee from the machine, talked about the weather and left. Then I got my butt up, signed myself out and went to find you guys."

We both got up and gave her another hug.

"You shouldn't have done that, You need to rest up, but I'm glad you did," I said.

"You'll like this next bit." Her smile curled up on one side, her eyes glistening. "Before I came here, I went into work to sort a few things. Then I went up three floors to McGoohan's office, told him he was an asshole and quit."

"Wow," Brandon said.

"Damn," I ran a hand through my hair. I grinned and jiggled my leg excitably. I necked my whiskey.

It all felt so weird. Everything. I couldn't process it all. Never mind that I was already half cut. I was worried that she'd quit her job, but ten minutes ago I thought she was dead. So, I guess it was more than cancelled out. But still.

"Are you sure you want to do that? I don't want you to…" I babbled.

She held up a hand. "It's not just because of you guys. I'm done with it all. I'm done."

"Well, I'm just glad you're here." I broke into a laugh. "I can't believe this," I got up on my feet again. "Celebratory drinks?"

"Thought you'd never offer," Amy said.

Chapter 46

We stayed up half the night. It was wonderful.

The partial drunkenness had deserted me and the more I drank, the more sober I became. That was fine by me. I didn't need any extra buzz. I was enjoying drinking with my friends, half of whom I never expected to see again. Ever.

Amy was curled up on one sofa with a tartan blanket over her. Her eyes had taken on a slightly inebriated, dreamy quality. She had no makeup on. I could see bare the recent strain on her face, but she was still very beautiful. To me she had been dead, so now she was truly some kind of angel.

"So now you know it all," Amy said. "Are you still going through with it tomorrow? After all that they've done?"

She reached awkwardly for her wine glass. Clearly she was still in substantial pain. Brandon hopped off the sofa beside me and passed her the glass.

"Thanks, Brandon," she said.

I nodded my head, lighting up another cancer stick that I really didn't need. "We'll still do it. Yeah?" I looked towards Brandon. He nodded as well. "All in all, it needs done. In an ideal world, no. But it'll get us our money, then we're out of here. I want an escape route. I told McGoohan that already."

"He walloped him on his head too," Brandon added with a grin.

"You hit him?" Amy covered her mouth and swallowed the wine down, her eyes growing wide.

"Yeah, I gave him a wee slap. Just a backhand. I didn't want to knock the little prick out. I don't want them to stiff me afterwards. So, I'll play ball, I'll give them what they want. But I don't have to be nice about it." I licked my lips, "You see, I've got a theory."

"Oh?"

I told her about it. About McGoohan, Kate, Isiah, all of it. Amy listened carefully, adjusted her position, grimaced, then looked up at the ceiling. She chewed her bottom lip.

"Wow," she said. "Yeah, I guess I wouldn't put it past him. I mean, they're all capable of it. But they've created a ton of trouble they didn't count on if they did."

"That's what we reckon," I said.

Amy looked thoughtful again. "God. All of this, so they can meet their own political ends."

She held her side again. The poor woman looked shattered.

"I need to go to bed," she said. "Is there somewhere I can crash?"

"Of course. You take the bigger room on the left there," I said. "We'd better call it a night too. I'll take the sofa." I locked eyes with Brandon and he nodded. He slotted a freshly made spliff into his top pocket. One for bed.

We all got to our feet. Brandon and I took turns to give Amy another hug. She lingered when my arms were around her and pulled her head back to look at me.

"Y'know that if you're doing this, I'm coming with you, right?"

I felt my thick eyebrows almost meet. "You're not well enough, Amy. You can't."

"No Aims. C'mon," Brandon said.

She looked between the two of us, shook her head and smiled. "I'm not asking your permission. Fit or sick, you two still wouldn't have a chance of stopping me."

***

I managed a very deep, dreamless sleep. I had been zonked. I'd thought it'd take a while to get over, but I went out like a light. Probably the codeine. We all slept in. At about ten I heard someone firing up the kettle and I forced myself out of bed. It felt like Christmas morning. As a kid I was always scared that Santa hadn't come. Not that he ever left much. Now I was genuinely scared that last night had all been a dream.

I was relieved to find Amy in the kitchenette, lifting out plates, freshly showered with her hair tied back in a bun. A few minutes later Brandon shuffled in, bleary eyed. We had a little breakfast and nursed our hangovers. Despite that we all were full of smiles. Amy and I took turns to go to the bathroom to see to our bandages. Brandon said he felt left out. I told him not to speak too soon. When Amy came back in, she asked if I'd put a little tape around the gauze on her back. I said I would. She hiked her top halfway up her torso and turned around. Brandon smirked a little and turned his back. I fumbled with the tape, presented with Amy's toned, mocha skin and a glimpse of her bra straps. I hurriedly

199

sorted her out, not wanting to take too long and have her think me a creepy perv.

"Thanks, Michael," she said and gave me a peck on the cheek. "I'm going to finish getting ready." She headed back to her room.

Brandon turned back around, finishing a cup of coffee, a cheeky look on his face.

"Shut up," I said.

***

I didn't want us to sit around and fret all day, so I suggested we go out for a while. I drove us into the city proper, which was a little scary itself. The traffic was hectic. We visited a few record shops, a couple of bookstores. We had some coffee. Brandon bought a new cap with NYC embroidered on it. Then we went to the Hard Rock Café' on Times Square. It was amazing. I walked around every inch of the place, not caring if I was annoying some of the diners talking quietly at their tables. I'd probably never be there again. Hell, I didn't know if I'd make it through the night. There were all sorts there: Elton John's hand-painted piano, original Jimi Hendrix lyrics, one of Flea's basses.

They used to have original Beatles' suits, a Fedora hat that Elvis once wore, even Howlin' Wolf's guitar. But they'd all been nicked in a robbery about ten years earlier.

Metallica pumped out of the stereo and on the many mounted TVs. Not really my thing, but ZZ Top came on after, which was better. Brandon and I got a couple of huge cheeseburgers and shared a plate of nachos. Amy just had a salad. Each to their own. For drinks we just had Cokes for a change. Hair of the dog wouldn't have been a good idea.

On the way back to the apartment I put on one of the new CDs I'd picked up. It was Dylan's *Time Out of Mind* released a few years before, but I hadn't gotten around to it yet. The first track began with lone organ stabs. It was called *Lovesick*. It was a good track, and I couldn't help but wonder if I was a little lovesick myself. But now wasn't the time for that either.

Back home again, we drifted off to our separate spots for a nap. We had a big night ahead of us. At about seven, we reconvened around the small table with cartons of Chinese food and a map of the area.

"This curry tastes weird," Brandon said.

"That's my black bean chicken, you eejit," I said reaching over.

We talked through the plan as we ate.

"Amy, are you sure that…" I began.

"I'm fine." Amy cut me off by raising a hand, her eyes still on the map. "That reminds me…" She lifted her handbag and rummaged through it, took out a pack of painkillers and popped two. Then she offered me some.

"Are they strong?"

"Pretty strong. They take the edge off, but they don't mess with your head."

"Okay, thanks." I took one with a slug of lemonade.

Afterwards, we went through the plan a couple of times. I brewed a big cup of coffee and Amy said she'd get her gear from the car. Brandon gave her a hand and they returned with two bulging gym bags.

"Just a sec." I'd already cleared the food away and now I moved our cups to one side, and they set the bags down on the table.

Amy pulled the zips back on them.

Brandon gave a low whistle. "Damn."

"I signed out this little lot before I saw McGoohan. I don't plan on returning them. You'd be surprised how loose the FBI is about some things."

I dug through the bags. The first one was mostly filled with an array of ammo. There were also a few knives, slings, belts and five handguns. All Glocks. The second packed an even bigger punch; a shotgun, the large machine gun from the night in the church yard, and three M16 assault rifles.

"Jesus," I said.

"We forming an army?" Brandon asked.

"You guys wanna trade up?" Amy asked lightly.

"Well, I'll take one of these." I lifted a knife and a belt. "Thanks, Amy." I grabbed up some ammo, careful to get the right magazines.

"You don't want anything else?"

"I'm kinda happy with my old Colt," I said.

"Stuck in your ways. Okay, cool. What about you, Brandon?" She held one of the semis aloft.

"I'll try one of those things," Brandon said with a wide smile.

***

After choosing our weapons, we sat with the TV on low and had another brew. We were keeping a clear head, and everyone seemed to be coping with the stress okay. Brandon was even sticking to plain old tobacco. I sat on the sofa cleaning out the Colt. Amy went through the workings of the M16 with Brandon on the other sofa. We were silent for a few minutes, except for the gentle murmur from CNN, my shuffling of the metal components of my gun and Brandon dry firing the rifle.

At about nine I said, "Right, will we get loaded up?"

"Yep, sounds good." Amy popped another pain killer with a swig of Coke.

We loaded what we needed into the bags, with some spare ammo. The rest we hid under one of the beds. We each dressed in dark coats with jackets, spare ammo stuffed in our pockets. By ten we were in my Hornet, sweeping through the streets. Amy sat up front beside me. Brandon rode in the back. I left the stereo off.

"You guys all good?" I asked when we were about a mile from the house.

"Yep." Amy pulled her hair back and tied up a high ponytail.

"For sure." Brandon patted one of the bags.

"We do this and we're home free," I said.

They both nodded. Amy set a black baseball cap on her head and threaded the ponytail out over the adjustable band. Brandon had on his new NYC one.

"I'm odd man out then," I said, patting my head.

"Ain't a ski mask more your thing?" Brandon asked from the back. I saw him flash a grin in the rearview mirror.

"Wee fecker," I half-turned and gave him a dig on his leg. "We wore balaclavas actually."

"Boys, boys, settle down, would you?" Amy said.

"Yes Ma'am," Brandon said.

I gave a little salute.

Eamonn Boyle's home, and the apparent head of operations, was in the suburbs out past Brooklyn. The streets here were wide, houses spread out and lined with mature trees. Boyle's place was at the end of a cul-de-sac on the left. As we'd been told, the other side of his house had a large lawn with an eight-foot fence separating the property from a small public wooded area. There was only one way out of the street. It was almost eleven and the streetlights illuminated the start of the road. I killed my lights and let the engine purr gently. We passed a few houses at a crawl; all were lit dimly behind thick curtains and expensive looking blinds. Top end cars were parked in driveways, ignoring the double garages. Maybe they were left out as status symbols. Maybe the garages were already full of even better models. The houses were mostly red brick, huge and impressive. An army of gardeners and maintenance men would be making a good living off this one exclusive street.

I parked up six houses down the street, under an overhanging birch tree, away from the reach of the street lighting. We got out and took what we needed with us. I already had my Colt down my jeans. Brandon and Amy slipped their rifles inside their jackets. I looked them up and down as we began walking back the way we had come. A close inspection and it would be pretty obvious that they were armed, but anyone walking a dog across the road, or somebody arriving home from the office, hopefully wouldn't notice.

We took the next left at a steady clip, just half a mile taking us to the entrance to the little wood. The gate was locked as we knew it would be. We paused and scanned about. So far, we hadn't encountered one sinner. It was all clear. Nobody in their gardens, no traffic. The fence was only four or so feet tall, so we took turns to scramble over it. I told Brandon to go, then Amy. I noticed Amy wince as she hopped down at the other side. I had a last check over my shoulder and followed suit.

"We got this," Amy said and led the way into the blackness of the trees beyond.

Chapter 47

"You ever seen Predator?" Brandon asked.

"Never saw it." Amy pointed the barrel of her gun left and right as we made our way through the woods, forging our own path away from the gravel lane.

"Aye, I have. You fancy yourself like Predator?" I asked, giving him a wink.

"No, just like Arnie." He pulled a pose with the M16 across his chest.

"Yeah, maybe Arnold from *Happy Days*," I said.

"What's *Happy Days*?"

I gave an eye roll. It was probably too dark to see it. Such a waste.

"Aww come on." Amy looked at him with surprise. "*The Fonz* and the gang?"

He shook his head.

Amy sighed.

We moved on, our eyes adjusting to the darkness. The fence outside Boyle's house was now only a hundred metres off to our left.

"Did you hear Stanley Kubrick died?" Amy asked.

"Damn. That sucks," said Brandon. "I love *Space Odyssey*."

I stopped. "You've seen *Space Odyssey*, but you've never heard of *Happy Days*?"

"Nope."

I shook my head. "Well, if you two are finished with your T.V and film trivia, can we get this thing done?"

"Sure." Amy brushed past me and led the way again.

We kept low, each with our guns out, Brandon bringing up the rear. We were almost at the fence now. The trees stopped about a metre from it, though they towered above the house, some branches hanging over the property. There was a security light illuminating the back of the house. There were a few flowerbeds and small trees breaking up the expansive lawn, but not much else. It was tidy. There was a shed off to one side and a small fountain.

I could make out a little paved area beyond the east side of the house. We made it to the fence and got down on our hunkers.

We crouched there and watched.

Amy pulled out a set of binoculars and adjusted them as she swept from one side of the house to the other. She pointed to a faint light cast behind a curtain in a room upstairs. "I think that's his office there. According to the intel."

"Yeah, looks about the right spot," I agreed. "It's hard to tell if anyone's downstairs. Lights are on in most rooms anyway."

Amy nodded.

We'd been told that there had been regular observation of the house. Estimates from the FBI said they thought that aside from Boyle and Sullivan, there'd probably be three or four others, but there could just as easily be more. That was the average over months of surveillance. There would be no observations tonight, they were keeping well away.

"Let's sit tight a while," I said. "See if anyone walks the perimeter."

"Agreed," Amy said.

Brandon looked on, adjusting his awkward crouch and setting his gun across his knees. The barrel pointed towards my legs. I pushed it away with two fingers.

"Just in case." I raised an eyebrow.

"I'm a pro now, don't ya know?" Brandon said.

"Well even pros can sometimes accidentally shoot their buddies."

We kept watch.

We didn't have long to wait.

Less than ten minutes later, the smell of tobacco floated towards us. Then we saw a wisp of a dark figure appear around the corner and walk around the back of the house, past what seemed to be a large kitchen. The figure ambled along, smoking, a rifle slung across his back.

Then he looked towards us. We all pressed ourselves down into the dirt. When I looked up again, he was ambling towards the east side and away from us. He hadn't seen us. He'd just been looking out into the woods.

"You think there's just one outside?" Brandon whispered.

"I'm not sure," I said.

We waited a few more minutes but didn't see anyone else.

"C'mon let's make a move," Amy said.

I took out a small set of wire cutters from my back pocket and began snipping the fencing from the bottom up. It sliced through with a satisfying *clip, clip*. The noise was minor, but we all kept a close look out just the same. After a couple of minutes, I'd cut a big enough gap that we should all be able to crawl through. I held it open for Amy and she squeezed inside, gritting her teeth. Brandon and I slipped through afterwards. We stayed low. We crept across the grass and hid behind the shed.

"I'll take the first guy." Amy slipped off to the side and hurried across the lawn. She went and hid beside a small coal bunker near the doorway at the back of the house.

The plan was to do everything as quietly as possible for as long as possible, but there was no way of knowing how long that could last for.

We waited.

Then the smell of tobacco smoke drifted towards me again, followed closely by the figure. As he passed just beyond the backdoor, Amy sprang up, her rifle across her shoulder, a knife in her hand. I saw her face set, but strained as she plunged the knife into his chest and then pulled it free. She put her other hand over his mouth as slit his throat. She lowered him to the ground. He bled out with a sickly gurgling sound.

I heard another set of footsteps coming from around the bend. I signalled for Brandon to wait there as I padded off towards the corner. As the second man came around, I smacked him in the face with the butt of my gun. He had a rifle on his shoulder too. I hit him hard in the stomach, winding him. Then I grabbed his head and a handful of hair and twisted it hard to the side until I heard it crack. He was already dead when he crumpled to the ground.

Amy and I both crouched down and listened.

Nothing.

I pointed at Brandon and beckoned him over.

He came across, clinging to his gun, his face pale. He looked at the two bodies, sweat on his brow.

"You okay?" I asked.

He nodded.

"Alright. Let's go."

I hid down behind the back door, then raised myself up. The top third of the door was made of glass. I peeped in. There was a modern, classy kitchen beyond, lit by downlighting. There was some kind of living room on past it. I stood back up and tried the handle. The door opened with a thin, high squeak. I went in first, the other two quickly behind me. Our guns pointed wherever we looked. The kitchen was clear. I pointed my gun at the room beyond and moved into it.

We went in as one. It was a large living room with red leather sofas, heavy framed artwork, lots of antique wood and dim Tiffany lamps. I could see the hallway outside it and a staircase beyond that. Amy went to the window and parted the blinds to have a look outside. Brandon stood beside me.

All at once there was a middle-aged man in the doorway with an M16. His face was flushed, his eyes fearful. Immediately he sprayed bullets at me with a deafening roar. I threw myself down behind a table. Brandon swivelled and spewed bullets at the man. The man cried out before falling to the ground, dead, his body peppered with hot lead. I stared up at Brandon, then got to my feet. Amy ran over.

"Jesus, I guess you *do* know how to use that then," I said.

Brandon's eyes remained on the sorry sight of a dead man, riddled with his bullets.

"I suppose we don't need to worry about being quiet anymore." Amy moved to the side of the door. There were voices from upstairs, then feet on the stairs.

"Get back!" Amy hissed. Then she swung out into the doorway and began pumping rapid fire towards the staircase. She ducked back into the room as a barrage of shots was returned, smashing into wood and plaster around the doorway. We ran for cover.

More footsteps on the stairs.

I crawled behind the door, then stretched around and plunged off a few shots from my Colt. A fresh volley of shots was returned as I swung back around.

"Cover me," I whispered. "Aim high."

Amy and Brandon took aim from their crouched positions and emptied the rest of their clips through the doorway. I scrambled around Brandon's kill and gingerly crawled out. My eyes locked on a man, lying on the stairs, bleeding from his arm and neck. He attempted to aim a shotgun at me. I unloaded the rest of my Colt into his midsection. Then a hail of bullets rained down from above. I sprinted back into the room. Amy had finished reloading the two M16s. She snapped hers shut. Then she handed the other back to Brandon and threw me a clip for my Colt.

"Cheers." I ejected the spent clip, reloaded and slid a round into the chamber.

"Let's take them from two sides," she said.

Amy jogged towards the doorway. She hopped over the body, threw the assault rifle into the room opposite and forward rolled into the room behind it. Another barrage of bullets chased her. She disappeared around the door jam, unhit. The woman was a force of nature. Some bullets must have hit the baby grand piano in there. It leaked a dissonant, low rumble of impossible chords.

Then there was silence.

A very unnatural kind of quiet, with a haze of cordite in the air and the heaviness of death.

We waited some more.

"Be ready for my say so," I whispered in Brandon's ear, then gestured with the gun for us to take up position on either side of the doorway.

There was a creak at the top of the stairs.

I could hear somebody breathing hard.

I squinted around the doorway. The guy I'd killed was three quarters of the way up. Maybe six steps from the top. He'd be a challenge to get around.

I listened hard.

Somebody was coming.

Three steps?

Now four?

"Now!"

I swung around the door. Brandon moved only a millisecond behind. Half a second later we fired in unison up the stairs at two new figures with guns. Amy was out too, standing in a perfect shooting stance, riddling them both with bullets.

The bodies literally piled up on the wide polished oak staircase and began to slide and wedge together. We held fire. Six down. But how many left?

We looked each other up and down through the fog of smoke. Checked that we were all okay.

Then we made a move upstairs.

Chapter 48

At the top of the staircase, there were only three ways to go.

"I think it's this one." I pointed down the first corridor.

"Yeah, I think so, too. We should split up a minute anyway. See if there's many more."

Amy marched off and gestured to Brandon to follow her He raised his gun up into combat position. I knew this was all too much for him. The lad had done brilliant, but he hadn't seen half the violence that Amy and I had.

"We'll check these two halls first anyway." She kicked open the first door.

I set off down the first hallway. There were only two rooms. I turned the handle, pushed it open, then stepped to the side. From my angle I could see it was a plush little games room. I saw a poker table, wooden chairs with soft fabric covers and a small corner bar. I went inside, walked a loop. All clear.

I paused, took a deep breath and had a think.

Two outside, one in the living room, three on the stairs. Six so far. But none of them had been Sullivan or Boyle.

Surely it was just them left. But where were they?

The second room should be his office. It'd be the right size and position according to the info from McGoohan. I exited the room and sidled silently towards the second door. It was dark stained wood with brass fittings. There was a plaque about six inches long, three quarters of the way up. 'OUR DAY WILL COME', it proclaimed in Irish. *Tiocfaidh ár lá*, indeed.

I heard the heavy tread of footsteps down the hall. I raised my gun and jogged towards the noise. Amy and Brandon came around the corner. I lowered my gun and blew out my cheeks.

"Frig me," I said. "Anything?"

"All empty." Amy bent forwards slightly, catching her breath.

"Just bedrooms," Brandon added.

"You guys okay?" I mostly meant Amy. She looked like she was weakening. Even *she* couldn't completely recover from getting shot in only a few of weeks. Brandon nodded and Amy tipped me a wink. *We go on, then.*

"That one's empty." I pointed my gun at the first room. "I think the other one's his office. They're both probably inside."

"Okay." Amy straightened and set off in front.

"Ever let a guy lead?" I jogged lightly up to her. "You'd be a rubbish dance partner."

"Not if I led and twirled *you* around." She raised her rifle in front of her.

Brandon took up position just behind us. He trained his weapon on the door through the gap between me and Amy.

"After you." Amy gestured with a flourish towards the doorway.

"Thank you." I put my back to the wall and reached around with my left hand to try the handle.

Locked.

Amy raised an eyebrow at me.

"Right, hold on a sec," I whispered. "I'll kick it in. Get ready."

I took a step back before launching my foot at the door, kicking to the right of the lock.

It didn't budge.

My leg juddered. I stumbled backwards, feeling like an idiot.

Amy smirked.

"Shut up." I poked my tongue out. "Right, then. You two shoot the hell out of it, then I'll try again. Okay?"

"Cool," Brandon said.

I stepped to the side. They aimed their guns.

"On three." Amy looked at Brandon. "One... two... three!"

The noise was horrific as they riddled the door with bullets. Amy paid special attention to the wood around the lock.

They stopped. The door was a state. The thick cloud of gun smoke diffused towards the staircase.

"No point in anything subtle. I'll kick it in. You two then fire right away. Sure as hell, someone's gonna fire back, so be careful"

I stepped away again, then launched a kick. This one connected even harder, right where the lock would be weakest.

The door broke free with a crack. I sidestepped. Amy and Brandon fired through the doorway. The room was longer than it was wide. An olive green-painted and wood panelled room.

We inched inside.

There was a large mahogany desk at the far end. The window behind it was part-stained glass. The barrel of a magnum hung over the top of the desk. Two loud rounds zipped from it. We dove for cover and opened fire towards the desk.

A shaken voice cried over the din. "Okay, okay!" The magnum was tossed away to the side and bounced across the thick carpet.

We stopped shooting.

Two raised hands appeared from beneath the desk.

"I'm coming out," croaked a man's voice. "I'm unarmed."

I wondered if Magnum had a recent sale on.

We trained our guns on Boyle as he stood up to his full height. That was just under six feet. He was quite thin but looked strong. Maybe just shy of sixty. His navy suit looked expensive, as did the black dye job he had treated his beard and receding hairline to.

"I'm unarmed," he said again.

"You are now." Amy pointed her long barrel at his head.

We both took a step forwards. Brandon slung his gun behind his back and stood near the doorway.

"Michael, we can work something out…" His voice rasped, but still boomed with substantial confidence.

I raised my free hand. "I've heard all this before. I suppose you're going to tell me it was some other guy who ordered the hit next."

He rolled his tongue over his front teeth. They'd had work done to them. His face had an odd shape to it as well. I guessed it had been nipped and tucked within an inch of its life.

"No, I'm not going to say that." He let his hands drop slowly to his sides. "Yes, it was me. I'm the top man. But still, there's always a deal that can be done."

My eyes widened as his left hand whipped down for something. Before I could react, Amy pumped a single round through his skull. He fell back into his chair. His upper half flopped down across the desk.

I breathed out.

Amy and I shared a brief look. We walked over to the body to check that he was dead.

There was no doubt about that.

"Don't fucking move," snarled a voice behind us.

Sullivan.

I spun around into a shooting position.

Amy pivoted too, this time a fraction slower than me.

Neither of us fired.

Sullivan's arm was draped around Brandon's shoulder, with a gun against his temple.

Chapter 49

"Let him go," I growled.

"I don't think I will, mate." Sullivan's smug voice dripped thick with a broad Belfast twang.

"There's two of us," Amy said.

"Aye, but neither of you want me to shoot this young fella first now, do you?"

I licked my lips.

I wasn't a good enough shot to avoid Brandon with any certainty. I flexed my fingers.

"Here's how this is going to go," Sullivan said. "Me and him'll back out of here and take a little drive. Nobody's gonna get shot. Nobody else, anyway." He nodded his head toward Boyle.

Sullivan started to back out of the doorway. He pulled Brandon with him. Brandon's gun dangled impotently over his shoulder. His eyes were wide with terror. The kid was trembling. Amy and I each took a step forwards, our guns trained on Sullivan's conceited face. There was no way he was letting Brandon go. And there was no way he was giving up on killing me either. But I had to choose my moment.

"That's close enough," Sullivan warned. He backed away towards the staircase.

Amy advanced to the door ahead of me and I stayed out of view behind her.

"Keep your gun on him," I whispered. "Don't scare him or get too close. I'm going to try something else."

Amy gave the faintest of nods.

"That's it. Nice and easy," I heard Sullivan say. His voice echoed down the hallway.

I stuck my Colt down the back of my jeans and crossed to the desk. I squeezed past the body, pulled up the window and looked down.

I could hear my blood rush in my ears. I struggled to steady my breathing.

HUNTED

Far below were the two bodies of the men we had killed first at the rear of the house. To the side of the ledge, about two feet down, was a black drainpipe. It led all the way to the ground, though it didn't look the sturdiest.

Nothing else for it.

I pulled the window up further, all the way to the top. I climbed out and swung my body around so that I could grip the ledge. My legs dangled below me. I got some momentum going and leaped off. My hands reached for the pipe. I made it. Both hands clung tight. The drainpipe buckled and a couple of nails flew out as it inched from the wall, threatening to pull away completely.

"Stay where you are, ye wee bollix," I mumbled to it.

I quickly started to descend. My hands burned and the pipe pulled away further from the wall. More nails pinged out. About ten feet from the bottom, I could feel the whole thing give, as whole brackets tore away.

I jumped.

I landed awkwardly. Piping fell around me. I hobbled off around the side of the house and drew my gun. I kept low and swept through the patio area towards the front. I hoped the noise hadn't been loud inside the house.

I made it to the front before the door opened. I knelt behind the wall of the tile-roofed porch. Listening hard, I could hear the muffled sound of Sullivan's voice from within, then the door eased. Sullivan backed out, still clutching Brandon in front of him. He shouted to Amy to stay back. I could make out her shape at the far end of the hallway. I was so close. Only a few feet away. Brandon's head looked wildly all around. Then he glanced over his shoulder and his eyes locked with mine.

I widened my eyes and nodded.

I silently mouthed, *"One... two... three."*

On three, Brandon whipped his arm out and elbowed Sullivan in the stomach, lessening his grip. The barrel of Sullivan's gun pointed skyward. I took careful aim and shot Sullivan in the back of his right knee.

Sullivan cried out, dropped his gun and faltered. I took a step forwards. Brandon broke free and ran back into the house. I stood and took aim for Sullivan's head. Somehow, he managed to stay on his feet and chopped at my hand. The gun was knocked from my grip. Then he was on me, despite the blood spurting from his busted knee. We tumbled to the gravel, his weight heavy on me and his breath foul.

"I'll kill you, fuckin' traitor!" He roared right into my ear.

Sullivan clawed at me, too close for proper punches. I jabbed him in the ribs, then kicked out at his injured knee. He yelped, allowing me some traction. We tumbled about the ground. I could see out of the corner of my eye that Amy and Brandon were in the doorway, guns aimed at our writhing bodies, both unable to take a clear shot.

"I'm not the traitor," I said through gritted teeth.

My hand slipped inside my jacket, my free hand still grappling with him.

"I want an Ireland where kids aren't blown up. Not one where everyone lives in fear. Where there aren't assholes like you, Sullivan. That's what *I* fought for. *You're* the traitor."

I tore my knife free from my jacket and plunged it into his chest.

Sullivan stopped fighting and fell back on the hard gravel. He flailed like a wood louse on its back in a puddle. Blood gushed from his chest. He looked down at the terrible wound in anguish.

I pulled the knife out, stared him in the eye, then stabbed him through the centre of his rotten heart.

***

We glided through the night, safe and warm inside the Hornet. It responded to my every move. Everything felt natural. Man and machine in perfect harmony. Every nut and bolt exactly where they ought to be.

We had done it. We had bloody done it. And we'd survived to tell the tale.

Brandon and Amy huddled close for comfort on the back seat. They were both shaken, but holding up. Three streets away I slowed as we passed by a cortege of police cars and ambulances, sirens wailing. Then I sped up again as we headed off the intersection for the apartment.

HUNTED

The apartment, where there would be warmth, safety, cigarettes and drinks. Somewhere that we could take stock, check on one another properly and think about the future. We might have a future now.

"Are you guys okay? We did it."

I smiled at them in the rear-view. Amy's arm half hugged Brandon in close. They nodded.

"You both were incredible," I said. "You did good."

"Yeah, I know we did," Amy said.

I held the wheel with one hand and with practiced dexterity, I produced a cigarette from my pocket, set it in my mouth and picked up my lighter. There was next to no traffic in this part of the city that supposedly never sleeps. I crossed to the next lane for the Meatpacking District and blew smoke towards the half-open window.

"At least it's done now," Brandon said. He pulled off his cap and gave himself a little fan with it.

"It is mate, it is," I said.

Our eyes met in the mirror. I nodded. He gave me the thumbs up.

Amy bent forwards. "And the world is maybe a tiny bit better for it." She leaned back and kissed the top of Brandon's head.

I couldn't hold back a grin.

"'The whole worl's in a state o' chassis,'" I said.

Printed by Amazon Italia Logistica S.r.l.
Torrazza Piemonte (TO), Italy

54326362R00127